# Snowed

# Snowed

## Maria Alexander

RAW DOG
SCREAMING
PRESS

Snowed © 2016
by Maria Alexander

Published by Raw Dog Screaming Press
Bowie, MD

First Edition

Cover Image: Daniele Serra
Book Design: M. Garrow Bourke

Printed in the United States of America

ISBN: 978-1-935738-89-3

Library of Congress Control Number: 2016949775

www.RawDogScreaming.com

*For Bret*

*You will always be my Aidan.*

# Chapter 1

I want to kill the person who tore down my flyer.

The torn blue corners of my flyer are stuck under the brass thumbtacks, surrounded by cheery posters for bible studies and prayer meetings. We're in a public high school, but nobody complains. Nobody but me, of course: Charity Jones. Eleventh-grade troublemaker.

Anger mushrooms inside of me. Bell's about to ring and the meeting is this afternoon. People rush past me on their way to class, bursts of cold white mist escaping their mouths.

Screw this.

The backpack slides from my shoulder to the icy pavement. I dig into it for a spare flyer. I posted the information on the school's online activity board last week but nobody checks that. I tack up the new flyer and stand back to examine it.

> 'Tis the Season for Reason!
> Have Doubts?
> You're Not Alone
> Join the Skeptics Club
> In the Library
> Thursday, November 6 at 2:30pm

My back bumps into a solid mass. The campus gorilla.

"Awwww, did someone tear down your Satan Club sign?"

Darren Jacobs. Blond-haired, broad-shouldered, senior quarterback. Leader of what I call the American Teen Taliban aka the "BFJs" — Bullies for Jesus. My throat tightens with fury. The gorilla's girlfriend, Beth Addison, sneers at his side. She's the cheerleading captain and editor of the yearbook.

My face burns as I heave the backpack up over my shoulder. I know I shouldn't answer. "No. But someone did tear down my anti-idiot sign."

As Beth scowls at me, Darren tosses the crumpled blue flyer over his shoulder. So *he's* the one who tore it down. "You're going to hell, fatso. You and everyone in your little club."

I plunge into the crowd and head over the dead winter grass. Why can't they leave me alone? For years at other schools I was teased for my smarts until I finally got into a magnet school, although sometimes I was still teased for being chubby. But now that we live here in Hickville? I get tormented for being a skeptic—*and* smart *and* chubby—but mostly for not backing down.

Thanks to the flyer drama, I stagger into first period AP Calculus late, as everyone is already passing forward last night's homework.

"You okay?" Keiko asks as I drop into my seat and slip off my ski jacket.

"Douchebags tore down the sign." My face feels hotter and now leaky.

"Seriously? Isn't that vandalism? I told you we shouldn't have advertised."

Keiko's Smithsonian-grade brains and ethnicity provoke a lot of teasing, which sucks because she's already painfully shy. Her parents moved here from Japan when she was 8 years old. They converted from nothing to being Southern Baptists for unknown reasons. Maybe to fit in? It makes no sense. A non-believer, Keiko has suffered from the endless sermons and restrictions ever since.

As for "diversity," Keiko and I are pretty much it. Hey, at least today no one's called me a "jelly beaner" yet. I'm actually mixed — my dad's black and my mom's white. I wouldn't mind people getting my ethnicity wrong if they weren't such racist jerks about it.

It's California, right? The home of hipsters, homeopaths and tech startups? Not here. Thanks to my dad's new job, we're stuck in the foothills of Sacramento — Oak County — where guns and God overrule science and compassion, and there's a church on every corner. No one here has voted Democrat in at least half a century.

"Charity? Five points off of homework for being late."

Crap.

Mrs. Stewart wrangles the homework into one papery heap. "Everyone take out a pencil for the not-so-pop quiz. Come on, come on."

We settle down for the test. The only sound is Michael Allured sniffing. I once asked him what he was allergic to. He said, "Only two things."

"Only two?"

"Yeah. The air and the ground."

I've had a crush on Michael since I arrived last year. Like most of the guys I have crushes on, he doesn't know this. Also, he's the smartest guy in school. I don't have a chance. He's always been involved with older girls or someone outside of school. Or so I've been told. I like his dark brown eyes and how his mousey brown hair splays forward over his forehead. His decided lack of athleticism hasn't won him much favor with the girls here, but it scores with me for sure.

I make good progress on the quiz before I hear a buzzing in my bag. It's my cell phone on vibrate. It buzzes. And buzzes. Mrs. Stewart glares at me over her reading glasses. Keiko's bag is buzzing out of control, too. We're only required to mute the ring tone, not turn off the phone, but this is distracting.

"Turn it off, Charity," Mrs. Stewart orders. "You too, Keiko."

We shut off our phones.

After class is over, we compare text messages in the hallway. Multiple unknown phone numbers were texting us over and over: *Satan. Burn in hell.* And various bible verses. Fifty-six messages so far…

I turn off my phone, wondering if I'll ever be able to use it again.

Keiko looks like she's going to cry.

The day rattles on until the last bell rings. I shuffle down the hallways, slouching as if an extra inch of protruding scapula will somehow keep people from staring at me. My younger brother Charles tumbles past me, a flash of white paper between his fingers as he pulls it from his leather jacket. He passes a cigarette to a friend as he presses one between his lips. One of his friends croons, "Hey, man! It's Cherry!"

I walk faster.

"Hey! Shit stirrer!" Charles runs up alongside, cigarette dangling between his lips, his black hair wild. His Vin Diesel complexion and light green eyes are a total win with the chicks. His sloped forehead and permanent squint remind *me* of a demonic hedgehog.

"What do you want, hoodlum?"

"What the hell did you do to the library?"

I slow down. "What?"

"You can stop embarrassing me any day now, loser." He spits on the ground and marches off.

I hear Christmas caroling. Who is singing? I hurry toward the noise.

*Silent night, holy night. All is calm. All is bright.*

As I round the music building, I see the library. The carolers flank the front door, holding signs.

JESUS (HEART) YOU
ATHIESM = SATANESM
JESUS IS THE REASON FOR THE SEASON
STOP MILITENT ATHEISM

The crowd shoves signs in the faces of entering kids. Everyone is annoyed, both sign feeders and eaters. As I approach the scene, I vow to be cool, even though I just want to die. I started this fight. I've got to finish it.

I've got to be brave.

A murmur of recognition. They've noticed me. Darren and his church friends are no longer singing "Silent Night" but "Onward Christian Soldier."

"Stop persecuting Christians! *You're going to hell, you atheist whore…*"

It's not all sweet church words like those.

The shouts are deafening. My whole body feels like collapsing into itself to escape the thousand prickly pins of red-hot hate. I concentrate on putting one foot in front of the other, on not caring, on knowing I'm right. On anything except the crowd.

And then I notice her.

# Chapter 2

Judy LaHart stands off to the side, twirling one of her purple pigtails. Everyone says she's a fantastic artist. But since she's a total misanthrope, no one knows much else about her. As soon as she sees me, she sidles up to me. "Hey, are you Charity? I'd like to go to your club, but this is a little scary."

"We'll go in together. Safety in numbers." This is the first time we've ever spoken to one another. We're from two different worlds, art and math.

Judy studies me and then smiles. "I kind of suck at numbers, but okay." We press forward together to the heavy glass library doors.

The crowd has decided we're lesbians and now shouts homophobic slurs.

"Where are all the 'peaceful' Christians?" Judy asks.

"Home praying for this crowd," I reply. "And us."

Judy makes a pouty face at the signs. "Awwww! It's so cute when they try to spell."

The library doors shut behind us. No one follows—probably because Mr. Vittorio is standing on the other side, glaring at the commotion. He holds open the door and yells: "Get out of here! You're disturbing students who are studying! If you don't leave, I'm calling the police!"

I sometimes wish Mr. Vittorio were more like Giles the cool British Librarian-Watcher dude from *Buffy the Vampire Slayer*. But today I'm glad he's more like a brooding Italian Mafioso with his thick black moustache and sharp eyes. He guards the library as if it were the mob's safe house.

"Sorry, Mr. V," I say, as if it's my fault.

"You've got serious guts, kid," he growls, peering out the glass doors at the dispersing crowd. "You realize I have to report this to the administration. The new policy's to protect you."

Trembling, I unwind the scarf from my neck and let my backpack slide off my aching shoulder. "Do you really think that's going to help? Won't it just make things worse for me?"

Mr. Vittorio picks up a stack of books and hauls them to the back room. "You've got to trust someone, kid."

I look around the main room.

A few people are gathered at one of the long tables near the periodicals. My pal Leo Donatti waves to me. A skinny band geek and Michael's BFF, he sits with his trumpet case standing next to his chair. We've played D&D together many times at Michael's house, bonding over our mutual love of peanut M&Ms. He should be famous for his talent on the horn, but he's more famous for his big nose. Judy has already joined the table. The rest are sophomores and freshmen. No seniors. Everyone waves.

"Hey, everybody. Leo! Where's Michael?"

"He's not interested," Leo replies, leaning back in his seat. Judy has planted herself right next to him. "Something about being a cat who walks alone? He was quoting crazy stuff."

"'The cat that walked by himself, and all places were alike to him,'" I recite as I dump my backpack on the floor. It's from a Rudyard Kipling poem Michael's obsessed with. I memorized part of it to impress him.

"That's him!" Leo says. I can't tell if he's ignoring Judy as she checks him out or if he honestly doesn't notice.

"I'm not an atheist," Judy says, hunching forward. Her large hazel eyes are perfectly winged with black eyeliner. Her gaze sweeps the participants before landing on me. "I just like to question stuff. I hope that's okay."

"Totally! The only requirement is that you have a thinking problem," I reply. "Or actually, that others have a problem with your thinking."

As people chatter about how they each have a "thinking" problem, two words shout in my mind:

*Where's Keiko?*

There's a blur between the book stacks.

"Excuse me. I'll be right back."

I follow the blur. It's definitely Keiko. She stops at a dead end in the Reference section, wiping her eyes on her jacket sleeve.

"Keiko, what's wrong?"

"I told you we shouldn't have advertised!" She sobs, her eyes red with tears, nose running.

"We had to put up flyers. It's the best way to reach people who need us."

"Making people walk through an angry crowd is cruel. And all those text messages! I have like almost a hundred! My parents are going to kill me for going over the limit." The tears come in a torrent now. "And if they make me show them the texts…I don't know what I'll do."

She sobs harder.

"I'm sorry," I say, my throat tightening. I want to say something noble about how this is what happens when you stand up for what you believe in — or, in our case, don't — but those words sit like bricks in my mouth. Also, I forgot she has a text limit. That's cruel in and of itself.

"If this was really about helping people and not about your *ego*…" she says.

"My ego?"

"You always have to be right." Her voice raises a notch. "Well, maybe this is wrong. Maybe people should be allowed to think whatever they want instead of being told they're wrong."

Okay, now I'm mad.

"Keiko, the only people who aren't allowed to think whatever they want are you and me! We rationalists need to stick together."

"If thinking 'rationally' means you don't think about putting your friends through hell, then *count me out*!"

She pushes past me and storms out of the library.

I sink down onto the floor between the book stacks. What just happened? I've never seen Keiko that mad before. Is this just about me and her feeling embarrassed? Or is something else going on?

As soon as I can collect myself, I return to the group. The meeting attendees list the threats they've gotten from the vociferous religious/conservative/whatever faction of our school. It's only a segment of the school population that's a problem, but it's still an issue.

"We've got to support each other," I say as the meeting draws to a close.

"Seriously," Judy says, although the younger members already seem like they might bail.

I exchange phone numbers with Judy.

As we head to the door, Leo hangs back as he digs into his backpack. "Hey, Charity?"

"Yeah?"

Before he can answer, Judy stuffs a piece of paper in Leo's jacket pocket, giving him a look like she could eat him alive. "Just, you know, if you want to call me to study or anything." She winks at him—"Nice to meet you guys!"— and disappears out the door.

Leo watches her in a nervous stupor. "Did she just give me her phone number?" He digs the paper out of his pocket to check. He shakes his head, as if to wake up his brain. "Um…wait. Here." He hands me something in a colorful wrapper. "I can tell you need this more than I do."

It's a bag of peanut M&Ms. My favorite candy in the world.

"Thanks, Leo." I would hug him but he's already running out the door. That gesture means more to me than he could possibly know. Or maybe he does. For the first time all day I feel warm and fuzzy inside.

They say bad news comes in threes. The first was the angry mob and the second was the fight with Keiko. I'm not superstitious, but I can't help but wonder what's next.

I was supposed to go home with Keiko and her mother, but that plan has clearly fallen through. The crowd's dispersed and the school is nearly empty as I wander toward the parking lot. Just as I pass the music building, Matt Swain is exiting the band room, trombone case in hand. He's always friendly, so I ask him for a ride. A freakishly tall senior with a kind face, Matt's the eldest of six kids in a super Catholic family. He's also one of the nicest people I've ever met. He drives a beat-up yellow pickup and is far more preoccupied with the upcoming Winter Musical than with whatever else is going on at school. He was blasting away on his trombone in the band room, unaware of the library drama. As I recount the event, I tell him about the Skeptic's Club meeting.

"So, you don't believe in God?" he asks. "How come?"

"Why should I believe in someone I've never seen? It's like believing in Santa Claus or the Easter Bunny. No one has ever produced the 'real' Santa Claus or Easter Bunny, and no one believes in them—except kids, of course. If you can produce God, I'll believe."

"Yeah, but God isn't a person. He's everywhere. In everything. You can see him in the trees and newborn babies and people in love. He had a body, but… you know."

"When I see trees and newborn babies and people in love, that's exactly what I see. Not God. That's an interpretation of what you're seeing. I get why people feel that way. It's cool, but I'm just one of those people who needs proof. And I want to make that okay. Like, it's okay to believe. Why isn't it okay not to believe?"

Matt looks thoughtful. "Well, because you're insulting people when you say you don't believe."

I can see where this is going, but I. Can't. Shut. Up!

"Why is it an insult? Because I disagree? I don't get it. We should value what we see, not what we don't see. It's like the person who is *not* gullible is persecuted."

Matt's face pales.

Oops.

We drive on in awkward silence. By now, we're three miles from school, way up in the hills where scraggly blackberry bushes line the crumbling roads and shaggy old trees crowd around rambling houses. He turns onto the gravel road that winds deeper into the woods, leading off to a cluster of small houses where our olive two-story sits. The window screen to Charles' bedroom always catches my eye. It's slightly bent up from him sneaking out at night.

Both Mom's red Camry and Dad's blue Prius are in the driveway. It's 5:30 p.m. Something's wrong. Did Charles get picked up by the police again? Maybe the school officials told them about what happened today.

I apologize and thank Matt for the lift. He nods, lips tight. I slip out of the truck and he takes off. I remember that I turned off my phone in math class. First period. Hours ago. I find my phone and turn it on. A bazillion harassing voice messages from the BFJs. I scroll through until I find one from my mom and listen.

"Hi, honey! Please come home ASAP after school, okay? Oh—if you see your brother? Remind him, too. We need to have a family meeting. Love you!"

Great. Here's "thing" number three.

# Chapter 3

I can hear Mom and Dad chatting in the living room, asking questions. Another softer voice with a strange accent gives staccato answers.

"Charity?" Mom calls out. She sounds annoyed.

I shuffle through the foyer, inhaling the smell of baking lasagna. When I enter the family room, Mom and Dad are sitting on the couch with mugs, tea bag tags draped over the edges. Some guy I don't know sits with them in the easy chair. I can't help checking him out. He's my age, average height, with skin pale as cream and wavy ebony hair. His light blue eyes shimmer under long, inky lashes. His wrinkled, striped dress shirt is much too big for his narrow shoulders, and his scuffed black boots with pointed toes peek out from the cuffs of his baggy jeans. He gives off a weird vibe, like he's been in prison or working for suicide bombers.

He must be a stray.

My mom's a social worker. She's always bringing home people for meals. Damaged people.

Mom wraps an arm around my shoulders, kissing my ear. "Where have you been? Did you get my message?"

I shake my head.

"Hey. How'd it go?" Dad hugs me as well. I kiss his big scruffy face.

They are being *very* nice. Something's up.

"Not great. I'll tell you later." I stare at our visitor.

"Charity, this is Aidan MacNichol. Aidan, this is my daughter, Charity."

"How do you do?" He holds out his hand. His eyes barely meet mine. His voice is a notch higher than I expect and kind of sing-song. What century is this guy from? Who says stuff like that?

"Hi," I say and give him The Boneless Hand. *I'm touching you but I'm not happy about it.*

Except I am. His skin is incredibly soft, like my mom's charmeuse dress. He lets go. At the last second, I almost don't.

And he almost doesn't, either.

"Where's your brother?" Dad asks.

"I don't know. In jail?"

"Charity, stop it," Mom sighs.

"What? I never know where he is."

A car roars into the gravel driveway. It must be Charles' ride. The music escaping the car windows sounds like someone is grinding the air into steel shavings. As the car retreats, Charles bursts through the front door and makes for the staircase.

"Hey! Charles, come here." Dad motions to him.

Charles looks as if he'd rather snack on rat poison than join us, but he does.

"Hey." Charles lifts his chin at Aidan. Aidan nods back.

"We want to talk to you guys." Mom puts her hand on Aidan's shoulder. "Aidan is going to be staying with us for a little while."

"This is bullshit," Charles announces and heads for the staircase. He looks at Aidan. "No offense."

"Hey, get back here!" Dad yells.

"No family meeting? You just drop this on us?" I ask.

Mom looks mortally offended. "Charity!"

"It's not fair. We never get a say in anything that happens around here. Not about Aunt Bulimia—"

"Aunt *Bellina.*"

"Or the dog I wanted?"

"Honey, you know Charles is allergic."

"The only thing he's allergic to is school!"

"Shut up, Cherry." Charles glares at me, his hamster face squinching up.

"We have guests from my work all the time," Mom says, "and you've never cared before."

"Yeah, for *dinner.*"

Aidan slinks back, hands in his pants pockets. He watches the sky through the sliding glass door on the far wall of the living room. He's humming a familiar tune under his breath. I can't quite place it.

"I should go."

Aidan's announcement cuts through the room. Everyone falls silent.

"I can't stay here," he says. "I'm sorry, Mr. Jones. You've been very kind."

"You're not going anywhere, Aidan." Mom invokes The Voice. It's from her days as a trial lawyer. "If you leave, I have to call the authorities. You're underage, your legal residency is in question, and the county has put you in our care. You can stay with us or you can go to juvy." Mom darkened. "I don't recommend juvy."

"Neither does Charles," I say.

"Shut *up*, Cherry!"

Aidan sighs. "I don't know what this 'juvy' is but I suppose I don't want to go."

"Are you from like England or something?" Charles asks.

Aidan looks confused. "I beg your pardon?"

"Where is he sleeping?" I ask.

"Your room," Dad says.

My face heats with horror. I bury it in my hands.

"Kidding!" Dad says, throwing an arm around me for a bear squeeze. "Sewing room. Now let's have some chow."

Mom shuttles us to the dining table. She interrogates Charles as to why he stinks like cigarette smoke, but he claims it's from riding with his friend Noah. I say nothing. As we set the table, she brings out the salad and lasagna, which smells heavenly.

Humiliation and disappointment haven't affected my appetite at all, apparently. I wish *something* would.

I notice that Aidan holds the fork like he's strangling it. He scrapes the plate. Everyone winces. Where is this guy from? And why is he so strange? Who doesn't know how to use a fork?

I want to flee to my room to cry but I can't. I want to make up with Keiko. I feel terrible about that fight. But Mom has laid down the law: No running off before the meal is over. Supposedly this encourages Charles to stay put and bond with us. If I ran upstairs and flung myself onto the bed now, I'd be doubly busted because we have a guest. I just want to be alone and this weird stranger is keeping me from my snug room where I can just melt down.

"Are you all right?" Aidan looks at me, concerned. "Don't worry. It wasn't you who misbehaved at school today."

Wait—what? How could he know? Or does he?

Mom shoots Aidan an anxious look, then me. "Honey, is there something going on?"

"Cherry started a riot at school today," Charles offers.

"A riot?" Dad eyes me with disbelief.

"Shut up! That's not what happened!"

"And then she made the Christian girls cry."

"Charity!" Mom says. "Was this your club?"

"Mom, I didn't do anything to anyone."

"Then they sent Cherry like a million text messages so she can't use her phone anymore." Charles beams with triumph.

I want to slam his face into the Pyrex dish. "*You!* Did *you* give them my cell number?" My face heats with the rage. My hand balls into a fist on the table.

"That's enough." Dad points at Charles. "Did you give out your sister's cell number?"

"Of course not," Charles says, indignant. Dad eyes him suspiciously, but lets it drop. There is no justice.

Mom wearily passes Dad the wine bottle. "Charity, what happened?"

"Nothing. I put up a flyer about the Skeptic's Club and the BFJs picketed my meeting, calling me a lot of unspeakable names. They harassed everyone who was there. They were harassing me with texts calling me a Satanist even before the club meeting. I had to turn off my phone. That's why I didn't get your call."

Tears scald the corners of my eyes.

"Where were the school officials?" Mom asks. "I can't believe they let this happen!"

"Don't worry. Mr. Vittorio told me he's reporting it. He's the librarian."

Aidan sits with his hands folded in his lap, eyes trailing to the window.

Mom narrows her eyes at Dad and polishes off her glass of wine.

And then there's Keiko… I can't take it anymore. I manage to stand up and choke out, "Excuse me," before dashing for my room.

I hear Charles complaining behind me. "So Cherry gets to have a tampon tizzy and get out of dishes?"

I slam the door and the tears spill out. As I fall on the bed, I look to Mr. Spotty and Miss Yoyodyne, who squat beside my desk. These aren't stuffed animals. They're robots I built. I feel like kicking one of my plastic component bins but I hurt so much, I just double over on the bed.

Footsteps pound up the stairs and Mom taps on my door. I know her knock.

"Come in."

Mom sits on the bed and hugs me. Between sobs, I tell her what happened with Keiko.

"Honey, these people are serious bullies. Do you want me and Dad to talk to the principal?"

"*No.* That'll only make it worse. Besides, the school says they'll deal with it. Can we wait and see what happens?"

She looks unconvinced, wiping hair out of my eyes. "If they lay a hand on you…"

"…I have a good lawyer."

After Mom leaves, I text Keiko.

*I'm so sorry, K. Please don't be mad. I won't put up any more flyers. I promise! Xoxo*

As I read *One Hundred Years of Solitude* for AP English, I can hear the bumps and scrapes of Dad and Charles setting up the cot in the sewing room. Despite his protests, Charles enjoys showing off that he can lift more than Dad, who had back surgery several months ago. Mom digs through the sewing room closet. "We'll get you more clothes this weekend," I hear her tell Aidan. They wish each other a good night.

After two long hours of AP Calculus followed by Honors Chemistry and French, I eventually crawl into bed, exhausted and wishing that I believed in something—anything—that I could pray to and make things okay with Keiko.

Everything falls quiet except for Aidan. I hear him humming. The wall is thin between us.

I remember hearing Mom crying in the sewing room after we first moved here. She and Dad weren't getting along. I hate thinking of my mom being weak. She has to be strong, the badass lawyer who torches anything in her way with her words. I love her for that. To hear her sobbing was haunting.

Aidan keeps humming. It's that same tune as before but this time I know what it is.

*Carol of the Bells.*

A Christmas song.

# Chapter 4

I open my eyes the next morning to the sight of Mr. Spotty's yellow oval eyes. Mr. Spotty's grounded because I used his catapult arm to throw rocks at Charles. I didn't mean to hurt him. He was hiding in the bushes with his friends smoking pot. I just wanted to startle them, not take a hunk of flesh out of my brother's forehead.

Although, I'm kinda glad I did.

The other two robots aren't grounded, just temporarily decommissioned as I work on a new, far more sophisticated robot. Her name is Les Femmes Nikitas and she flies. In three parts. She could seriously wreck the house — even the garage — so I only test her outside.

Still feeling like crap, I slip out of bed and check my phone. No texts from Keiko, just the BFJs. It's quieted down a bit, though. I go online. Keiko has unfriended me everywhere. I slouch over the keyboard, wishing I were dead.

I claim the bathroom before the boys can. As I brush my teeth, I glower at my ridiculous hair in the mirror. My dad is black. My mom is a ginger. My hair is doomed. By the time I'm out of the shower, Charles is banging on the bathroom door.

"Innaminute!" I yell.

Charles continues to assault the door. Mom chimes in. "What's going on in there?"

"Just doing my fracking hair!"

Mom yells, "Some women would kill for your hair! Ask Alex Kingston! You look just like her."

"Alex Kingston," I yell back, "is perfect in every way and is married to The Doctor." I punish the rebellious strands with more conditioner, tie them back, and apply mascara.

My dad shouts from the master bathroom, "River Song is *not* married to The Doctor, honey. That was in a timeline that no longer exists."

"River Song is totally married to The Doctor!" I burst out of the bathroom. "Love is—"

Aidan stands there, toothbrush in hand.

"—forever."

His eyes are a milky blue color, like that neon fluid you find inside glow sticks. Otherworldly. Alien. Beautiful. I fall into them for a moment.

I then realize my bathrobe is open. I clutch the collar closed and feel embarrassment burning up to my earlobes.

"I'm so sorry," he says. "Your mother said to wait here."

"It's okay," I sputter. Did he already shower? He smells good. I can't even look at him, I'm so mortified that I might have flashed him. "I'm done."

"Thank you," he mutters. As if paralyzed, he doesn't move until I try to step past.

Dad drives us to school. He insists. I'd rather risk the bus than be seen with my loser brother and Aidan, who looks dweeby in one of Dad's shirts and old gray ski jacket. He grips the straps of a sagging backpack Mom dug up from the garage. Before I can get out of the car, Dad taps his cheek and grins.

"Forgetting something?"

I lean over and give him a kiss. To my surprise, he gets out with us.

"I want you guys to help Aidan today, okay? Make sure he gets on the right bus and everything."

"Sure." How in the world can I help anyone today when I can't help myself? At least it's Friday. Just have to make it through one more day. Sometimes the weekend can reboot and correct social disk errors.

"Great. Catch you guys later." Dad waves to us as he walks Aidan to the school office. If only he hadn't gotten that job transfer a year ago, we'd still be in Woodland Hills. At my old school near Los Angeles. There were kids like me — multiracial, hella smart. No bullies.

The hallways are socially chilly. No one says "hey" or anything.

In AP Calculus, Keiko ignores me. She sits toward the back of the room when I enter, pretending to study. Even Michael Allured doesn't notice me, but he's enrapt with his latest gadget, an app for his tablet that lets him draw equations and store them. Not that he cares about getting tainted by my friendship. Michael couldn't care less about social status, which is partly why I like him.

When class ends, Keiko races out without looking at me.

No one talks to me all day except Darren and his crew. They hiss "You're going to hell!" even at lunch as I huddle over a ham and cheese sandwich I bought off the food truck.

Alone.

They're wrong. I'm already in hell.

By the time I get to fifth period American History, I slouch forward in my chair and rest my forehead in my hand. I had a lot of friends back at Willow High. The Math and D&D Clubs. The robotics team. But here? Nothing. I'm on a robotics team but it's made up of students from the surrounding schools, some outside of the county. No one school out here has enough engineering wannabes to make a whole team. Our team does okay, but I miss my old team so much. We're still connected on all of our phone apps, but I think they've forgotten me. It's been too long since we've seen each other. Out of sight, out of mind, I guess.

People file into class, including Aidan.

He seems distracted by the walls. Mr. Reilly's entire classroom is papered with "Wanted" posters of famous historical figures. It would be cool except Mr. Reilly seems to be permanently displeased with us, making us feel like we're the ones on the posters.

Aidan notices me and stares.

"Sit," I stage whisper.

Thankfully, he sits over a couple of rows, behind and out of sight. At least I don't have to look at him. It's super cold outside and Dad's coat has been draped over his arm all day. What the hell is wrong with him?

Mr. Reilly addresses the class. "As we discussed last week, the Industrial Revolution fundamentally changed the way we harvested food, made clothing, even structured our society. It all started about eighteen hundred—"

"I beg to differ, sir," Aidan says. Mr. Reilly keeps talking but Aidan continues. "One could argue it began nearly two hundred years before, as the ideas of many famous philosophers trickled down into popular thinking."

Oh, god.

Mr. Reilly scribbles something in his notebook. "As I was saying, the Industrial Revolution changed lives in a fundamental way. Can someone tell me how manufacturing changed?"

It's silent for a moment. Usually I raise my hand whenever I can but today I feel like rolling up like a pill bug.

"Standardization and the steam engine. They changed everything."

Why can't Aidan shut up? *Why?*

"Mister…MacNichol, we raise our hands when we wish to be recognized so that we may speak. Do you understand?"

"Charity? Is this some sort of ritual?"

"Cherry's got a boyfriend," Darren singsongs. People laugh. It's that mean laugh, the one you know you're going to hear later in the hallways. "Cherry loves gargling his Jizzterine." Darren throws back his head, his bottom lip curling into his mouth as he nods. Like he's just scored big. He runs a hand through his buzz cut.

My head drops to the desktop. I don't care. They can call me a Satanist—it's not like Satan even exists—but *this* is too much.

Mr. Reilly's eyebrows rise. "Mr. Jacobs!" He scribbles in his attendance book on the podium. "Report directly to the principal's office after class."

Darren groans. "Seriously?"

"Say another word and go directly to the principal with possible suspension." He directs his next comment to Aidan. "We'll talk after class. Please hold your comments until then."

And he does. But as soon as class lets out, taunts and kissing noises fly through the room. I swear, you'd think it was junior high. As Mr. Reilly calls Aidan to his desk, I duck out. The eyes of the "Joan of Arc—Wanted for Heresy" poster seem to follow me out of the room under the thundering of the bell.

As soon as I'm outside, Darren Jacobs grabs my rear end and yanks up my underwear. The fabric cuts into my crotch. I fall forward, sprawling on the pavement.

"Bet he loves that watermelon ass!" Darren yells. A chorus of hoarse laughter follows.

I struggle to sit up, hands and knees stinging.

A hand extends to me. It's Aidan's. Those milky blue eyes are watery with concern. Can't he see how it's only going to get worse if we touch? I try to stand on my own.

"Charity, I'm so sorry."

"Don't be!"

I grab my bag and stomp off. I want Darren to die almost as much as I want to die myself.

# Chapter 5

It started drizzling during Music Appreciation. The droplets cling to the waves of my doomed hair. I shrink into my jacket collar, lowering my head. The sky rumbles like sheets of metal dragged over asphalt. I search for Bus 83 in the chaos of the parking lot. It's usually the last to show up.

Why didn't I take Drivers Ed this year? Oh, yeah. Stupid AP classes.

Aidan the "boyfriend" is nowhere in sight. He probably got detention for being a weirdo in one of his classes. Mom would want me to find him and haul his butt to the bus, like a foster care bounty hunter. Maybe I should screw up once in a while like my brother. Then they wouldn't expect so much of me.

My heart races. I have to make a decision. Number 83 is heading up the street. Mom will kill me if I don't take care of that guy.

I break away, running around the band room building and straight up to the quad, which is peppered with stragglers. I scan the hallways for that bulky gray ski jacket. *Rien*, as we'd say in French class.

*Aidan!*

A whisper on the wind. Or is it a scream?

Following the phantom noise, I walk out to the football field. Who knows where he could've gone? I call out his name again. Surrounding the empty field like a castle wall are the green and white bleachers. I approach them and step around the back of the stands.

"Aidan?"

Legs splay out from the bleacher underbelly. Someone's lying on the ground. Are they drunk? For such a "godly" school, there's lots of that.

"Hey! Dude! Get up!"

I draw closer. Dark fluid streaks the jean pant legs and Converse shoes. I crouch down to get a better look.

It's Darren Jacobs. His face is frozen in terror. A pool of blood seeps from his eviscerated body. One hand clutches the ground as the other protects his gored stomach. His face is slashed and bleeding.

I turn away and retch, acid hot in my throat. Shaking and gasping. Knees wobbling.

We've had some pretty major stuff happen with Charles. My parents often didn't believe me whenever I would tell them something was happening. Would anyone believe this? I can't stand the thought of being called a liar again. Not about something this serious.

There's one way to make sure I'll be believed.

I pull out my phone, hands trembling, and take a deep breath before I snap a photo.

A sick shiver rushes over me.

And then I run.

# Chapter 6

I search frantically for a teacher, terrified that whatever attacked Darren is silently loping after me. Clubs of every description meet after school: drama, choir, jazz band, debate, and more. Mr. Reilly is the first teacher I find. He's standing with Aidan in the quad. My heart pounds between my ears as I yell, "Mr. Reilly! It's an emergency!"

He withers as I describe what I found. Before I can show him the photo, he puts his arms around Aidan and me, rushing us to his classroom.

"Get inside! It's a lockdown!"

Mr. Reilly shuts the door and locks us inside before sprinting toward the office. Within moments the school fire alarm goes off, followed by an announcement on the intercom system.

"*Attention all students and teachers. Emergency lockdown. emergency lockdown. Immediately go to the nearest classroom and lock yourself inside. If you are already inside a classroom, lock the door. Avoid the windows. I repeat, avoid the windows. this is not a drill.*"

I grab Aidan's sleeve and pull him to the far side of the classroom, hunkering down to the right of the windows, out of sight. We hear the screams of other students. *Get inside! Quickly!* It's the most chaotic time of the day. At least some kids will be able to get away because they have cars. As I text Mom, a helicopter rumbles low overhead, louder than the thunder.

*Mom, we're in lockdown! I found Darren's body. He's been killed. We're at the school. Aidan and I are locked in Mr. Reilly's room.*

I then text Dad and tell him the same.

And finally Charles.

*Where are you?*
        WHO WANTS TO KNOW
*School is in lockdown. Are you okay?*
        YEAH. AT MIKE'S HOUSE

*Good*
> DID YOU SHOOT SOMEONE?

*Shut up*
> I KNEW IT!

I click the phone screen to black, tears pouring down my face, and put the phone on vibrate. My head's a jumble of shock and fear.

"Are you all right?" Aidan whispers.

The floor is freezing. I feel sick. I want to go home. I wished Darren to be dead and now he is. What I saw is going to keep me awake forever. Who could do something like that? Or was it an animal? What could overpower Darren unless it was a big person? He's—I mean, he was—one of the strongest boys in school. He must've been taken by surprise.

Police sirens slice through the air and eventually officers flood the school. We don't see them but we can hear the *scraaaawwsh* of their radios, footsteps pounding through the open halls. Unfamiliar voices and words.

I bury my face in my arms as I pull my knees against my chest, tears soaking my coat sleeves. To my surprise, Aidan gently puts his arm around my shoulders. "Are you all right?" he asks. "Can I help?"

Aidan's warmth is hypnotic. The scents of cinnamon and rose and nutmeg waft from his collar. An unusual cologne, especially for a guy. Did Mom buy it for him? It suits him, whatever it is.

"I don't think anyone can help," I say. "I don't think I'll ever sleep again." The fright of seeing Darren's bloody body, the pain of fighting with Keiko, the terror of the bullies, the aggravation of being DNA-bonded to Charles. Everything feels dark and heavy.

"I feel a little responsible. I hope you'll forgive me for invading your home."

"It's not your fault. Your timing isn't great, I'll admit, but it's not like you could help that, either."

"Perhaps. But I could have chosen to be someone else's problem. Not yours."

More helicopters now. Shouts in the distance.

"Where are you from?"

Aidan takes away his arm. I miss it immediately. "From up north."

"You mean, like Canada? Or somewhere closer, like Oregon?"

"Like Canada, I suppose."

"You suppose?"

"Why does it matter, Charity Jones?"

I suddenly feel cold. "It matters because I feel uncomfortable living with someone I don't know."

"I don't know anything about you, and yet I feel perfectly comfortable living with you."

"Really? Even after the terrible welcome we gave you?" I smile wryly. "You're running from someone or something, aren't you?" My chest tightens.

Aidan sighs, turning toward me as he rests his head against the wall. Those eyes. They're impossibly beautiful. They look into mine as he talks. "My father is an evil, powerful man who seems to have terrible sway over his children, as well as many others. He'll stop at nothing to find me, and I don't want him to harm anyone in the process. Like your parents. Or you and your brother. I know you don't like your brother. I don't like my brothers and sisters, either. But I'd never forgive myself if my father hurt you or your family."

A lump in my throat. Could this be true? "Why didn't you call the police on your dad? Don't they have laws against child abuse in Canada?"

"There are no police where I'm from. And besides, everyone loves my father. I even think some of my siblings love him despite who and what he is. When your heart is black as coal, you can love dark things. But I'm not like them. I don't even look like them."

"Maybe you're the milkman's." I wink. Aidan furrows his brow. "What I mean is, maybe he isn't really your dad."

"Oh, he is. There's no denying."

"Then you *should* keep running. You should never stop." *But I'm glad you're here. Please don't leave.*

"But then, like your mother said, more people will be after me than my father. Although, technically, he shouldn't be able to find me."

"How come?"

Aidan is silent for a moment. "I'm the only one not on the list."

"What list?"

"It's a long story. I'll tell you another time. But he has a way of learning things and he has a lot of friends. I don't like to take chances."

"But you must've come a long way without getting into trouble. How did you get caught?"

"I was famished. I can go for a while without eating. I guess I attracted attention scavenging for food. And then the police picked me up. They seemed very nice at first, but when I refused to tell them who I was and I admitted I was sixteen, they called your mother. Or at least someone who knew her."

The images of Darren swim up unbidden into my mind. I shudder, squeezing my eyes shut. Aidan puts a hand on my arm.

"You've had a terrible shock. Let me help to take your mind off things. Tell me, what's your favorite class?"

The honest answer is none of them. I like to build things. I tell him about the *first* robotics competitions where we have to build a robot to certain specifications so that it can perform in a big contest against other robots. And the coolest part is that we are encouraged to cooperate with other teams. It's not about winning as much as it is about learning how to exchange ideas with other people.

More helicopter noise and police chatter. I huddle against the wall, nausea knuckling my stomach. Aidan holds me gently. "Go on. Tell me more about the robots."

"My dad works at Aerojet."

"What's that?"

"It's an aerospace company. My dad builds rockets that go to space. And other things."

"To space." He whispers to himself as if remembering something. "And other things? Like what?"

My phone buzzes. Mom's picture appears.

"Mom!"

"Honey, are you safe? We got the robocall from your school. I can't reach you until the police release the lockdown. It might be awhile."

"I know. I'm okay. We're locked in Mr. Reilly's classroom."

"Where's your brother and Aidan?"

"Aidan's with me. Charles *says* he's at Mike's." That's Mike "Pulp Fiction" Palmer, whose dad has an arsenal of guns that would embarrass an army base. The thought of Charles around guns terrifies me.

"Okay. We'll be waiting for you when they lift lockdown. Just be safe, okay? Keep your voices down and do whatever the police say."

"Will do. I love you."

"I love you, too."

We sit quietly for a while, listening to the sounds of chaos outside. Then, the intercom makes a new announcement.

"*When your door is opened, put your hands on your head and exit slowly. You will be escorted out by police officers. Follow their instructions.*"

"That wasn't very long," Aidan says.

"It only seems that way because we talked the whole time."

"Which was easy," he replies. "You are far prettier than Mr. Reilly. And smarter, too."

"*Everybody* is prettier than Mr. Reilly." No one except my parents and a boy named Rizwan in junior high has ever said I was pretty. Smart, yes. Pretty? Almost never. And I don't realize how much I want that until Aidan says it. Or almost says it—he said prettier, not pretty. Aidan, who talks like an escapee from a Jane Austen novel. Of course only the oddest guy at school thinks I'm pretty.

I take his hand and squeeze it. He winds his velvety soft fingers with mine. It's the most delicious sensation I've ever felt. I never want to stop touching him. Ever.

"I mean it. You are," he says. "Pretty."

I wish I didn't have barf breath. As I study his lips and hold his warm hand, wondering what it would be like to kiss him, the custodian keys rattle in the lock and someone throws open the door. Cold air blasts the stuffy room, bringing with it the smell of rain-soaked earth. Aidan and I stand, jostle our backpacks and, hands on head, we exit the room.

Students stream from other rooms, dazed as the police corral us toward the parking lot, which is crowded with cop cars and news vans.

As soon as students spill into the parking lot, reporters pull them aside and question them, the glassy Cyclops eye of a TV camera aimed at their faces.

"Aidan! Put up your hood!"

"What?"

I grab his hood and yank it up onto his head. "You don't want to be on TV. Your dad will see you."

Aidan looks confused but lets me cinch his hood in place. We lock eyes, the conspiracy sealed for no other reason than that I want to kiss him. And he looks at me like he might have if the situation were different. He gives the hood an extra tug forward.

A policeman stops us as we wade through the crowd. "Are you Charity Jones? Come with me."

# Chapter 7

My heart feels like it's being squeezed in my chest as the officer leads me and Aidan to the music building. The police have commandeered the band room for a temporary headquarters as they debrief school officials and get statements from other kids. Music stands have been shuffled aside and chairs clumped together wherever people talk.

"You wait outside." The officer indicates Aidan as we cross the threshold.

"I'll see you soon," Aidan says, his eyes locking on me until the band door shuts.

The chaos of police radios and uniforms scares me in a whole new way. The officer strides toward a clean-cut, brown-haired man in a suit and trench coat. He talks on his phone as he straddles a backwards chair in one of the practice rooms. We enter, his dark eyes fixed on me. To my surprise, the officer shuts the practice room door.

"Charity Jones?" The trench coat man offers me his hand and clicks off his phone. "I'm Detective Jim Bristow. I'm a homicide investigator for the county. Can I ask you some questions?" He pulls a notepad and pen from one of his inner coat pockets. "Have a seat."

I awkwardly sit in the chair and shift so that I'm facing him, letting my backpack slide to the floor. He smells like coffee and cigarette smoke, his trench spotted with dampness from the rain.

"Now, don't be scared. You haven't been arrested or anything like that. I'm just going to take your statement and ask you some questions, okay?" He asks for my age, address, parents' names and phone numbers. I give him everything. "You found the body, correct? Can you tell me exactly how that came about? No detail is too small."

My mouth is dry as I recount finding Darren under the bleachers. He listens as he leans forward, taking notes, and then interrupts.

"So, why were you out at the bleachers? Doesn't seem like a place I'd find someone like you." He studies me. "No offense if you like sports. My wife loves sports, and she's a doctor."

"I was looking for Aidan."

"Aidan—?"

"MacNichol." My heart skips a beat as he writes down Aidan's name. "He just came to live with us, and since today is his first day at our school, Mom said to make sure he didn't miss the bus. I didn't see him anywhere and Mom would have killed me—so to speak—if I didn't get him on the bus. When I couldn't find him, I became desperate, wondering if maybe he'd wandered off." I don't tell him about the whispers I heard. I'm not even sure anymore that I heard them.

Detective Bristow stares at his notepad for a moment, rubbing his eyes. "And did you find Aidan?"

I nod. "He was with Mr. Reilly, our history teacher."

"The teacher you reported the death to."

"Yeah."

His pen scratches his notepad some more.

"Did you know Darren? What was your relationship like with him?"

"He was a bully," I say, voice low. "He harassed me. A lot of the jocks taunt me." My voice cracks and then I add quickly, "I'm not the only one, though. They pick on my friend Keiko and the other honors students, too. Especially anyone who is overweight." I hope Keiko and I are still friends, anyway.

He kicks at some dust on the laminate floor. "Do you know anyone who would want to hurt him?"

"Sure. But no one would want to *kill* him. Maybe just see him get a dose of his own medicine." Okay, that's not entirely true. There was a time I thought I'd love to see him dead, but when I actually *did* see him dead, it was a different story.

"Fair enough," the detective says. His mouth upturns at the corners, a dim smile. "Thanks, Charity. I might need to talk to you again at some point." He hands me his card. "If you think of anything else I might need to know, please don't hesitate to call."

As Dad drives, Mom grills me even more than Detective Bristow did. Aidan and I sit behind them. "Honey, why did you think Aidan would be in the football field?"

I shrug. "I don't know. I was frantic. And then I thought I heard something."

"Like what?" Mom asks.

"I'm not sure. A voice maybe? I thought I heard it behind the bleachers, so I went to check and that's where I found him."

Mom's phone rings. "Hello? Speaking." I can hear a man's voice on the other end. "We've been trying to get ahold of him, Officer Polk." She shoots an angry look at Dad. "He told Charity that he was at his friend Mike Palmer's house. No, I don't have that address."

Something is seriously wrong.

"You're welcome, officer. Thank you." She hangs up.

"So?" Dad says.

Mom's voice is shaky. "The police need to talk to Charles. He was one of the last people in contact with the boy before he died."

"Shit!" Dad strikes the steering wheel with his fist. "He better not be mixed up in this!"

Aidan seems to want to say something, but instead he closes his mouth and gazes out the window.

"Mom," I say, "if he doesn't already know, Charles can't know I'm the one who found the body, okay? He'll tell the kids at school and my life will be even more over." I wonder if anyone saw me talking to Mr. Reilly.

Mom's eyes wrinkle with sadness. "He won't know, baby." She reaches back and caresses my hand. "I love you so much."

"I love you, too, Mom."

As soon as we get home, Mom attempts to establish normalcy. I'm not hungry at all, but she heats up dinner for everyone else. Dad breaks out his tablet and iPhone in the living room, trying to find where Mike Palmer lives. He intermittently calls Charles, leaving increasingly angrier voicemail messages.

Aidan's presence is comforting, so I help him set the table, smoothing a fresh green tablecloth over the surface. When he puts all the silverware on the right, I explain that the knife and spoon go on the right on top of the napkin and the fork goes on the left. He pays close attention, like someone studying for a test. I'm careful not to touch him, but I want to more than anything. I stand close to him as he rearranges the silverware and I inhale that strange, sweet smell. The knots in my stomach start to relax.

Then we hear it: Charles' hooligan friends peeling out in the driveway, his footsteps crunching up to the front door.

Dad lurches to his feet when the door opens. "Give me one good reason I shouldn't give you to the police forever!"

Mom rushes past us, wiping her hands on a kitchen towel. "You're in serious trouble. I've had enough of your tough guy bullshit."

"Get off my back! What the hell is your problem, anyway?"

"Listen, you're going to cut that shit talk right now because I am not saving your ass this time. The sheriff wants to talk to you about the murder at your school," Mom says. "And since you didn't have the decency to return our calls, I can only conclude that you are mixed up in this somehow."

I move slowly into a position where I can see into the living room. Charles looks aghast.

"Me? Why would they want to talk to me? I didn't do anything!"

Mom grabs his arm, her eyes searing his face. "Do you think we're idiots? You know Darren Jacobs was killed today at school. What do you know about this? Tell me now before I drive you to the station."

Charles shakes, his mouth open, eyes wide. He notices me watching from the dining room. His look hardens and he points at me. "If anyone had a reason to kill him, it was her."

"Don't change the subject!" Dad barks.

"I'm not! Darren totally humiliated her today. She probably went Columbine on him."

Both Mom and Dad turn to look at me expectantly. I tremble. "He's lying. It was no big deal."

Charles is undaunted. "Darren was also leading the torch and pitchfork brigade on her club."

Mom explodes. "*Your sister did not kill anybody.* And you have set off my bullshit meter." She pulls the phone from her pocket and starts dialing.

"Okay! Okay, I'll tell you what I know. I just don't want to get into more trouble."

"You are already in more trouble," Mom says, phone to her ear.

Charles slumps, his expression helpless. "We were supposed to meet Darren after school."

Mom pulls the phone away from her ear and pushes the end call button. She focuses on him like a laser beam.

"We were supposed to meet him behind the bleachers so that Noah could sell him some molly. But then Zachary was all, 'Dude is a narc,' so we bailed. We were going to text him to cancel but we got distracted."

Mom's face is flushed with rage. "You're hanging out with drug dealers?"

She's coming totally unglued. "You are not only talking to the cops but you are busted forever."

Dad grabs him, mad as hell. "You think you're a tough guy? Let's go. Your Mom will take you."

"I can't narc out my friends!" Charles protests.

"You tell the truth," Mom yells. "No more. No less."

Charles' gaze drops to the floor.

Dad wraps his arms around me. I shed my stoicism, tears soaking his sweater.

I barely hear the front door open and shut as she and Charles leave.

Looking stricken, Aidan turns and stares out the window as if searching for something. Or someone.


After dinner, I spend the rest of the night in my room trying not to think about the blood. I wonder how long I can keep the secret. It feels impossibly heavy. It would help to tell a friend.

Maybe I could tell Michael?

I'm not nearly as close to Michael as I am—was—with Keiko. We're friends. Heck, his mom is friends with my mom. But there's this wall of mystery between us. He turns every serious question into a joke and never gives a straight answer. I just don't know how he'd react. And maybe that makes me hesitate. I don't think he'd betray me, but he's enough of a question mark that I'll have to find some other way to deal with the secret for now.

Mom and Charles eventually come home. They confer with Dad. The cops say Charles needs to stick around. For the first time in a long time I feel sorry for my brother. I can't believe he would have anything the do with this. I check online for news reports and find only one, but they don't say it was Darren. Everyone will figure it out soon, though, if they haven't already. They must have. Someone would notice immediately if he was missing, and they'd put it together.

Before I go to sleep, I wander to Mom and Dad's room, and knock on the door.

"Mom? Dad? Can I ask you a question?"

"Sure, my Power Puff. Come in." That's my dad. Did I mention he's a dork? "Are you okay?"

I close the door behind me. "Yeah. I'm okay," I lie. "I had the weirdest conversation with Aidan."

"Weird? What do you mean, weird?" Mom asks.

"Well, Aidan was telling me today about his dad. I wasn't sure I should believe him."

Mom and Dad both lean forward, hungry for any information about Aidan's family.

"I think his dad might be somebody important, even respected, but really dangerous. I'm worried about him. If we give him up, something terrible will happen to him. We can't let that happen. Can we?"

"Come here, sweetheart." Mom makes room for me on the bed. Dad reaches for a glass of water on the nightstand and swallows his medication for the night. He doesn't seem to be healing from that back surgery very well. They think I don't know, but I see how he moves and I Googled the names of the medicines he takes. He's in a lot of pain. "Sometimes when kids are severely abused, they make up stories to make their life seem more interesting than it really is. Aidan might be telling the truth about his dad being an important or powerful person. But he might be making his family sound better in some way to cover his pain. Are you okay? You've had a terrible shock today. I'll arrange for a counseling session, okay?"

I shake my head. "Do I have to? I just want to forget it. Aidan helped today, by the way. He's kind of strange, but he's really nice."

"He seems like such a sweet boy. If his family turns up, I'd love to throttle them. We think he's very far away from home because of his accent. He might have hitched a ride or two as far away as Vancouver. Or maybe he ran away from his family while they were visiting the States on vacation. We're not sure. Just don't get too attached, okay?"

"*Mom*, I'm not getting attached."

Dad lies back on his pillows, blinking.

I should leave them alone. I wrap my arms around her. "I'll see you guys in the morning."

Mom hugs me and kisses me on the forehead. For some reason, when she hugs me my chest feels like it's full of hot coals. The sadness floods back. "Good night." I kiss Dad and leave.

I tiptoe back to my room—not because I don't want to disturb anyone, but because I'm trying to hear my brother in his room. He's quiet. Maybe he's already asleep. Or he's sneaked out.

The sewing room door is open a crack. The light is on. I hear Aidan humming again. It's that Christmas carol. It's hypnotic. I'm drawn to the door opening. My feet take me there even though I don't want to go. I want to go back to my room and climb into bed. It's cool. And dark. I've forgotten about Charles. All I can think about is how Aidan's hand felt in mine. That silkiness. I can't resist peeking into his room.

Aidan's back is to the door. His hands are in front of his chest. He unbuttons his shirt and shrugs it off.

His pale, muscular back is carved up with long, angry scars. Like he's been brutally whipped.

I clamp my hands over my mouth to keep from gasping out loud and dive into my room.

# Chapter 8

Remember that disabled girl who recorded her sheriff father on a webcam as he beat her viciously for downloading video games? When I watched that viral video, I felt sick. My own father is so sweet. I think the angriest I've ever seen him was the night Charles was arrested for shoplifting. His face was sweating, his teeth clenched as we waited in the lobby of the jail. Once we got Charles home, he raised his voice and threatened to leave Charles in jail next time, but he never totally lost it like that dad in the video.

He tends to give in to my mother, who usually has the strongest opinions. But even she isn't explosive or violent. If I'm afraid of anything, it's the moment when she transforms from super-nice social worker into soulless, hyper-rational Terminator. Her mind is terrifying. I've had some smart teachers, but my mother is brilliant.

So, it's hard to believe a parent would be so cruel, but Mom has told me stories from work and I've heard whispers at school about it happening to other kids. It's real. But I have never seen anything up close and personal like what I saw last night on Aidan's back. Between Darren's eviscerated body and those scars, I had the worst nightmares I've ever had. I dreamed about goblins clawing at my window. I dreamed about cobwebs falling on me from the sky. I dreamed about so many horrible, painful things.

I can only imagine what Aidan must dream at night. No wonder he won't tell anyone where he's from.

And now Darren doesn't dream at all.

I wonder if my mom saw those scars. Maybe that's why she took him in. That and because he was so polite.

Now I can't look at Aidan without thinking about the ruined flesh snaking up his back.

It's the weekend. When Aidan isn't eagerly helping mom or dad with something like one of the servants on *Downton Abbey*, he sits in his room reading and humming Christmas carols.

He also watches TV, his jaw slack. Dad tries to show him episodes of the original *The Twilight Zone*, but Aidan asks only to watch things made in the last sixteen years. Dad keeps it light. *The Simpsons, Friends, Big Bang Theory.* As the laugh tracks trickle up the staircase, I wonder what he thinks.

Dad set up a spare computer in Aidan's room Saturday night. I overheard him explaining what a computer was and how to use it for his schoolwork. Despite Aidan's complete ignorance, he rapidly picked up the technology, especially email. Nobody at school uses email unless it's for school or parents. I only found the message that Aidan sent me Saturday night because I had to pick up some homework for Economics.

His email comprised just one line: *You have the best father in the world.*

I do. Because now we can talk without anyone knowing.

I wrote back. *He is, isn't he? Too bad he didn't give you a phone.*

Aidan replied almost immediately.

*Dear Charity,*

*It doesn't matter to me what device I use. I was wishing I could write you a letter, and here we are. You're the only person to whom I wish to speak. I know you've been through trauma, but when you're feeling better, I'd like to know more about you. Where you were born. What you like to eat. Your favorite books. These "shows" I was watching. Do you like them? If so, which ones? Can you recommend something? This is all very new to me, I'm afraid.*

*I hope you do not see this as an inquisition. Please tell me and I shall cease asking. You are kind, beautiful and intelligent. The last thing I wish to do is offend you.*

*With admiration,*

*Aidan*

Okay, he's still weird. And so is email. But does he like me? Is he trying to decide if he does? I'm so excited that I quickly reply.

*Dear Aidan,*

*I'm not offended! Not at all. I was born in San Diego. My parents moved to Los Angeles after Charles was born. I really miss L.A. I had more friends and everything was easier. My favorite food, no question, is pepperoni and mushroom pizza. LOVE IT. And chocolate, especially peanut M&Ms, but anything chocolate is good. My favorite TV show is Doctor Who. I'm sure if you ask my dad to show it to you, he will. Both he and Mom love it, too. But, like, new Who, not old Who. Old Doctor Who is kind of cheesy.*

I agonize how to sign off. Yours? (Too forward.) Sincerely? (Too formal.) Squealing Silently with Excitement Because You Might Like Me? (Too honest.) I decide to mirror his signoff.

*Also with admiration,*

*Charity Jones*

Aidan's reply is simple and elegant. The only other email I receive from him that Sunday afternoon.

*Dear Charity Jones,*

*Your candor is delightful. Thank you so much. I shall sleep better this evening knowing I have even a shred of your admiration. It means so much to me.*

*As ever,*

*Aidan*

I check online for updates on Darren's case. The story has spread to national news. If the police have any leads, they aren't saying anything.

*Slain student's body was discovered by another Oakwood High School student... The bloodied body of an Oakwood High School student... Police have been questioning students, but so far there are no suspects... Investigators are baffled by the brutal slaying of an Oakwood High School student.*

They aren't releasing any details yet. I find the latest news article, and at last they identify the body as Darren Jacobs. I then check Twitter and discover I was right: Charles told his friends who it was, and they spread the news over social media before the authorities even confirmed it with Darren's family. His poor parents.

That ghastly photo both haunts me and calls to me. I need to see it.

Connecting my iPhone to my computer, I turn it on and tap through the latest harassing text notifications, hoping against hope to see something from Keiko. (Nothing.) I then download my recent photos. Once I find the folder, I open the photo in an image viewer. It's somewhat murkier than the scene actually looked, shadows layering Darren's body. One hand clutches the ground as the other protects his gored stomach, his pants soiled with blood and mud.

Those once-mocking eyes are glazed with horror.

And then I see something I didn't see before. Hating myself, I zoom in until I can see the grisly details: Two bright blue orbs of light glimmer beyond Darren's body.

Watching me.

I must not have noticed when I took the picture because I was fixated on Darren's corpse. Could it be the animal that hurt him?

If so, why didn't it hurt me?

I'm probably experiencing a form of pareidolia. That's when people see significant forms in random images. Like the man in the moon. Or "the face" on Mars. Yet my skin crawls.

As if the eyes still watch me.

A thorough search online of Oak County's fauna turns up nothing with reflective blue eyes. If it hadn't been the middle of the day, I would guess it was an owl or a cat. Or maybe it was a possum, but the eyes are too large, too far apart. Now that I think about it, I wasn't shining a flashlight under the bleachers and it wasn't sunny. My phone camera didn't use a flash. So, maybe the eyes weren't reflecting light at all, but rather glowing…

Should I tell the police? But then I would have to explain this photo. I can barely explain this photo to myself, much less someone who might think I had something to do with the murder. They might think it's some kind of trophy or something.

Shivering with horror, I fall asleep with the light on, imagining a swarm of deadly insects pelting my bedroom window until their bodies crust over the glass.

# Chapter 9

Monday morning.

The bus wheels grind up the wet gravel, the smell of last night's rain blossoming from the asphalt. My stomach tightens as I step on board, Aidan climbing up behind me. He eyes the vehicle like Mr. Spock assessing some new alien species. Dad's old ski jacket consumes him, hiding the goofy new shirt that Mom bought him when she dragged him to Ross. Mom has no fashion sense, and apparently neither does Aidan. They came back with ugly green sweaters, hideous striped dress shirts, long johns, and baggy jeans. I think socks and underwear were in the equation, but thankfully she didn't parade those out.

They came back laughing. Mom looked smitten with his archaic jargon.

I have a feeling that the ride will be worse than usual.

I'm not wrong.

As I approach a seat with just a chunky, freckled freshman and his gym bag, he puts his arm over the bag as if it was a girlfriend. "No way," the boy says. "You can't sit here, Satan Claus." Someone snickers. "Your boyfriend can't sit here either."

I hadn't anticipated this kind of fallout from Thursday's demonstration, but someone's got to move over. I look to the seat across the aisle, this one with a boy and a girl who look bored, shoulders slumped, busily texting on their phones, trying to keep at least six inches between them because god forbid someone should think they were a couple. Many people are already sitting three to a seat. It's tight, but they could fit another person. They have to. The girl sits closest to the aisle. I try to meet her eyes, but she shakes her head, massive hoop earrings wagging.

I turn to another seat, where a sullen sophomore in skinny jeans sits with his legs spread, eyes closed as the ear buds implanted in his head make loud crunching noises. He doesn't acknowledge me when I talk to him. Not even when I touch his leg with my foot. He's pretending he can't hear me.

The bus driver yells, "Sit down so we can get going!"

"Oh, this is absurd."

Aidan says this. Aidan! I glance back at him, those eyes blazing with ire. He points at the freckled freshman. "*You*," he says with shocking authority. "Do you *really* want the new Xbox for Christmas? And a copy of your favorite game, *Road Kill*, which you've only played at your cousin Tyler's house?"

The boy gapes at Aidan as if he were an ancient Egyptian god.

The bus driver shouts, "Sit. Down!"

Aidan then turns to the girl with the hoop earrings. "And *you*—do you *really* want your father to buy you that bright yellow Volkswagen bug for Christmas? That is, if you pass your driver's test on this third try?"

The girl's eyes widen. "What? How did you…?"

"*Then move over. Both of you.*"

They scoot aside in unison. The freshman drops his bag to his feet. Aidan sits beside him, extending his hand to the seat created by the frightened girl, inviting me to sit. He turns to the boy. "Satan Claus?" Aidan looks away and laughs. "If you only knew."

I sit down. Aidan is freaking me out. Yet at this moment, he looks peaceful, even happy as he watches the scenery slip past. What just happened? Was it like the dinner table incident? Did he really know things about these two people? Or was it just bluster? He just learned about computers. How does he know about Xboxes? And of all things, what they want for Christmas? That commanding voice—it came out of nowhere.

Since ours was the last stop before school, we reach our destination twenty minutes later.

Charles isn't with us. His loser friends used to pick him up but they didn't always make it to school. After that day the truancy officer visited, everything changed—for a while, anyway. Dad usually leaves too early to take us to school, but today he took Charles because he's now forbidden to hang out with Noah. Aidan and I opted for the bus because it meant we got to sleep in later.

We pull up and everyone pours off the bus. Two police cars are parked along the front curb with a gray Mustang. A news van lurks in the parking lot, a reporter talking to the camera. Teachers wearing black armbands usher arriving students to the gymnasium. The assistant principal's voice echoes over the outdoor intercom. "Please join us in the gymnasium for first period. Attendance is mandatory."

Pulling up his hood, Aidan says nothing as we plod toward the gym. Girls dressed in black sob with Beth Addison outside the entrance, comforted by a number of broad-shouldered football players. They are too absorbed in their grief to notice us slipping inside with the torrent. I don't know how they're going to fit the entire school in here. Since I've been coming here, we've never had a full student assembly. I notice a couple of kids from the bus chattering and pointing at Aidan. He breaks away from me and moves to a section higher up on the bleachers. Maybe he's trying to draw attention away from me, but I can't shake the feeling that he's scouting the crowd.

My chest aches as I notice Keiko sitting with a couple of girls I don't know. I desperately want to reconnect with her. I slip my phone out of my pocket. The texts have already started. "You suck Satan" and "atheist bitch." I blow past those charming messages and compose a new one to Keiko.

*I'm sorry I hurt you.*

No response. She doesn't take out her phone.

I compose another text. Something that is sure to get her attention and tickle her curiosity.

*I know who found the body.*

Nothing. She doesn't even check her phone. It then occurs to me that her parents have probably confiscated it.

Crap. Now they'll know if they read it.

Mrs. Cartwright, our principal, speaks into a microphone. "Everyone take a seat so we can get started!" A lot older than my mom, yet somehow not nearly as intimidating, she towers over the spindly assistant principal, Mr. Landau, who stands at the doorway, directing stragglers. The first period bell rings. Beside Mrs. Cartwright is Detective Bristow wearing a dark brown suit and striped tie under his trench coat. Behind him are two police officers. I recognize one from Friday.

"Good morning, everyone," Mrs. Cartwright says. "I know that news gets around and that many of you already know about the tragedy, but for the rest of you I'm sorry to be the bearer of bad tidings. Darren Jacobs, one of our star athletes, passed away in a senseless act of violence this last Friday."

A low roar ripples through in the gymnasium. The drama queens swoon, people text madly on their smartphones, others merely gawk with disbelief.

"We're going to miss Darren very much. Some students are organizing a candlelight vigil for Thursday night. Check the website for event details. Today, with the exception of first period, we're having a regular school day but tomorrow is Veterans Day and the school will be closed. We have counselors in the office if you feel like you need to speak with someone. You can also talk to me, Mr. Reilly, or Mr. Landau. And do talk about this—with your friends, your family, your clergy. Right now, you might be in shock. This deeply affects all of us." Mrs. Cartwright looks troubled. I've never seen her so serious. "I want to introduce you to Detective Bristow from the Oak County Sheriff's Department. Listen very carefully to what he has to say. Your life might be at stake. Thank you." She hands the microphone to the detective.

"Good morning," he says, sounding exhausted. "I'm Detective Jim Bristow. First I want to say how sorry I am for your loss. It's a tragedy to lose a good friend, teammate, and fellow student who contributed so much to his school."

Clearly the detective never knew Darren. He was a mediocre student, a bully, and a closet druggie.

"As you probably read in the news, Darren Jacobs' body was found behind the bleachers on the sports field. We're conducting an investigation and we need your help. If you have any information about Darren's death, please do not hesitate to contact me or anyone else at the Sheriff's Office. Contact information will be distributed in your homeroom classes, including an anonymous tip line that you can call twenty-four-seven. Officers Wasnowski and Polk will be patrolling campus for the next few weeks.

"In the meantime, it is extremely important that you be alert and travel in groups. You have a beautiful school here with open hallways, surrounded by nature, but that makes it very hard to secure against threats. So, please follow some basic safety procedures. If you venture beyond the classrooms, do not walk alone. That's not just for the athletic teams and other folk who use the football field. That also goes for those of you who walk to and from school. Stay together. Stay safe. And if you see anything suspicious, contact a school official right away. Lastly, do not try to engage with a suspicious person or animal. If you feel threatened, call nine-one-one and get out of there. Darren was a big guy. I hear that he scored, what, seventy touchdown passes last season? And rushed almost four hundred and seventy yards? Yet he was no match for his assailant. No matter how tough you think you are, or how tempting it might be, disengage, okay? And call the authorities. Thank you."

He's not calling it a homicide. Maybe they're not allowed to say until they know for sure.

The photo. Should I show it to him? Maybe they know what has glowing blue eyes. But will I get into trouble for having taken the photo?

In homeroom, I fold up the flyer with the hotline number and stick it in my backpack. The detective's card is tucked in one of the zippered pockets. Mrs. Linklater announces that the Winter Dance will take place but not until the weekend after Thanksgiving, and that it will include a fundraiser for Darren's favorite charity—his youth group, Inspiration International.

I never go to dances. I'm especially glad I'm not going to this one.

Those glowing blue eyes and Darren's dead body haunt me through the day. A smoky gray sky promises a downpour as we head for homeroom. A crowd converges in the hallway. The only person who acknowledges I exist is Michael Allured.

"So, you staying safe with your mad nunchuk skills?"

He makes a noise that sounds like an asthmatic ninja whipping around invisible nunchuks.

"Michael, if I could wield nunchuks, I would have used them already on certain BFJs."

"True. Your lack of mad nunchuk skills is concerning."

And then he takes off. I have no idea what that was supposed to mean. Michael then sends me these odd texts:

> Is your Aidan friend in the mafia?
>> ?
> Or is he John Edward's secret love child?
>> ??!
> Personally, methinks he's related to Sherlock Holmes aka Benedict Cumberbutt.

Apparently Michael's hearing gossip from our fellow bus riders. On the bus this morning, I tried not to stare at Aidan's hair. He caught me looking and mouthed, "What?" I shrugged, feigning ignorance while I almost died of embarrassment. I then tried not to stare at his perfectly sculpted nose. It contrasts with the lazy waves of sable hair falling over his forehead.

This crush is ridiculous.

Mr. Reilly's class rolls around. Without their leader, Darren's followers fail to find a voice. Mr. Reilly appears more serious than usual, which is quite a feat.

"I've set aside the curriculum I'd planned for today in favor of something a little lighter." He approaches the chalkboard and picks up a piece of chalk.

"I realize it's a cardinal sin to talk about Christmas before Thanksgiving, but since we have entered the Industrial Age in our reading, let's talk about modern American cultural values and ideas that stem from that time period. A little history-lite, if you will. But I assure you it ties into what we've been studying."

He writes: *A Visit from Saint Nicholas*

Oh, great. Another one of Mr. Reilly's *tangents*. I'm pretty sure no one else talks about this stuff in their American history classes.

"The American poet Clement Clarke Moore published this poem anonymously in eighteen twenty-three. What else was happening that year? Anyone?"

No answer. He writes on the board: *The Monroe Doctrine.*

"In early December of that year, President James Monroe declares America's neutrality in European conflicts. Step-by-step, America continues to distance itself from the UK and Europe, further establishing its independence. Meanwhile, this poem single-handedly established Christmas culture in America, distinguishing it from British and European customs and traditions. To this day, this depiction of Saint Nicholas remains the dominant iconography for the American celebration of the holiday."

I recall Aidan humming Christmas music in his room. He must be loving this lecture. I glance at him and discover that he's slumped backward, arms crossed, his features locked in fury. I look away quickly. What could he possibly be so pissed about?

Mr. Reilly continues, "Can anyone tell me the origins of Christmas?"

One of the BFJs raises his hand. "It's a celebration of the birth of our Lord and Savior, Jesus Christ."

"That is a correct statement, but it is not the correct answer," Mr. Reilly says, much to my relief.

Another BFJ raises her hand. "But the word 'Christ' is in the word. You can't ignore that. There's this whole war on Christmas by people like you trying to deny that fact."

"I did not deny it, Ms. Barnsworth. I asked, what is the origin of the holiday? In other words, what else is happening at this time of year that humanity has celebrated?"

I raise my hand.

"Yes, Ms. Jones."

"The winter solstice. It was a time of feasting for ancient cultures. They'd slaughter their cattle so they wouldn't have to feed them during winter and eat the meat in preparation for the next four months of possible starvation."

"Very good."

Another BFJ complains. "Oh, just ask Satan. She's sure to tell you the truth. Not."

Mr. Reilly walks to his podium and scribbles something in his book. "Mr. Katz, you have detention. Bullying is not tolerated in my classroom. Report to the office after class immediately."

Gasps of disbelief. Even I can't believe that Mr. Reilly did that. The administration is definitely on the move. My cell phone buzzes with more texts. I turn it off.

Aidan raises his hand. He's learned the ritual. Mr. Reilly calls on him. "The feasting originally occurred at the ancient Roman festival of *Natalis Invicti*, also known as The Birth of the Unconquerable Sun. As for December 25 being about the birth of Jesus, some scholars claim it was first the birth date of Mithras, a god worshipped by a Roman cult that rivaled Christianity for the first four centuries. The birth of Mithras may or may not have been linked to *Natalis Invicti*—it might not be in December at all—but one thing is for certain: the word 'Christ' does *not* appear in the word 'Sunday,' which was a sacred day to Mithras and other sun worshipers long before Constantine the First declared Christianity to be the official religion of Rome."

He flashes me the biggest grin.

The classroom is silent.

I'm stunned, too. Not just because of that jaw-dropping response, but because no one has *ever* backed me up before. Teachers sometimes. Students never. Since I first arrived at Oakwood, I've felt like I'm from another planet. No one speaks my language.

I suddenly have a crush on Aidan so fast and so huge that it feels like a hockey player slamming into me. My heart swells so tight, I think my ribcage is going to explode.

Mr. Reilly grins, returning to the chalkboard. "Mr. MacNichol is correct." He then writes: *Myth. History.*

"Where does one end and the other begin? And who determines which is which?"

# Chapter 10

The day is about to end with AP English Literature and Composition for what promises to be a heavy discussion about *One Hundred Years of Solitude*. Mauricio Babilonia's yellow butterflies are already suffocating my thoughts. Or are they Aidan's butterflies? Is that what I imagine I hear at my window at night? Butterflies rather than bugbears?

But as I'm on my way to English, another text appears from Michael. *Can you come over to consci? NOW?!? Holy crap!*

The Consumer Science building is on the far side of campus at the border of the thick forest that hedges the northernmost part of the school. I might not manage to evade Officers Wasnowski and Polk patrolling, and I might get in trouble for being late to discuss the butterflies. Screw it. I take off for the Consumer Science building, a fire in my legs. It's a crazy day. Surely Mrs. Hohlwein will overlook a lapse or two.

I try to maintain a casual air, pretending I belong on *that* side of campus—the side where people take classes about baking, basic computer skills and setting up checking accounts. Why is Michael over here?

And why does he need me?

Officer Polk (or Wasnowski?) rounds the corner of my Economics class, which is halfway between English and Consumer Science. I can't control my face, and I wince when I see him, surprised. I notice for the first time the arsenal on his duty belt: gun, Taser, ammo clips, Maglite, handcuffs, pepper spray, baton. I keep walking, flashing him a weak grin that I hope says, *Hi. Sucks that you're here but glad you are.*

He passes with a nod.

Skirting the outer end of the ConSci building, I turn the corner and stop. I don't see Michael anywhere.

Is this a setup? I'm out of sight. Anyone wanting to jump me could do it here. Michael would never do such a thing. But what if they're forcing him or they've stolen his phone?

*It's a setup! Run!*

I spin around to head back to English when I hear Michael's voice.

"Hey! CJ!"

He leans out from the trees, scanning for teachers and cops. Two others trail him. Judy coughs. Leo makes faces, pinching the bridge of his nose. Nice to see those two got together after the meeting. Or did they? Or maybe she and Michael are together? Regardless, it looks like Judy's clicked with the guys the way I have, which makes me happy.

I dive into the forest with them.

"You won't believe this," Michael says, stomping into the foliage. "I wanted you to see it before The Expendables find it."

Prickly fir branches swipe our faces, damp needles dusting the grassy ground. The scent of broken flora underfoot soon gives way to an overwhelming stench. Leo and Michael raise their shirts over their faces like bandits, revealing their thermal undershirts. Judy just coughs more and pinches her nose. "Get ready," Michael says, voice muffled.

Covering my nose with my arm, I nod. We step into a tight cluster of cedars. Michael points at a half-eaten possum on the bloodstained ground, lips drawn back and teeth bared, flies crawling over its gaping belly.

I shrug. "Nasty. Looks like bobcats got it."

Michael shakes his head. He steps between the trees and points at another mutilated possum. And another. Four altogether, two draped over the branches.

"Bobcats don't do this."

"People do this," Leo says. "Sick people."

He's right. A person like the one who killed Darren.

We pull away from the site. Michael continues. "What can you tell us about Aidan?"

"What?"

"Your *friend*," Leo says.

"Is this why you texted me? Silly me. I thought maybe it was because you respected my thoughts about this or something."

Michael kicks a pinecone out of his path. "No, no! I totally respect your thoughts! But don't you think it's weird? Your friend shows up, sees you humiliated by Darren, and then said jock is ripped apart?"

"How do you know he was ripped apart?"

Leo holds up his phone to show me the news article online.

*The Oak County coroner reports the Oakwood High School student died of massive blood loss due to deep lacerations to his throat and torso.*

"Something is stalking the school," I say as I take a hard look at the forest around us. Leaves quiver as the wind hisses through the branches.

"I don't trust these meatballs with badges," Michael says. The others nod. "They had all weekend to scour the school and crime scene. If they didn't find this, they won't find anything."

"Agreed," I say, thinking about Detective Bristow and the photo that's haunting me. "Maybe we should hunt this thing. Before it hunts us down, one by one."

Michael stops. "Us? The four of us. Are you crazy?"

"Maybe."

The branches wave in the wind as it picks up. I picture Darren's ruined body and the eyes under the bleachers. It isn't a person. Not even a sick person. It's a *thing*. And some primitive, caveman instinct surges deep in my skull, hollering to preserve hearth and harvest against the predator. Is this what my father feels when he's designing one of his war machines? I may never know. But right now, I want nothing more than to stop this thing before it gets another chance at me or my family.

"We don't have to confront it," I continue. "Let's just see if we can get more information about it." That's what my mouth says, as my brain screams: *Kill it. Kill it with fire!*

"How do we do that?" Judy asks, pushing her hands deep in her coat pockets. The chill cuts my cheeks.

"We monitor the local news. Listen in the hallways. Pick up anything we can. Dog injuries. Missing cats. Anything. It could be biding its time before it kills another student." Turning to Michael, I continue. "And it's *not* Aidan, okay? He's sweet and kind and eats lasagna and spaghetti. Not possum. Even if he had wanted to for some reason, he didn't have any opportunity to kill Darren. He was talking to Mr. Reilly after school. I know. I saw him." A slight lie. Also, wouldn't Aidan have had blood all over him? I don't even want to go there…

Michael looks rueful. "I'm sorry I cast suspicions on your friend. He's your foster brother now, isn't he? I had to ask, though."

"I know," I reply.

It's quiet for a moment. Michael and Leo pull the shirts from their faces.

"I predict tomorrow numerous kids are pulled out of school," Leo says.

"Would your parents pull you out?" Judy asks. "Mine might let me do online school, but I doubt it. There really aren't any other schools to go to up here."

Michael shakes his head. "We're trapped here, dear friends." A drizzle passes through the branches onto us. "Maybe there's a beast," he quotes, "maybe it's only us."

*Lord of the Flies*. Jesus, he's scaring me more than I already was.

Mrs. Hohlwein is not remotely happy that I'm late, but she grudgingly lets me in without a write-up when I whisper that I was in the restroom having "stomach problems." She proceeds to grind away at the history of Columbia and how the story represents history repeating itself. That's all I hear, thanks to the terrible images of death in the forest and Darren's body. Eventually they give way to the crush rumbling in my head. A thought can't cross from one side of my head to the other without bumping into Aidan. How does he know the things he seems to know? Maybe he's a genius like Sherlock Holmes who can guess things about people based on subtle physical clues. He's a lot nicer than Sherlock on TV. That's for sure.

My concerns melt away when I see him waiting to board the bus. He drops his backpack and peels off his heavy jacket.

"So, how do you know so much about Constantine and Mithras?" I ask, sidling up to him in line.

Aidan smiles enigmatically. "I'll send you an email."

I feel lightheaded. It's a crush, I tell myself. Nothing more. I always fall for the smartest guy in school. But I should know better. No one ever likes me back. He was just being nice to me when I was having a horrible day. And those emails. Just nice.

No one gives us any trouble on the bus home. Everyone is too busy talking about the murder or texting with friends. I sneak peeks at Aidan as we ride, sitting across the aisle from one another. I want to ask him what he's thinking, but I kind of like just being near him.

The sun burns through the clouds, spilling golden light on the gravel road and soggy leaves that litter the surface. The whole world brightens, which almost makes me sad because I love the rain, despite what it does to my hair. The trees, mailboxes and house eaves still drip with dampness. The storm is merely napping. When the bus drops us off at the end of our road, I walk beside Aidan. "Why aren't you wearing your jacket? It's freezing!"

"On the contrary, it's unbearably hot! Remember, it's much colder where I'm from."

"Which is?"

"Nice try, Charity Jones."

"Well, maybe you're sick. Stop. Hold still. I'll take your temperature."

We stop at the roadside, cool breezes licking our noses. I reach up and put my hand on his forehead. His skin feels comfortably warm, not fevered. "Not bad. Not on death's door, anyway." I can't take away my hand. Instead, my fingers brush his impossibly soft cheek. The black pinpricks of his pupils float in the ghostly blue of his irises as he watches me. He gently grasps my hand. *I've gone too far.*

Aidan closes his eyes and continues to move my fingertips over his face, onto his neck and into his hair. He brings my fingertips at last to his lips and kisses them sweetly. He then turns over my hand to warm my cold palm with his moist mouth. I feel like I'm going to die, heart racing, breathing shallow. I have never felt anything this intense in my life. I raise my other hand to his face. He takes it, kissing that one as well. He releases my hands and I stroke his neck. His skin might be silky, but he is solid muscle underneath. About five thousand volts of pure bliss course through my body as he bends, hesitating, his lips finding mine. I have never been kissed before, not like this. In Woodland Hills, a boy in junior high liked me but I didn't like him. Still, I'd wanted to know what making out was like. His slobbery lips smushed mine until my mouth ached. I hated it. After that, I wasn't sure I ever wanted to kiss anyone again.

But *this*. He brushes his lips against mine, like he's not sure where they should land. I'm not, either. All I know is to tilt my head. And I do. I bring my mouth to his, and time slows. All of my questions about him dissolve as I reach up and wrap my hands behind his neck, burying my fingers in his wavy hair. He slips his hands under my coat and caresses my back, pulling me against him.

I have never felt anything so perfect as this.

# Chapter 11

*Dear Charity,*

*Back home, all I had were books. No television or radio. Just Father's library, which is set deep into the ice, endless shelves packed with yellowing tomes. Most are stolen. Many are beautiful. Surrounded by snow my whole life, I've had little contact with your world except through these books. Your friend Michael called me Sherlock today. While I'm not entirely sure why he did that, I was relieved to know who Sherlock even was. I'm confused whenever anyone speaks to me. But Sherlock... I've read those stories. They're in my father's library. (Michael called me something else. Benedict? Do you know what he's talking about?) Sherlock Holmes is my hero. I love his mind.*

*Constantine. Julius Caesar. The Gallic Wars. Scholarly commentary about the Gospels. Colonialism and industrialism. The Phoenicians, ancient Carthage, the Saxons. I've read about these and much more. The great wars of Earth's history rage in my memory as if I'd been there, these history books are so much a part of me. The occasional journal drifts in, often damaged by bad weather or temper. But I read everything. Unlike my brothers and sisters, I love to read. I might be the only one who can read besides father. I can thank my departed mother for that.*

*I spent as much time as possible in the library. My refuge. Sometimes I'd hide from my father there, crouching behind the bookshelves as he hunted for me, lash in hand, howling my name until he gave up.*

*After each vernal equinox, I'd sneak to the surface to bask in the ribbon of sunlight as it struck the bluish-white snow. Everything dazzles like diamonds, even the forest of wind-carved ice sculptures that surrounds our compound, dimpled by shadows as the sun emerges from its long hibernation. When I was little, I imagined these icy giants were guardians of our strange life, shielding us from the sight of the great red Russian ships cutting through the ice. Not that anyone would bother us. Everyone loves Father. Later, as Father's abuses worsened—or did I simply become more aware of them?—I realized that the giants were our gaolers. I begged them every night to let me slip past their ranks to freedom. But no luck.*

*And then one day they did. After the vernal equinox, I escaped, leaving behind the library. I found some Canadian scientists who were happy to bring me to the mainland.*

*But thanks to your father, I now have a greater library than ever before. After I finished reading my textbooks a few days ago, I started reading online newspapers, government websites, scholarly journals, even articles about my father.*

*The lies and misrepresentations are worse than I ever imagined. I try not to think about it.*

*In fact, I try not to think about him or my family at all. Instead, I marvel at my new life. The raindrops beading on your eyelashes are far more beautiful than the glistening snow drifts. I have never met anyone like you, Charity Jones. And I never will again should The Fates separate us. Whatever you ask, whatever pleases you, anything it takes for us to be together, just tell me and I will do it.*

*With great affection,*

*Aidan*

Tuesday. Veterans Day.

I forgot to turn off my alarm. I was up half the night either crazed over Aidan or struggling with what to do about the photo. But even as I close my eyes again and drift back to sleep, I have made up my mind.

As I eat breakfast downstairs, I consider how to answer Aidan's email. It's bizarre. I don't know how much of it is true, but how can I resist his final declaration? I want to rush to him this morning, but I can't. Yesterday, Aidan wanted to kiss upstairs, but I cautioned him that my parents would be upset if they knew we liked each other. If they find out, they won't let him live here anymore. This would have to be a secret. And we would have to be very careful of Charles. Aidan didn't understand but said he would respect my wishes.

Mercifully, Aidan is tucked in his room studying when I emerge this morning. Charles is doing god-knows-what, but at least he's quiet. Even though Mom shouldn't be working, she's out on an emergency call. Dad's at work. I go into the garage and, keeping my voice low, I call the Sheriff's office. Detective Bristow isn't in, so I leave a message.

"I have something to tell you," I say. "It might be nothing or it might be very important. But I don't have a car or license. So, if you want to come by, that would be awesome."

And then I wait.

I spend the afternoon in nervous distraction, expecting the detective to call me back right away, but he doesn't. I'm counting on him coming by *before* my parents get home so that they won't know about the photo.

But he doesn't.

I have zero appetite. I mean, nothing. You could put a mushroom and pepperoni pizza in front of me and I wouldn't eat it. I have never lost my appetite like this before. At dinner, Mom watches me poke at her soggy salad when Aidan makes a surprising announcement.

"Mr. and Mrs. Jones, I would like to get a job."

Charles chokes on his mashed potatoes. Mom drops her fork and pounds on Charles' back. Dad is the only one who seems unfazed. "Do you think you can handle a job in addition to school? You've got a lot to catch up on."

"Actually, Mr. Jones, I'm well ahead already. And I was thinking of asking to take more advanced maths and perhaps physics. I'm only slightly behind in chemistry. I was hoping perhaps you could help me with that tonight."

"Sure." Dad gestures at me with his fork. "How many classes do you have with Aidan?"

"Only American History. And I think he's going to get pantsed. He's worse than I am." I grin conspiratorially.

"Pantsed?" Aidan looks troubled.

"Teased for being smart," I say. "They call it pantsing because they pull down your pants to embarrass you when you embarrass them."

"But they were wrong. And Mr. Reilly wasn't correcting them. If anyone should be *pantsed* it should be them or Mr. Reilly."

Dad laughs. "Evelyn, are you sure he isn't really yours?" He isn't just referring to Aidan's pasty Celtic complexion. Although Mom is what the Brits would call "ginger" and Aidan is more black Irish, I do see a certain clan resemblance.

Mom shakes her head, amused. "Like attracts like. We're not the most diplomatic bunch, are we?"

Dad sips his wine, thinking. "I'll have a talk with your teachers about making sure you're properly placed. If they think you can handle it, maybe you could work part-time at the Gold Country Christmas tree farm. It's within biking distance."

Charles drops his silverware onto his plate, glowering. "Dad, *I* want to work at the Christmas tree farm."

"Your job is to ace your classes, and you've got a long way to go. Besides, you're not old enough."

"I'm fifteen!"

"And your grades aren't good enough. If you get your grades up by the end of the semester, we'll talk about a job next year."

Charles shoves his plate away, rocking the table. "Bullshit!" He stands up and glares at Aidan, but doesn't say anything. I know that look. It's a dire warning.

"You! Settle down. Now!" Dad says. Charles stays, but looks like he's about to morph into a tornado. Dad continues. "What do you think, Evelyn?"

"I need to find out what the legal implications are. We don't even know how old you are, Aidan, or if you're from this country. Why do you want to work?"

Aidan's face saddens, but he remains polite. "I have always worked. It's just proper. And I'd like to have my own money. To not be a burden to you." Aidan's eyes land on me. There is nothing in this world except those eyes, those lips and his delicate skin. My breath thickens. I can't look away.

Mom sighs. "That's very thoughtful, sweetie, but you're not a burden."

There's a knock on the door. Everyone looks surprised but says nothing.

Dad answers. It's the detective. Dad invites him in.

If Aidan is worried, he doesn't look it.

Dad and the detective enter the family room.

"I'm so sorry. I didn't mean to interrupt your dinner," Detective Bristow says. He looks exhausted.

Charles yelps, "I didn't do anything!"

"Um, actually, I need to speak with Charity."

Crap.

Mom raises her eyebrows at me. "Is there something you want to tell us?"

Fingering the phone in my hoodie pocket, I reassure her. "It's okay, Mom. I need to talk to Detective Bristow." I look at the detective. "Alone."

"Are you sure? I'm right here, you know."

"Mom! It's okay. And if it's not, I know where to find you." I force a smile.

Dad drops his fork. "What on earth?"

"It's fine," Mom tells him. "She's not been Mirandized and she's not a person of interest." Mom looks tired. "Let me know if you need me, sweetheart."

Smelling of aftershave, coffee and sweat, the detective follows me out to the garage. "What are those?" he asks, pointing at the robots in the corner of the garage. I tell him about the robotics competitions, showing him the extensive electronics and equipment, but anxiety dampens my normal enthusiasm. He seems impressed nonetheless.

He's not a jerk, but he *is* a police officer. He could arrest me right now, just for wasting his time. "Detective Bristow, I just want to tell you first that I'm not sure what scares me more—the thought of what's going to happen if anyone at school finds out that I found Darren's body, or the thing I'm about to show you."

"Wait—you want to *show* me something? Does your mom know about this?"

I shake my head. "It'll only scare her more than she is already. Do I have to tell her?"

He shrugs. "It's up to you." He points back inside the house. "Was that Aidan MacNichol, the runaway?" There's something about the way he says the word "runaway" that makes me feel protective of Aidan. "Was he at the dinner table?"

"Yeah. But he's very nice. I mean, he's a little weird, but he's okay. And he's doing really well at school." He's also intoxicating, but Detective Bristow doesn't need to know about that, either.

The detective grins. "I'm glad to hear it. So, what was it that you wanted to show me?"

I take the phone out of my pocket. Detective Bristow's face lights up.

"I know this is super weird," I say. "But when I found Darren's body, I didn't think anyone would believe me. My parents used to never believe me when I told them things happening with Charles, so I guess I have a complex about that. Anyway, even though it was gross, I took a picture. And then when I was looking at it later thinking I'd delete it, I discovered something odd about it."

The detective really looks interested now. I call up the photo from my photo stream and hand the phone to him.

"There's something in the background under the bleachers. Its eyes are reflective, I think. Do you see the blue? I don't know anything with eyes like that. A cat? Aren't they usually green? Maybe it's an owl, but the eyes are too large. Do you see that hulking shape in the shadows? It's more like a small person."

He focuses on the photo, zooming in, making it larger with each sweep of his fingers. Eyes widening. Sweat beading at his temple. Lips parting. Without taking his eyes off of the photo, he asks, "Have you told anyone about this?"

I feel a wave of relief that he hasn't dismissed the photo out of hand, but panic then surges through me. "No. Why?"

He types on my phone.

"What are you doing?"

"Emailing myself a copy. It's good to have on file a photo taken before everyone arrived." The whites of his eyes remain wide.

"What is it, Detective Bristow? I'm really scared."

"I don't know yet." He hands me back the phone. The phone makes the "sent mail" tone. "But, Charity, this photo is evidence in a homicide investigation. You can't tell anyone about it. If you do, you could jeopardize our investigation. And if we find out, you'll be in major trouble. Do you understand?"

I nod.

"Good. You're a very smart young woman. Thanks so much for your help."

"Sure," I squeak.

He charges out of the garage. I follow him. In the house, the whole family stirs from the table as the detective rushes to the front door.

"Thank you, everyone. Thanks, Charity. Good night," is all he says coolly as he exits.

I chase after him. He slips inside his gray Mustang, lights and engine jumping to life. "It's what killed him, isn't it?"

The detective says nothing and drives off.

I hold myself together just long enough to excuse myself from dinner. I feel the darkness at my back, snarling and snapping. Behind the closed door of my bedroom, my face cracks with fear. Whatever killed Darren was right there. It could have killed me, too.

And it's still out there.

# Chapter 12

The next morning. Wednesday. In the kitchen, I cram a piece of toast with peanut butter and jelly in my mouth, trying to get out of the house. Aidan nibbles on buttered toast. Charles makes himself a sandwich. He's probably grateful that he isn't the target this morning.

Mom is sulking because I won't tell her whatever I told Detective Bristow. "You can tell me what's going on, honey. It's okay."

"I'm not in trouble, Mom. I just remembered something I'd forgotten to tell him on Friday. He told me not to discuss it with anyone, okay? Please."

"If that's all, then okay. Don't forget that I can help."

*No, Mom. You can't. No more than you can protect me from whatever is out there.*

Dad lays a hand on her arm and kisses her cheek hard. "Damn, you're beautiful when you're mad." He winks at me. He knows how it is to have Mom the Lawyer barking at you. "Let's get out of here."

Mom bristles, glaring at him for undermining her. "We have *a lot* to talk about."

I am dying to touch Aidan every moment in the car on the way to school today, as Dad insists on driving us three. I ride shotgun, with Aidan sitting behind me. *Dying.*

School happens without me. I drift from classroom to classroom, my brain far off in Aidanland, dreaming of snow giants, a cavernous library, and Russian ice ships sailing to Greenland. If anyone is harassing me, I don't notice.

I feel a faint pang when I see Keiko. I miss her but not like I did. Not like I should. She snatches glances at me as I pass. I wonder if she ever got my texts. I feel a prick of regret as I realize I never want anyone to know I found Darren. Not even Keiko.

"I want to show you something."

Aidan and I are in the driveway. We've spent the last half hour somewhere next door on the Burnetts' wildly forested property, picking through the blackberry bushes, hopping over puddles and snogging. (I like that word. I got it watching *Doc Martin* with Mom. It's the perfect word for kissing.) Maybe it would be safer to lock ourselves in my bedroom, but that feels ten times more dangerous.

But now it's time that he met my best friends.

I tell him to put his hands over his eyes. "Do *not* peek!" I yell. It takes several minutes as I fly around my room and the garage looking for remotes, but I'm finally ready. "Okay," I say at last, having arranged everything outside. "You can look now!"

Aidan uncovers his eyes and looks confused at the two robots sitting before him on the gravel.

I introduce them. "First, meet Mr. Spotty." Using my remote, I make Mr. Spotty roll around Aidan in a figure-8 with the other robot. His collapsible, crane-like body extends upward to his full height of four feet; his boxy head is perched on a platform atop the extension bars. He stops in front of a wide-eyed Aidan.

"Salutations!" Mr. Spotty says. His head turns slightly, as if looking over Aidan's shoulder, and his body follows. "Danger! Danger!" The motor whirrs ominously as Mr. Spotty cranks back his loaded firing arm and fires a tennis ball into the air, smashing into a tree branch across the road.

Aidan backs away quickly.

"It's okay. He's completely under my control." I collapse Mr. Spotty's body about one-third and move him back in line.

Miss Yoyodyne moves forward a few steps, her wide, articulated legs carrying her smoothly as she walks. Her head is a round black sphere with a white plastic hood. While I make some of my robot parts, most of them come from discarded toys and broken appliances. I sometimes beg Mom and Dad to buy me more sophisticated pieces. Rarely, Dad can even get a spare from work. But many parts for Miss Yoyodyne came from a movie studio through my friend and *first* teammate Mark Kabuto. Mark's dad was a prop master for a couple of major science fiction movies. A lot of the material he gave us wasn't strong enough, but some pieces worked very well. While Mr. Spotty looks vaguely like a retractable desk lamp, Miss Yoyodyne more closely resembles a robot in a Japanese sci-fi movie.

"Pick up that rock at your feet," I instruct Aidan. He does. "Now offer it to her."

Aidan watches the robot like a rattlesnake, but he does as I tell him. Miss Yoyodyne strolls up to him and takes the rock from his hand with her two fingers and opposable thumb. She then comes to me and drops the rock in my hand. Like Mr. Spotty, she's a one trick pony, but very good at what she does. We had to master that particular motion in our last competition—picking up a small item. But Miss Yoyodyne's dexterity is ten times better.

"You make toys?"

"They're not toys," I say, annoyed. "They're robots. It's what I do. Remember? I told you about it during the lockdown. And lots of times since."

I send Miss Yoyodyne back to Aidan. "Go ahead. Shake her hand." The robot extends her hand and Aidan takes it. They shake like good comrades.

"You did that?"

"Not exactly. She has a program and a sensor to detect the handshake."

He looks deeply puzzled.

"I have one more person for you to meet. She kind of has a split personality, so to speak." I'm so excited, I nearly miss the switch on the console, which was a pain in the butt to hack, let me tell you. "Aidan, I'd like to meet Nikita. Nikita? Will you come out?"

From the open garage door fly three quadcopters. They resemble small helicopters, but with four separate rotor blades. I control them with my motion-controlled game console, guiding them with my hands. There's a way for them to fly indoors using GPS. I just haven't figured out the algorithms yet. Aidan watches with awe. The Nikitas fly over him in formation, swooping and tumbling at my command. They weren't hard to make, but they are hard to control. They should be autonomous, but I guess that's what college is for, right? I've posted videos of each of them on YouTube. No one believes a sixteen-year-old girl made these. I had to turn off the video comments because they were so nasty. It makes me really mad.

"I named her after that old French movie, *La Femme Nikita*, because Nikita lives different lives—although, that's technically only two, I guess."

Aidan watches with awe as I land the Nikitas in front of me. "Is this your magic?" he asks. "I didn't think anyone had magic here."

"It's not magic. It's math." I frown at him. "Magic isn't real. Math is, and almost anyone can learn it. Math and physics."

Aidan's face is a storm of silence. "*You* are magic," he says at last, taking my hands. "You are the single most amazing person I have ever met. You're not only beautiful and funny, but you're a genius. How are you even possible?"

"You're amazing, too," I say quietly. "More than I can say."

Aidan squeezes my hands. "Charity, I want to ask you something."

Oh, no. What now?

"May I…can I take you…to the dance?"

I squint at Aidan, not comprehending.

"Are you all right?" he asks.

I nod.

"I did this incorrectly." He looks pained. He lets go of my hands and starts pacing. "I'm so sorry, Charity. I'm a blithering idiot. I just thought that I could somehow pick up the nuances of custom and carry on as if—"

"Stop already! You didn't do anything wrong." I pick up the Nikitas' quadcopters and put them in the garage. Aidan won't look at me. "It's just that we can't go to the dance together. I told you, my folks won't let you live here if they think we're into each other. And I can't stand the idea of them taking you away. Besides, you might wind up in a foster home where really bad things happen. And believe me," I said, guiding Miss Yoyodyne back to her perch, "you could wind up in some pretty horrible places. They could even send you to juvenile hall until you decide to cooperate with the police about your immigration status. You think you've got problems with customs?" I give the last word rabbit ears. "Just wait until you get thrown into a cell with some redneck kid who punches you to death for talking like a Jane Austen character. At least you're safe here."

Aidan's gaze falls to the ground. "What's wrong with Jane Austen?"

I sigh at him.

"I'm the heir to a vast empire, and I can't take someone I like to a dance." He kicks the gravel, spraying rocks everywhere, and then seems to immediately regret it. "You're right. I'm lucky. And I'm being childish. I can't jeopardize what I have."

Suddenly, it occurs to me that I might be wrong. There might be a way. "Maybe we could spin it."

He looks up at me, questioning.

"Maybe we could put it to Mom and Dad in such a way that it doesn't sound like we're going as boyfriend and girlfriend. You could be more of an escort. They might go for that. Of course, I've never been to a dance before and have always said that I hate them, so that might set off some alarms. But we could try it."

Aidan brightens.

"However," I continue, "only under one condition."

He raises an eyebrow. "Only one? What is it, pray tell?"

I run my hands over his ridiculous striped shirt. "Let me show you how to dress. You'll fit in better. And the better you fit in, the less likely anyone is going to find you here."

The air is cooling, but my heart swells against my ribcage. Aidan has a fire in his eyes.

"So, does this mean we might go to the dance? If we 'spin' things to your mother and father?"

"Yes."

"And if I allow you to renovate me?"

I laugh. "You mean make over—"

He embraces me with a fiery kiss.

I talk through the smooches. "So, that means yes, right?"

He nods, still kissing me.

A car erupts from the road beyond, startling us. We jump apart. The car turns into our driveway and is about to run over Mr. Spotty…

I cry out.

Aidan thrusts out his hand in a "stop" gesture.

The car *crashes* to a halt just two feet in front of Mr. Spotty. The sudden stop kills the engine. Inside, Charles and his friends shout, tumbling in their seats. The car grill is crumpled.

The driver's eyes widen with panic. It's Zachary. He throws open the driver's door, cursing. "Motherfucker! What did we hit?"

I scoop up Mr. Spotty and carry him back to the garage. "It's what you almost hit. You need to slow down."

Everyone piles out of the car. Charles throws an accusatory look at Aidan. "You did something! You made a motion with your hand. Like you were triggering something!" He searches the dirt and gravel for this alleged trigger.

"I was signaling for you to stop," Aidan says calmly. "That was all."

"But something pushed back, asshole!" Charles clenches his fists.

Zachary examines the front of the car, head in hands. "It's wrecked!" The damage extends across the front of the vehicle. "How is that possible? We didn't hit anything. My old man is going to kill me! Fuck!" He kicks the wheel.

Noah just shakes his head and repeats, "Fuuuuuuck!"

"You probably crashed your car driving drunk and are just now noticing the damage," I say, not fully accepting this explanation, either. Regardless, I hope they didn't see us kissing. If I weren't an atheist, I'd be praying.

"You probably rigged some kind of barrier or something, techno-bitch," Noah sneered. "It must've retracted into the ground, or some shit. We all felt it." He kicks at the ground with the toe of his military boot, looking for the imaginary mechanism. I then remember that Charles is forbidden from seeing Noah. Fingering the phone in my pocket, I realize that, if by some chance they did see us kissing, I can blackmail them.

"That's insane!" I pull my phone out, hands shaking. "If you don't leave, I'm going to call the police. I'm pretty sure you have to report damage over five hundred dollars, and I'm also sure you don't want anything to do with the cops. Correction: anything *more* to do with the cops."

"Have fun with Bitch Face," Zachary says to Charles, climbing back in the driver's seat. "And the freak."

Charles stalks off into the house as the car peels away. Before he goes inside, he turns back to Aidan. "I'm gonna find out what happened. And when I do, you're gonna be sorry you ever stepped foot in this house."

# Chapter 13

*Dear Aidan,*

*Thanks for being cool about Charles. My brother has anger management and impulse control problems. He's supposed to be taking medication but he doesn't always. He was arrested for stealing last year. Despite being on probation, he hangs out with the school drug dealers. If Charles lands in jail again, Mom and Dad are going to lose it. What's worse is that I always seem to make him mad. So far, he's all bark and no bite, but I dread the day something pushes him over the edge.*

*Your old life sounds so lonely and terrifying. I now understand why you ran so far to get away from your father. I mean, really far—it sounds like you lived in Greenland or Iceland. I won't tell anyone, of course. It does explain a lot, however.*

*I'm sorry we have to sneak around. Losing you would be pretty much the worst thing that could ever happen to me.*

*Yours,*

*Charity*

It's Thursday. A week since Aidan first came to live with us. Keiko's birthday is this weekend and I have a plan.

With everything that's been going on, I miss my best friend more than ever. I want to tell her how that first kiss felt, to gossip about his skin and hair and startling intelligence. I want to complain about calculus and Mrs. Stewart, to hear about her Driver's Ed lesson. It's only been a week, but I already miss hearing about her Golden Retriever, Jackson, and the crazy things she overhears from her room when her Mom's bible study group meets downstairs. I have no one to complain to about my hair. It's the exact opposite of Keiko's, which is as smooth and flat as silk (which she hates). I could complain about it online to other mixed girls (and I do), but it's not the same.

Keiko isn't a citizen. We don't talk about it much, but I can tell she's worried about her future. Even if she makes it to MIT and gets the degree she wants, unless she and her parents become citizens, she might not get hired. She might have to return to Japan to work.

This morning, the administrative building swarms with parents trying to remove their children, lobbying for teachers to carry weapons, freaking out (legitimately) about Darren's coroner report.

In the swarm, I tie three foil balloons to Keiko's school locker and attach a card.

*Happy birthday, Keiko!*
*Love, CJ*

Okay, so, I'm not very creative. Sue me. (Actually, my hair is kind of creative this morning. I styled it in a crescent roll at the base of my neck. I like it a lot.) Dad and I bought the balloons last night, and he then brought us here early so that we could tie up the balloons before she arrives. Aidan buries his nose in his chemistry book as he waits around the corner. He's wearing one of Dad's old black sweaters. He absolutely hates it and almost refused, but I told him that his eyes are now so stunning in contrast that he's irresistible. That convinced him to keep the sweater. That, and our deal.

My phone buzzes. It's Michael.

Data for you techno-ninja!
    Cool. What?
Two dogs killed last night. Maybe mountain lion or coyote. Got the kill addresses.
    Mountain lion? Again?
Right? But not impossible. More likely to attack a pet than a human.

Michael texts me the two addresses and I map them. That area looks familiar.

Both addresses are really close to Keiko's house.

"Isn't there a helium shortage?" Aidan asks. "Should we be using it for fun?"

"Keiko is worth it."

The sky drizzles on the school, but the foil balloon bouquet rises safely beneath the building overhang covering the lockers. They're shrinking and sagging a bit because it's cold, but when she brings them inside, they'll return to normal. The foil should resist the rain pretty well.

Buses and cars are arriving. I ditch the lockers, wondering if I should warn Keiko about her dog. Aidan wanders off to first period. I hide around the corner from the lockers, listening to the commotion about the balloons until Keiko herself arrives.

"Oh, wow!" she says. "You guys shouldn't have!"

"We didn't," someone replies. A pause. "Who's CJ?"

The cacophony of students swells in the hallway. Then someone says, "You're letting them go?"

My balloons drift over the school, wrinkled and forlorn. Someone throws a rock at one. It hits, pushing the balloon into a tangle of jagged tree branches.

I can't even look at Keiko in AP Calculus. I hate her. I pretend that it was that other CJ whose heart she broke as I slide into my seat at the back of the room. I stew in a black fog until I see Aidan in American History. I want to run away with him, to flee this joke of a school and the thing that's stalking us. We both need to run away from home. But we're trapped here.

Later, I text Michael.

*Let's form a patrol tonight. I have a plan.*

Mom and Dad wave as I leave the house. "Tell Michael's folks we said hi!" Mom says.

They think Michael, Leo, Judy, and I are going to Darren's vigil at school. Michael's old yellow Honda idles in the driveway. Leo gets out and lets me ride shotgun so he can sit with Judy. We all wear dark clothing, thick boots, and gloves. We look like a quartet of geek thugs.

Aidan has a job interview tonight. The owner of the Christmas tree farm told Dad he might pay Aidan under the table for some labor. I didn't tell Aidan about this. He'd have freaked out for sure and begged me not to go. We don't need any more drama than we already have. His butterflies constantly flutter around me.

Wearing fingerless gloves, Judy holds an extraordinary camera in her lap, the strap looped around her neck and under her armpit. It looks like something a war photographer would carry.

"Wow!" I say. "Check out your gear, Jay."

"It's my dad's," she says. "If we see anything, this'll get it. I've used it before." She shows it to Leo, who eyes it appreciatively. "Night vision."

The car peels out.

Leo looks uncomfortable. Poor Leo. Can't handle a cute punk girl flirting with him.

"You've got a nice dad," I say.

Judy nods, looking out the window.

I hold my purse close, feeling through the leather the box-cutting knife I use to strip wires. My foot hits a package on the floor.

"Careful," says Michael. "Actually, can you take those out?"

In the bag are the four heavy-duty flashlights I requested. I give one each to Leo and Judy, holding mine and Michael's.

Leo protests. "I don't need one. I've got a light app on my phone."

Michael glowers at him in the rearview mirror. "This can double as a weapon."

"But I don't like violence. It makes me nervous. And we're not going to get close enough—"

"*Take it*," Michael orders.

An inane pop song leaks from the speakers of Michael's car. I slip the blade into my right coat pocket. Michael doesn't seem to notice. He blows his nose and focuses on the road. "So, what's the plan again, CJ?"

"We're going to drive the roads and familiarize ourselves with the area. Once we find the midpoint between the two dog deaths, we'll park and go out on foot. Listen for dogs going wild. We might not see anything. And it might take hours. But it doesn't matter. We have to try. This is the only lead we have. And we need to be patient. If it's an animal, it'll probably be more afraid of us than we are of it."

"What if it's a human?" Leo asks.

I shrug. "I dunno. Run?"

Lonesome and shadowy, Keiko's house sits at the end of a long, rocky street with no lights. Silver Leaf Drive. Most of the streets are unlit, but the houses are at least close enough together that driveway floodlights illuminate the surrounding area. Keiko's street wanders farther into the sticks than most. They have their share of trouble from possums and the occasional bobcat scaring Jackson, with everyone being especially careful of rattlers during the summer. But that's it.

The Honda slips deeper into the hills, the headlights revealing not nearly enough. Judy and Leo memorize the roads, noting the turnouts and signs that read, "Private Drive—No Trespassers." My skin crawls as I clutch the blade in my pocket, Michael's flashlight heavy and cold in my lap.

We agree that the place where the paved road ends in the trident below Keiko's house is the best stopping place. Michael pulls off the road and parks by the bushes. The night squeezes everything in its blind fist until we pull out the flashlights. I'm sure everyone can hear the thudding in my chest over the crickets and owls. A wind cuts through my coat sleeves as the thick clouds drift apart to reveal an almost-full moon. The scents of wet leaves, damp rocks and Leo's antiperspirant mingle.

"This way," I stage whisper, marching down the leg farthest from Keiko's house. Golden Oak Road. The house at the end of this road isn't for another half mile. The moist wind howls, scraping my face and ears. Branches crackle. Gravel crunches under our feet.

"Let's split up," I say. "Boy/girl. Michael, you and I will find a spot on that side of the road behind the trees. Leo, you and Judy are going to move up the road closer to the house to find a place to sit and listen. And *no phone use* unless it's absolutely necessary. We don't want to draw attention to ourselves."

"I think it would be better if you and I go," Leo says, trembling. Maybe from the cold. Probably from something else.

"Really?" I was trying to pair him with Judy on purpose.

"Whatever," Michael says, impatient. "I'll go with Judy."

Judy looks disappointed. They take off into the brush.

A couple of weak lights peer over the drive of the house. If these people have a dog, they keep it inside. An engine rumbles in the distance but doesn't come near us. Leo nudges me. The mouth of a path opens off the road. I nod and we head down the path.

We're definitely trespassing. I hope no one has a shotgun.

We settle in a small clearing well away from the poison oak bushes. After half an hour, my rear end hurts from sitting on the cold, hard ground. I fidget. The tension is getting to me. A dog barks. It could be Jackson—it's a throaty, big dog voice. I don't pay much attention to it because dogs bark at anything. I also hope it's not Michael and Judy getting too close to one of the houses.

It's weird. I might have crushed on a guy like Leo about six months ago. Band geek. Comic book dork. Straight-A student. But here we are instead, sitting in the bushes on somebody's property, waiting for the worst.

"Are you going to the winter ball?" he whispers.

"Maybe," I reply. "Are you?"

"I never go to those things."

"Why not?"

He shrugs. "Girls freak me out."

"It's okay if you like guys," I tell him.

"I like girls. But they make me unbelievably nervous."

"Everything makes you nervous, Leo. You nearly wet yourself when I paired you with Judy."

Leo looks flustered. "That one is especially dangerous."

"Look, she's not a chainsaw. She's a cute, smart, talented girl. And I'm pretty sure she likes you, dummy."

"That is precisely why I'm afraid of her."

"Afraid of *her*? Or something else?"

He's quiet a moment. Just when I hope he's done talking, he says, "I'm afraid I'll disappoint her."

Oh, dear. "She's a big girl. Let her take that risk. Maybe you're wrong."

A dog barks in the distance and then stops. After listening for a few moments, Leo continues. "So, who are you going to the dance with?"

"I can't say." Literally. I hope he doesn't press me.

"A lot of guys have asked you, huh?"

"No. I don't get asked to things like that." I feel awash with self-pity.

"You're kidding, right?" Leo draws in the dirt with a stick.

I shrug. "No. I'm not exactly hot, so…"

Leo eyes me with disbelief. "Are you for real? Half the guys in band like you!"

"That's ridiculous!" I catch myself, lowering my voice. "Besides, if I'm supposedly so hot, why doesn't Michael like me?"

The dog barks louder. Fiercer. Another dog joins in. Snarling.

"Michael's a different story," Leo says. "He's—"

Savage, murderous barking.

Crap! We let ourselves get distracted. My phone buzzes. A text from Michael.

*CRAZY SHIT NNE*

I hear it! But what the heck is "NNE"? Ah! North by northeast. It's easier to follow the sound than use my compass app.

"Let's go!"

Even with our bright flashlights, the path toward the noise is treacherous. We stumble several times. The dogs' cries crescendo into high-pitched whines of terror. As we draw closer, a chain-link fence rattles. The woods clear to reveal a kennel full of panic-stricken dogs, barking and leaping.

And then I see it climbing up the chain-link fence. Something apelike. Bigger than a chimp with a thicker, goat-like snout and ears. Shaggy slate fur.

Glowing blue eyes.

"Shit!" Leo gasps. We scramble to hide behind a big tree. Can I trust my sight? It's dark. We press against each other. Should we run? I glance at the house. No lights on inside.

One of the creature's legs hangs oddly from its hip. Mangled. It continues to climb.

I can't stand here and do nothing. If these dogs die, I won't be able to live with myself. I pop out from behind the tree, aiming the light into the creature's eyes. "Hey! Possum killer! Leave them alone!"

The creature growls, clinging to the kennel fence. A mouth full of thorny teeth. Hands clawed like a sloth's.

I remove the knife from my pocket and open the blade.

The creature launches itself from the fence and disappears into the forest.

"Crap!"

Leo and I spin around, breathing heavily. We stand back to back, scanning the darkness. My legs feel rubbery.

"Way to go," Leo says bitterly.

"It's still here. I know it. Just keep the light moving."

The dogs jump and bark in a frenzy.

Leo shrieks.

I spin around. The creature dives at us, its bad leg hindering. Leo dodges, landing hard against a tree. I dive in the other direction and hit a different tree, gripping the light and knife for dear life. Pain sears my upper arm. The creature lopes like an ape, walking on its forepaws. If it were to stand, it couldn't be more than four feet tall. It bears down on me. I try to raise my arm to shine the light in its eyes, but my arm hurts too much. The creature hesitates, staring at me. Does it recognize me?

*Thunk.*

The creature sags. Leo has clobbered its head with his flashlight. That slows it down for a moment. I scramble to my feet as it howls with a renewed furor. I thrust the box cutter blade as it swipes at me. The blade is useless. The monster's claws have way too great a reach. I leap out of the way.

A car horn blares, the headlights of Michael's Honda flooding the kennel and the forest's edge. Judy jumps out of the car and goes to ground, snapping pictures.

A sharp croak escapes the creature's snout, its head jerking toward the car. It stops mid-swipe and flees into the forest darkness.

Leo and I dash to the car. We scramble inside and slam the doors shut.

"Let's go!" I yell.

We sit in the Denny's, Michael and I on one side, Leo and Judy on the other. Shaking. Sipping tea. We can barely look at one another. Judy's camera sits on the table beside her. My left upper arm hurts so badly I can barely lift it. My mind races with the implications of what we've seen.

"What will you do with the photos?" I ask Judy.

She hugs herself. "I want to delete them." A tear runs down her cheek. She wipes it away. "I want to delete everything that happened tonight."

Leo and I exchange a look. "No kidding," Leo says. "But we've got to do something."

"I'm not even sure anyone would believe those photos," I add. "But we need to store them somewhere. Judy, you have Dropbox, right? Put them there, please, and share the link with us?"

Judy nods. I study our little group of guerrilla journalists and make a hard decision. "I want to show you guys something. It's part of the investigation into Darren's death. Detective Bristow told me to keep it a secret. So, please don't tell a soul. I'll be incredibly busted if they find out I showed you."

Michael looks pissed. "You've been holding out on us?"

"I've been obeying a direct order from law enforcement. I live with the law, remember?"

Michael nods. "Ah, yes. Please continue."

I remove my phone from my purse, hands shaking. "I took this photo because I didn't think anyone would believe me when I found the body. It's given me nightmares ever since."

"You're the one?" Leo says with awe. "There were rumors, but your name's never come up."

Judy gives me a look of pity. Michael crosses his arms, raising an eyebrow.

I bring up the image on my phone that's haunted me until now. I hand the phone to Michael, and he passes it around.

"This is beyond intense," Michael says.

"I don't know what that thing was doing under the bleachers, but it surprised Darren, I think. Maybe Darren hurt its leg in the struggle. But those claws…" I can't continue. We all saw the claws—some of us better than others.

"But why was Darren hanging out behind the bleachers?" Judy asks. "It's so random."

"He was going to buy drugs from my brother's friends, but they stood him up," I respond. "The cops brought my brother in for questioning because he was one of the last people texting with Darren. He's no longer a person of interest. And that's fair because—I mean, you can see those eyes in the photo."

Leo shakes his head. "So Darren was a druggie, too. Figures. Freaking hypocrite."

Silence settles on the table. It's Judy who eventually breaks it. "What are we going to do?"

"We might not have to do anything," I say. "With all the gun-happy rednecks in this county? Someone is bound to kill it just because it's the wrong color." Wouldn't be the first time in history.

"It was a creature, right? Not a deformed person?" Leo asks. "I mean, it *looked* like a creature to me, anyway." Leo looks embarrassed. "I can't believe I hit it. I've never hit anything in my life."

"Well, that was the perfect time to start!" I reply. "Thanks, Leo. You saved my life."

Leo glows with the first hint of pride I've ever seen in him. He waves a hand at me as if to say, *It was nothing.*

"We should go to the cops," Judy says. Everyone looks at her like she's an idiot. "What? They've got guns. Right? Or maybe they can capture this thing."

"Sure. And what will we say? That we're trespassing and stalking people's dogs?" Michael asks.

"We could lie," she counters. "We could tell them we were out for a night walk and we heard all this barking."

"Would they believe that's what we were doing?" I ask. "That would put all four of us on their radar. Right now, I'm the only one involved with the police. I don't want you guys to be in any trouble. I totally understand if telling the cops makes you feel safer, but I'm telling you that it's a trade-off."

Michael finishes his tea. "Like I said, I don't trust those meatballs with badges. And this," he hands me back my phone. "This freaky monster movie stuff is *way* above their pay grade. I vote we keep quiet, keep our eyes open."

"And be better prepared for the next run," I say.

"But you know what we need next time?" Michael says. "A gun."

"No way," I say. "What we need is a better plan."

"And a gun?" Judy says hopefully.

"The Doctor doesn't use violence. And neither will we. Now that we've seen this thing, I think we can outsmart it."

"The Doctor?" Judy asks.

"The main character in *Doctor Who*. Don't you watch BBC America?"

She scrunches her face. "I don't watch TV."

"Neither do I. Except BBC. I mean, British TV doesn't count, does it? And *Big Bang Theory*."

Everybody nods.

"Anyway, we don't have to hunt this thing. We can make a trap and take it alive. If it's hurt, it's going to be easier to catch."

Michael waves away the waiter. "You're the engineering genius. If you think you can build a monster trap, I'll listen to you. But I'm telling you, we should all get our nunchuk skills up to snuff, my friends. I have a feeling we're going to need them."

# Chapter 14

I tell Mom that I was shoved against a building corner by some rambunctious kids. She ices my arm and gives me ibuprofen.

"If it gets worse, let me know. You'll need to see the doctor." She folds her arms in that badass pose she does so well. "Are those kids still bullying you?"

I shake my head. I'm not lying. The texts have stopped. Everyone is probably more wrapped up in the drama around Darren's death than with me. "No. This was just an accident."

She eyes me suspiciously but cuts the line of inquiry. "Well, try to be quiet up there. Aidan and your brother are already in bed."

"How did Aidan do?"

"That kid could charm a shark. Dad says he had Mr. Daniels at hello, he was so polite. Or should I say at 'Good evening, Mr. Daniels.'" Her imitation is spot on.

I throw my good arm around her, I'm so happy. "He's going to be great. You'll see."

She hugs me back. "I love you so much, my Little River."

"I love you, too, Mom."


If only I really were a time-traveling, regenerating, archaeological badass.

Aidan's light is on. I hear the usual humming. Mom's footfalls thump on the stairway. The light goes out.


I can't sleep.

I keep remembering that horrible thing climbing up the fence. Jagged teeth. Sloth claws. Gray fur. Blue glowing eyes.

Those eyes.

They must belong to something rational. An unfortunate. A DNA mutation. An animal. An ape?

It's 2:30 a.m.

I tuck my arm under my pillow, but I can't sleep because of the throbbing.

Wind howls outside. Rain splatters the window. I roll out of bed and, keeping out of sight, I shut the curtains so that nothing can peer inside.

What have we done?

And how will I tell Aidan?

He can't know. He'll leave for sure if he thinks something scary is stalking our area. He sent me a very happy email that I read before I went to bed saying how excited he was to have a job. To earn some money so that he could take me to that stupid dance. And when Dad realized that Aidan didn't know how to ride a bike, he pulled his own ten-speed out of the garage and fixed it for Aidan, who was already getting the hang of it before bedtime.

*I have read of such things in books in my father's library, but I had never seen one in person until I came here to your territory. The balance is tricky. I'll practice tomorrow after school. I'll master it by this weekend, which is when the job starts. I can hardly wait. Your intelligence, beauty and affection inspire me, Charity. I want to learn everything about your world so that I can be closer to you.*

It's definitely more than a crush. Am I in love with him? I can't be. It's only been a week. More like infatuation. But isn't love that feeling where you want to live and die at the same time? And you can't bear to be apart?

I wish I could tell him how I feel. Instead, I respond that I am completely thrilled and proud of him. I'd be happy to help him with the bike lessons. I don't tell him that I've never liked bike riding, but maybe it's better with the one you love?

Pushing aside books and computer parts, I sit against the wall shared with the sewing room. My wet cheek rests against the cool wall. This new secret aches, driving a wedge between us. I want him to wrap his arms around me, to assure me that I'll be safe. That we'll both be okay.

I hear rustling from the other room. A creak from the floor.

Slowly, the wall beneath my cheek seems to warm.

I pretend it's him sitting on the other side, his body magically warming me from the other room, as the tears flood my face in the darkness.


During what little sleep I get, I have nightmares about living in a house with a front door that has broken locks. The creature is trying to force the door in my dreams, to slash me with its claws.

On the way to school the next morning, while other kids on the bus chew gum and scrutinize their phones, I research how to create a DIY motion detector. It's not hard, it turns out. But I will need to hit Fry's for a couple of things I don't already have in my stash. Then again, would this even be useful? By the time that thing is on my side of the window, no indoor motion detector will matter. Perhaps what I need is an outdoor motion detector that switches on a floodlight.

Or a death laser.

No, no. I told everyone, no violence. But damn, it's tempting.

I look up at Aidan. He watches me with a sad look. I ask him what's wrong, but he doesn't respond.

After I deposit my books in my locker, I hear someone sobbing. Probably one of Darren's girlfriends. The vigil last night no doubt brought up oodles of drama.

But then the crowd stirs as I head toward class. "You!"

I ignore it. More drama.

"You killed my dog!"

It's Keiko. I'm stunned. This is so unlike her, to make a scene.

"Charity Jones, you killed my dog!"

# Chapter 15

One of Keiko's new friends shoves me.

I spin backward and hit the lockers, but my backpack absorbs the blow. They're not the girls I saw her with in the gymnasium when we met the cops. These are BFJs. I can't believe this is happening.

"This is insane! What are you talking about?" I say.

One of her friends speaks up. Her cheap perfume gags me, her makeup thick and bright. "You know perfectly well. She didn't like your birthday present, so you killed her dog, you crazy fucking bitch."

After what I went through last night, facing true danger, I can't take this stupid crap anymore.

"If *you* don't want to wind up in court for slander or to finish your days at Pondorado for bullying, I suggest you take your *lying asses* out of my sight. If you touch me again, I will have you arrested for assault and sue you until you are old and wrinkled. *Get out of my face!*"

Mouths open, the girls disperse. The crowd makes approving noises. I might have won this encounter—if winning is even possible.

Keiko lingers, studying me. Her eyes red. Lips and nose chapped.

I feel queasy and shaky, flushed with adrenaline. "You, too! Get away from me!"


Did I even really know Keiko?

We met at Mathcamp last year. I know how incredibly dorky that sounds and it really is, but it's super fun. They held it at Stanford University. If it weren't being held in California, my parents wouldn't have let me go. They could barely afford it as it was, what with having to cover Charles' legal expenses. At least Dad's job was covering the relocation costs. Anyway, I *loved* Stanford. It looked like Hogwarts for graduate witches—to me, anyway.

I didn't notice Keiko at first, even though only maybe a quarter of the students were girls. We wound up being roommates in the dorm. Nervous beyond belief, neither of us had ever been away from home on our own before.

But the fear didn't last. They kept us so busy with cool classes and games and singing and skits…I miss it just thinking about it! Neither of us had been anywhere where we weren't the smartest person in the room. It was kind of an ego blow at first, but also very liberating. We went off campus with some of the guys to San Francisco and visited The Haight, had crepes at Squat-n-Gobble, and got generally traumatized by the amount of incense in the shops and on the sidewalk. I'll never forget our conversation that night in our dorm room—lights out, window open to the Bay Area breezes—talking about our dreams. I wanted to build robots, no question, but *not* for the military. I'd never said that aloud before because I didn't want to hurt my dad's feelings. He comes from a military family, grew up a military brat moving around the world. It totally shaped his genius. I never want to disrespect that. But I don't like violence. My bots must have peaceful purposes.

Keiko wanted to teach. Or make spy satellites. Or save the whales.

Her mother had already told her that she'd die if Keiko married a white man. Any future husband also had to be both Japanese and Christian. Keiko was already crushing on three guys at camp: two were Midwestern, agnostic white dudes and one was Jewish.

I understood her angst and we bonded over it. Most of my mom's side of the family won't have anything to do with us. I've never met my grandparents or aunts and uncles. A couple of cousins have reached out to me online—my cousins Melissa and Josh, who are both in college at Texas A&M—but they're caught in the family drama. We want to be friends, but until they're no longer dependent on their parents for anything, it'll be pretty much impossible to have an IRL relationship.

Dad's family is more open, especially his sister Bellina. At least my parents are cool and don't care who I date or marry, as long as I'm happy.

Well, they almost don't care. This whole thing with Aidan would definitely freak them out. How did I manage to get in a relationship with the one boy they'd freak out over?

Anyway, Keiko and I bonded over that, math and the fact that we were both big-time Hermione Shippers.

We were both shocked that I would be going to Oakwood High School after winter break. She'd been going there since the beginning of her sophomore year. Obviously we were "meant" to be friends. She had very few friends at Oakwood High, but she chalked it up to being shy rather than shunned. She didn't seem shy to me. Maybe because at Mathcamp she felt less self-conscious about being smart. Or because she was so far away from home.

I don't understand the depth of Keiko's anger, why she cut me off. Did her parents have something to do with that?

And this—this is the lowest thing anyone has ever said or done to me. The taunting, the bullying—I can rise above that to a degree. I feel like a space alien at school most of the time, anyway. I'm getting used to it and the isolation. The internet helps. But not now. I'm actually too angry to get depressed.

At least it's Friday.

Michael texts me with more details confirming what I already feared. Apparently, after we drove the creature away from someone else's dogs, it later attacked Jackson instead when Keiko's parents let him out to do his business last night before bed.

In a way, I did kill her dog.

I head to AP English. Anger coils up inside of me, ready to strike at anyone in arm's reach. It's not fair. I couldn't have let the creature kill those dogs. Damned if I did, damned if I didn't. One thing is for certain: this thing has to be stopped before it kills again. But not with guns or any other weapon other than wits.

The question is: how?

After the bus pulls away, Aidan takes my hand. He's wearing a dark blue button-up shirt over a long-sleeved thermal shirt. Mom made him put the thermal shirt on under the dress shirt I picked out. Like the black, the blue makes his eyes shine like jewels. A couple of girls on the bus were gawking at him. He seemed clueless. "Something is wrong. Are you upset with me?"

"What? No!" The rain has let up. The smell of wet dirt and trees is sweet. My arm aches. The cold weather isn't helping. "I'm just going through a lot right now. I can't talk about it yet. But as soon as I can, I will. I promise."

"Is it about Keiko's dog? I heard there was a ruckus."

*Ruckus.* "Yeah. Keiko accused me of killing her dog."

"But that's absurd!"

"Right?"

"She's grieving. She wants to place blame."

"But why on me? Why not on the mountain lion or whatever it was that killed Darren? Maybe it killed her dog, too?"

"She's still angry at you. But I know you didn't do it."

He puts his arm around me and squeezes.

I yelp and pull away.

"Oh, no!" He looks panicked. "Did I hurt you? I'm so sorry!"

"It's nothing," I reply, wincing. "I hurt it last night. At the vigil. I fell against a wall." Worst. Liar. Ever.

He doesn't look convinced.

I bury my fingers in the hair on his neck. He shudders, closing his eyes. With a dramatic sweep, he dumps his backpack and takes me in his arms, kissing me deeply. His mouth tastes like grilled cheese and chips, but his lips are so soft that I want to die touching them. I avoid his back, ever aware of those horrific scars and the secrets they hold.

A rustling in the brush at the side of the road. My eyes snap open and I pull away again. "Let's go home."

His face darkens. "Home? But we can't be together there. What's wrong?"

I pause. What good is it being smart if you can't actually use your wits to get out of trouble with your boyfriend? "If there really is a dangerous animal around, then we shouldn't mess around outside. We need to be more careful. Physical safety first. And we'll figure out the rest."

A memory of the creature lunging at me surges forward. I suppress it, willing the nausea to subside, focusing instead on Aidan's eyes. My fingers brush his chalky cheek. While some acne lines his jaw, he has very little facial hair. Does he shave?

He scans the trees lining each side of the street. The foliage is sparse closer to the asphalt, thickening farther from the road. "You were both naughty and nice last night, weren't you?" he says at last, but there's nothing playful about his words. His fingers trace my lips.

"What the heck are you talking about?" I ask. "Ever since you first arrived, you've been saying things like this. What are you, some kind of moral savant? And whose moral compass are you using, anyway?"

He smiles the way Mr. Reilly does when someone asks a question he doesn't expect and takes my hands in his. "That is the question, isn't it, Charity Jones? Who gets to decide what is good and evil? Who makes the rules? Man or monster?" He kisses my fingertips, his ghostly eyes leveling with mine, and a shudder sweeps through me. "Who is to say which is which? I cannot tell you. Yet I know your heart. I can peer into it. It's as transparent as a glass of water.

And not just your heart. Everyone's heart. I can see what's in that glass. But how is a mystery. Since I left home, I've been inundated by these impressions from people." He brings my hands to his cheeks. "I try to stop them. Sometimes I can. Often I can't. I only say things to you because I feel that I can trust you. If you wish to condemn me for this, I accept that condemnation. I'll never speak of it again. Because I think I love you, Charity. And anything that brings you happiness brings me happiness. Even if it puts my very life in danger. I would give it for you."

He's an empath? Or a psychic? There's no evidence whatsoever for psychic activity. Michael is right. He must be some kind of Sherlock Holmes, making deductions from miniscule physical cues. I only take this speech seriously because he knew. *He knew.* He's scaring me a little, but I can't hold back the tidal wave of blazing emotion. He loves me. *He said it.* Granted, Mom has always said that guys will say this—or anything really—to get you into bed with them. She'd probably also say that you can't love a guy without knowing him. But right now, in this spectacular, dizzying moment, Mom's cynicism just doesn't ring true.

No one except my family has ever said "I love you" to me. Most of all, he's the one I've most wanted to say it.

I grab his bag with my good hand and break for the house. He chases me. "What are you doing?"

I laugh and run faster. He catches up with me, but I keep going. When I hit the front door, I listen for sounds of Charles rummaging in the kitchen or playing music in the garage, but the house is empty. Feet pounding upstairs, racing toward my room. I glance into Charles' room: he's gone. Aidan stops at the threshold of my room like a vampire needing an invite. As I dive inside, I grab his shirt and pull him with me, kissing, grasping and devouring him. We tear off our coats. My body drives against his, and I can feel the heat just below his belt. As he caresses me, he smells like rain, shampoo, sweat, starch, heat, hands, dirt, skin…

Fear ripples through me. Even though I want it, I'm not ready for what should come next. Or what other people say should come next. And I'm alone with Aidan, vulnerable if he should decide to take what he wants. We should really have a relationship talk about sex. When we're calmer.

I smother my chattering thoughts and kiss him. We fall to our knees and stretch out on the floor. I avoid lying on the arm that's hurt. His hands stroke my waist, hip, and thigh as I raise my leg up over him. His palm brushes the underside of my breast. My fingers dig into his shirt and pull it out of his pants so that I can massage the silky skin of his waist. I'm dying every time I look into his eyes. Fading in a blaze of light as I turn inside out with lust. His kisses move to my neck and up to my ear. "I love you, Charity Jones," he whispers and kisses my lobe.

My phone buzzes. I ignore it and instead throw Aidan on his back as I straddle him, heart pounding. I lean over him, French kissing him. My phone buzzes again.

And again.

And again.

Something tells me to stop. I place my hand on Aidan's chest—a "hold on" gesture—and put a finger to my lips. "It might be my mom."

I roll off of Aidan, who looks a thousand times more delicious with tousled hair and blushing cheeks. He sits up against the bedframe, watching me.

The phone lies on the floor under my coat. I pick it up and check the texts.

The heat drains from my body.

Aidan sits up. "What's wrong?"

I turn the phone toward him.

"Death threats."

# Chapter 16

Maybe I should go to the police, but part of me doesn't believe these threats are actually serious. People believe whatever they hear, and these people clearly believe I killed Keiko's dog. They want me to feel badly for it.

A dark suspicion blooms in my mind. Charles swore his vengeance and he's been unusually quiet. Invisible and silent last night behind his closed bedroom door. He came home and ate obediently with the family, keeping to himself. Totally out of character. He would never hurt me, of course, but he loves to incite a little of the old ultraviolence. He used to brag that he'd killed a pigeon by simply throwing a rock at it when we lived in Woodland Hills. He never says "I'm sorry" or feels guilty about anything.

I sometimes wonder if he's a sociopath, but never out loud.

The next morning is Saturday. Aidan writes me an impassioned email in the middle of the night imploring me to tell my parents. He mercifully lets the subject drop over the torturous weekend. We can't kiss or touch, and even trying seems like a disastrous idea. Aidan watches *Doctor Who*. He thinks it's the greatest thing he's ever seen, but says it makes absolutely no sense. I guess he can stay my boyfriend.

We still need to talk about sex stuff. Soon. Like, how we're not doing that. Or are we?

I block every number that has texted my phone in the last twenty-four hours except for my tight circle of friends. It's awesome that I now have a "circle" of friends.

Monday morning, Aidan watches me as I head to my first period class. His coat hood raised over his head. Breath white in the cold air. Brooding eyes blaze against the purple dress shirt tucked into his dark blue jeans. I glance back at him, and he barely breaks eye contact with me when a couple of girls flank him, asking his name.

He mastered the bike this weekend with Dad's help. He'll start working the weekend after next, on Thanksgiving weekend. It turns out Mr. Daniels really is paying him under the table in cash. He'll make a small fortune.

Somebody shoves me in the hallway, hurting my barely healed arm. Another shove. People I don't recognize push past. A bigger shove, and I stumble forward into someone else. I apologize but they yell at me anyway. Couple of people run away through the crowds, laughing, before I can confront them. I decide to avoid the walkway entirely and suffer the rain on my way to class.

No one shoves me in the rain.

The numbers in calculus soothe me. Dispassionate, nonjudgmental, unyielding. Math is the soul of machinery. It's the only soul I believe in.

I ignore Keiko, but my heart still stings with loss.

When class lets out, a girl I never talk to named Jill Swain stands by me as I gather up my belongings. She's Matt Swain's younger sister. Catholics are pariah out here in Evangelical Land. Many conservative Christians think Catholicism is a cult. I think she's in choir. Or is that drama club? Either way, she has a great voice—that is, when she speaks, which is rarely. Pale and retiring, she clears her throat. "Charity, can I ask you something?"

"Sure." I grit my teeth. She's probably going to proselytize to me. Maybe I should cut her off and leave, but I don't want to be mean if I don't have to.

She waits for people to pass before she speaks. "I know this sounds a little odd, but I was wondering." Her voice drops. "Are you still having those club meetings? Because I would sort of like to come. But I haven't heard anything on campus since the big scene. I thought maybe you had moved them to somewhere else. Is that true?"

I shake my head. One of the Swains? No way. "Sorry. I just don't have time right now. I'll let you know if they start up again."

"I can't wait," she says. "I mean, I really need the support. I'm having doubts, and I was hoping you could help. It's really hard, you know. Here, at this school. Could we have a short meeting? Just the two of us?"

Jill follows me out of the room and into the rain. Maybe she's serious. She peers at me through her long blonde lashes. What if she's really suffering? What if her family truly is persecuting her for not wanting to say the rosary or take communion? Or go to confession? I can't push her away. Not after how I've been pushed away. "What's your phone number? I'll text you when I'm free."

She scribbles it on her notebook and tears off the piece of paper for me. "Thank you. This is awesome. Can we meet soon?"

Her words are enthusiastic but her voice is tired. She seems down and anxious. It's a miracle that she and her siblings are in public school at all. But then, there might not be any parochial schools here.

"I'll try."

I text her from the bus.

> *This is Charity. Been thinking about your request. I can't get home if I miss the bus after school. Want to talk at lunch?*
>> No way. Too many people watching. If you stay after school, my brother can give us a ride.
> *Matt?*
>> Yes. I asked him already.

Maybe Matt has forgiven me. Or forgotten. Or just doesn't care.

I cast a longing glance at Aidan. We can be together this afternoon, but Thursday will be our last afternoon for over a week. The thought is agonizing. We won't be able to touch the entire weekend or the week after that, as it's Thanksgiving break. Mom says we're having Thanksgiving at home this year. No visitors. Aidan and I will have to plan time together somehow. After our experience in my bedroom, I fantasize constantly about going further. Aidan is so polite and old-fashioned. He might want to go further but won't.

I text Jill.

*I'll think about it. I have a lot of homework this week.*

It's true. Aidan and I are overwhelmed with assignments before the break. Not much happens over the next two days except reports that two more dogs are slaughtered. Kennel dogs. People are moving their dogs indoors. Judy sends us the link to the night photos of the creature. She and I text almost constantly now, mostly about encounters with the BFJs. It's not the same relationship I had with Keiko—no one could replace her—but it's cool. Judy is funny, sweet, and sarcastic.

Jill keeps texting me, too. Nice, sad texts about how much she needs to talk. I send her links to videos and sites that she might find helpful but she says talking is better. She really wants to meet.

On Thursday, I finally give in. I can't see Aidan Friday afternoon, anyway.

> *Hey Jill. I'll meet you after school tomorrow. Where do you want to talk?*
>
> Yay! Let's meet in the farmhouse. No one should be there. We can talk in private.

The farmhouse, as we call it, is located past the football field, a derelict building that is half gardener's shed, half 4-H club meeting room. She must be really scared. But why not just go on the internet? Hundreds of forums host doubters and freethinkers, people trying to break away from religion but who might be living in strict religious households. Kids who are so oppressed that they can't speak up at home without fear of retribution or abuse. Matt and his siblings don't seem abused. In fact, they seem quite happy. But I guess not everyone wears abuse on their sleeve.

Still, the building is far away from the rest of the school. What if that creature is roaming again? I don't think it would actually come back on campus, but it might be lurking in the forest beyond, waiting for an opportunity like this.

Then again, it'll be daylight. I think it got caught outside of its safety zone the first time, when it killed Darren. I can't imagine that it would do that again.

I respond.

*Cool. I'll meet you there after sixth period.*

After the bus drops us off at our usual stop, Aidan tears off his jacket, shoulders my backpack with his and holds my hand as we walk. "Did you get any more of those dreadful messages today?"

I shake my head. "Nothing since I installed an app to block everyone except a few friends."

He squeezes my hand. "I still say you should report them to the authorities. They threatened your life. I checked last night on the internet. That's illegal behavior."

Oh, god, he is so cute. "What your dad did to you was illegal, too," I reply. "But I don't see you going to the authorities."

"My father is too powerful for that. I told you. Besides, there aren't any authorities where I live. Even if there were, it would be meaningless to tell them anything. They wouldn't believe me. My father's reputation precedes him. If they only knew."

"Well, believe me," I explain, "in my world, kids do things like this all the time and they almost never get in trouble. There's always a lengthy investigation of some sort that goes nowhere. I've seen it on the news. I do think some people are intrinsically evil, but these guys who sent the texts, I honestly think they're cowards. They would never actually hurt someone 'because Jesus.' Or whatever. But threatening and fantasizing is okay somehow."

"What a humane world you live in. My father would not hesitate to destroy anyone who threatened his secrets."

I change the subject. As we reach the house, we talk about tomorrow and the week after. How it will be difficult to spend time together, especially given all the homework we have over Thanksgiving break and Aidan's new job.

"So, today will be our last time together, since I'll be working and you'll be doing homework?" he asks.

"Actually," I say, closing and locking the front door. "Remember the club I started but everything went insane?"

He climbs up the staircase. "You're starting it again? How wonderful! You're so brave. You really are a sort of Isabella Lucy Bird. Adventurous, I'd say."

"I'm going to pretend that I understood what you just said." I climb up the stairs after him. "But the answer to your question is no. I'm not restarting the club. There's somebody who wants to talk to me, so I'm going to spend some time with her. Her brother is going to give me a lift home. I'm not sure when that will be."

Aidan enters the sewing room and drops his book bag on the floor. "So, what do you want to do on our last afternoon together until after this thanking holiday I keep hearing about?"

My heart beats so hard as he approaches that it feels like the only organ in my body. He takes my chin in his hand. "You are always concerned for others, Charity Jones. That is one of many things that I love about you." He kisses my fingers. "I want to show you something. It's almost as beautiful as you are."

He leads me downstairs and outside. Cool breezes rifle the branches. I hesitate. "I don't want to spend time outside if we don't have to."

"We'll only be a few minutes," he says.

We walk around the back of the house. Aidan leads me to a patch just beyond Dad's new tool shed. It looks ridiculously artificial on the wilds of our property.

A dash of red catches my eye. A single, gorgeous rose growing miraculously in the mud, ruffled by the wind. Rain drops bead on the surface. The ground around it has not been disturbed. This wasn't planted. It *grew*.

"Where did this come from? We've never had roses back here. Or anywhere. They have to be cultivated by people with super green thumbs. We just…Mom doesn't. Dad…doesn't…"

Aidan draws me close to him. "It's a winter miracle. And I assure you, it won't be the last."

As he kisses me, our bodies warm together in the cold, I hear fluttering. A tiny wind. Motion surrounds me. My eyes open.

Several dozen radiant blue and gold butterflies flutter around us.

Aidan smiles. "It's what you want for Christmas, right?"

Laughter bubbles up from my throat. I can't stop laughing. Or crying. But I don't want to stop kissing him. "This isn't real. It just isn't."

He kisses me again. "It's a little early for Christmas presents, but there's no sense in waiting until Christmas when you can have roses and butterflies now."

In moments, we're back in the house, in his room, entangled on the floor. A couple of stray butterflies land on his computer monitor and book bag as we explore each other's bodies. Timidly, tentatively. Clothes on. My skin sweats with fear and desire. Touch me. Don't touch me. Here. Not there. Okay, there. I guide his hand, his eyes wild. His excitement and hunger obvious.

"Aidan, we need to talk about what we're doing. Or not doing."

His fingers brush stray hairs from my face. "I will do whatever you ask," he whispers. "And no more."

His lips find mine. Nothing could be holier in this world than his touch. I drink him in, my mind aflame with images not of movie love scenes but ivory drifts carved by blue shadows beneath a white sun. Bloody droplets falling into a sparkling stream with coppery fish. Smoke billowing from a house on a hillside blanketed with pines. My heart thunders in my ears. Two heartbeats. His mouth works down my neck. My breathing slows. Cold sunlight. Blinding.

Intoxicating.

The perfect azure sky is streaked with pink clouds. I tear away.

Falling.

I sit on the floor, blinking.

Charles yells at Aidan in the doorway. Aidan clutches my backpack and coat.

"She needs her goddamn cherry popped," Charles sneers. "But not by a faggot like you."

"You're disgusting," Aidan asserts. "There's nothing improper going on. Your sister is sick. Now get her a glass of water instead of standing there like a useless ass."

What did Charles see? Why didn't we hear him come home? Or did we? I can't remember what's happened the last—I check the wall clock—half an hour. My head feels like it's on fire.

"Fuck you, car smasher," Charles yells. "First you take my family, then my job, and now—" Charles' finger jabs Aidan's shirt, but stops inches away. He tries to push forward but can't. His hand trembles. He yanks it back like he touched a nest of hot wires. A shadow passes over his expression. "There is something deeply fucked up about you." He licks his lips, looks at me. "It's like fucking *Haven* around here or something. And you of all people are encouraging it! I'm telling Mom. You slut."

Scrambling to my feet, I get in Charles' face. "If you say one word to Mom and Dad about anything, I swear, I'll tell them about you being with Noah the other day *and* the accident. Who do you think they'll believe?"

Charles sears me with a dark, threatening look. I've never seen him so angry before. "So that's how you wanna play it? You're both gonna pay. Big."

A switch has been tripped in my brother. I can tell. I have no doubt I'll pay. I just don't know how.

# Chapter 17

*Dear Charity,*

*As I traveled through Washington State, I hurt myself hiking and couldn't go on. An older gentleman living in a cabin on a mint farm helped me get on my feet. In return for his care and healing supply of mint—he had several varieties, but peppermint was what I needed—I worked for him a few months, helping on the farm, cutting wood and hunting. I stayed long after I was healed. I didn't mind the hard work but I hated the rifle. I mastered it but ultimately had to reject it, as every time I pulled the trigger, I felt my father's blood coursing through me.*

*If only he would embrace the image of himself that the rest of the world treasures, he could bring unprecedented joy to humanity. Perhaps his nature is so wicked that he simply can't. His blood sour, his visage horrifying, his temper volcanic. He wishes only to punish and destroy, not to love and nurture. He loves my siblings because they're as monstrous as he is. He despises me because I resemble my mother. It's not that I look like her, but because I'm "weak" like her, uninterested in hurting others.*

*I'm not sure that's true. I felt my father's blood coursing in me when your brother threatened us yesterday. Hatred clouded my reasoning. It took all of my will to restrain my father's power within me, to keep from releasing his fearful gifts. Thankfully Charles chose silence last night when your parents came home. He'll probably blackmail us, but I'm sure we can counter him.*

*I have to leave as soon as school is over today to get to work. So please know that every moment I'm awake, I dream of feeling your touch. Everywhere.*

*Yours forever,*

*A-*

If Aidan and I stay together, he's got to get into therapy because he's got some serious daddy issues. No wonder he thinks my dad walks on water! And he kinda does. He was the one who fought for me to get into Mason Letters Charter, the awesome science magnet school in the Valley. The night after we were notified that I'd made it, he battled L.A. traffic to take us to Sweet Rose Creamery, where I devoured salted caramel ice cream to die for. Mom was supportive, for sure, but she didn't think a magnet school was as important as being in a good private school. She was wrong in my case.

Believe it or don't, I used to be pretty shy. That school inspired me to find my voice. I came out of my shell and started speaking up about things, although no one wanted to hear about things like how much it sucks being torn between which race box to check. You can never check both. And I hate choosing.

I guess I've always felt like a fish out of water. Or rather a whale on the beach.

I'm more worried about Charles than Aidan can imagine. He left the house this morning with Dad, glaring and slamming doors. I caught a glimpse of his leather jacket at school as he darted for the road to smoke a cigarette. He could get suspended for smoking on campus, but between the ongoing investigation of Darren's death, frantic parent calls, the withdrawal of students, and her own holiday plans, Mrs. Cartwright isn't paying attention. She's probably too worried that someone will finally open a charter school in the county.

Aidan rode his bike to school this morning so that he can leave right after for his new job. I saw it chained to the bike racks earlier today. I ached to see it because it heralded our hiatus. But when I realized this meant he would have the money he needs to take me to the winter dance, one of those butterflies fluttered in my stomach. Maybe I don't hate dances anymore.

I should be thinking about what I'm going to wear to that stupid dance, but Charles has once again peed on my peace of mind. Even though he hasn't said anything yet to Mom and Dad, it's a Damocles sword hanging over our heads.

At the end of the day, it's ridiculously cold, the clouds clearing to expose the bright blue sky. Aside from the occasional snarky text from Michael or Judy, and a check-in from Leo to let me know that he hasn't heard about any new killings, no one has spoken to me today. Trying to be inconspicuous, as if that were possible, I stand with my back against the wall of the English building, scanning the crowd for Jill.

Instead, Judy trots toward me, looking amazing in a mustard wool jacket and blue knit hat, her purple bangs escaping the brim in squiggles. "Hey, what's up? I don't usually see you after school."

I shrug. "I don't do much after school unless it's the robotics team, and we're on break until after the New Year." My eyes once again scan the thinning crowds. "Jill Swain wants me to meet her at the barn to talk about some stuff.

What's going on with you? Are you okay? Any news?"

"Jill Swain?" She frowns. "Seriously?"

"Why not?"

"She's uber Catholic. What if she's seen with you?"

"I think she wants to be one of our tribe, though. That's what we're going to talk about."

Judy looks skeptical. "I guess we've seen stranger things lately."

"Unfortunately. How are you doing?"

"I'm still kinda shaken, you know?" Her eyes dart around. "But I'm sleeping better. Leo and I are just doing some last-minute stuff for French club before we go on break."

I detect a faint blush in her cheeks. "Are you guys together? You are totally together."

A smile plays on her lips and she demurs. "Maybe. I think so. Things changed after that night."

Maybe my pep talk helped. Or maybe Leo has finally gotten a little YOLO in his diet. Either one would be awesome.

"I *hope* so! Well, don't let me keep you. Leo is super sweet and you guys make a cute couple. Have fun. Okay?"

She bear hugs me. Surprised, I hug back.

"You, too!" she says. She takes off with a wave.

I watch her leave, happiness—for her, for Leo, for all of us—bubbling inside of me.

Jill appears a couple of minutes later, looking pale and worried. "Come on," she says and we take off for the barn.

Fewer students are hanging around. I don't see Charles, but I do see Judy and Leo heading off toward the Foreign Language building. Jill is quiet, trudging forward with a purpose. I try some small talk. "So, what's your family doing for Thanksgiving?"

She looks confused for a moment. "Nothing special. Staying in town. I'm sure there'll be football or something."

I glance over at the bike racks. Aidan's bike is still here. Maybe I misunderstood. Of course, he could be chatting with Mr. Reilly again, but Aidan is such a perfectionist about everything that I can't imagine him losing track of time. I feel a scorch of disappointment. I hope he makes it to his first job on time.

I follow Jill from the main track of buildings into the grassy expanse that rests between the school proper and the 4-H building. Jill casts glances over her shoulder and speeds up. She's definitely nervous about this. I understand why.

The phone buzzes in my hand. I ignore it, as it's in the hand shielding my eyes from the searing sunlight. The crabgrass is mushy underfoot, mud oozing up around my boot soles. We're closing in on the building, the crude odor of hay mixing with clover and wet wood.

It buzzes again.

Jill hooks my arm in hers. "Thanks so much for meeting with me." We round the corner to the benches and tables.

"Sure," I say and drop my backpack on a damp bench. I check my phone. Jill starts to talk, but I don't hear her. My head's exploding as I read Judy's text:

> Aidan arguing with Charles! LOOKS REALLY BAD
> *Where?*
> POSSUMS

I grab my bag. "Sorry, Jill, but I've gotta go. I'll be back soon. I promise." I tear away across the wet grass, stumbling as my feet slide. That area is the one place that the kiddie cops don't patrol well, as evidenced by the undetected dead possums. The cops might not even be hanging around now that the break has officially started.

Crap! My backpack strap digs into my shoulder. My chest aches. I pass the bike rack: this time, the bike looks strange. Front wheel missing. Weird. I push forward. I race through the school to the English building. Listening. Stragglers wait for rides, joke in the halls.

The forest echoes with harsh voices. I halt, wondering if it's wise to interrupt. Maybe they need to have this fight. To settle things. I slow down, stepping carefully. Break no branch underfoot. Can't let them know I'm here.

Through the branches I see Aidan and Charles, facing off. Charles is so agitated that he's dancing from foot to foot, twitching and gesticulating with thrashing hands, face flushed and sweating. Madness flares in his eyes.

"You're a thief," Charles accuses. "You stole my job. You stole my family. You stole my life! You're an intruder. Nobody wants you around except my slut sister."

I lean against a wide tree and peer around. I only see the two. The 10-speed front wheel leans against a tree next to Charles.

"Cherry sucked my dick last summer," someone chortles. Whoever said that is hidden somewhere among the trees. I wonder if there are others I just can't see.

How did I go from school sacrificial virgin to Mary Mother of Whores? In a week, no less! I guess I get around. Who knew?

"So you have a choice, motherfucker," Charles continues. He wipes the sweat from his face with his coat sleeve. "You can walk away now and leave forever, or we'll fucking kill you. What'll it be?"

Aidan crosses his arms. Unflinching. His eyes are bright with anger but they aren't focused on Charles. Instead, his gaze moves around from tree to tree. "It seems you are not capable of handling this dispute on your own."

"Fuck you. You know why they're here. You're a sneaky freak!"

"Sneaky? It's sneakier to vandalize someone's mode of transportation and provoke a conflict."

Charles circles him. "Now it's an even fight. And I got six witnesses here who will testify that you tried to kill me in an argument. The cops will believe these homeboys before they believe a runaway freak from Canada or wherever the hell you're from." He steps away from Aidan with a maniacal grin.

"Is that so?" Aidan says. "Well, then…Game on."

A half-dozen guys leap from the surrounding woods. Toughs and creeps. A couple of jocks—Zander Wilson and Deacon Burr. The jocks are probably more "customers" of Charles doing him a solid. Zander carries a hammer. Deacon, a bat. Zachary, whose car was smashed, carries a tire iron. His buddy Noah, chains.

Charles steps back.

They swarm Aidan.

And then it's the end of the world.

Aidan flings out his arms. Deacon goes flying vertically, his head hitting a nearby tree. He slumps, unconscious. Zachary and his tire iron fly in the other direction, landing on his back, winded.

Noah hesitates, scuttles back and circles around, swinging the chains.

Meanwhile, Zander drops the hammer and runs. But he's barely taken a few steps when he rises straight up at least 20 feet as if lifted by an invisible hand, legs bicycling in the air like the coyote in the cartoons. He cries out, looking around desperately.

Noah lashes at Aidan, who catches the chain in his hand—or, at least appears to. The chain hovers a foot away from his fingers. He yanks his hand back and Noah stumbles toward him. The chain wraps itself around Noah's neck like a boa constrictor, squeezing until he just turns blue and drops. The chain loosens. He's breathing but unconscious.

Zachary sits up, muttering. Before he can take another breath, his body lifts and flings itself against a nearby tree, breaking the arm that holds the tire iron. He collapses, weeping and cursing, weapon released.

Zander shrieks at Aidan from the air. "I'm going to fucking kill you, freak!"

Aidan laughs in a voice I have never heard. About an octave lower, gravely and frightening. "Will you really?"

"Fuck you! I'll get my dad's rifle and blow your head off, asshole!" Zander yells, voice wavering.

"I'd like to see you try."

And at that, Aidan raises a fist to the jock, palm downward, and opens his hand. The jock plummets to the ground, hitting it with a *whump*. He howls like an animal, clutching his leg. The broken bone has ripped through muscle, skin and jeans. Blood soaks the ground.

*Click.*

Charles, who has been hanging back, steps forward. He aims a handgun at Aidan. Holy crap! *Pulp Fiction Palmer…*

Aidan sneers. "A gun? Really?"

"Get out of here, motherfucker. Or I'll shoot."

Aidan opens his arms and raises them up as he says, "Go ahead."

Charles pulls the trigger.

*Bam!*

My ears ring. But the bullet ricochets away from Aidan as if it hit an invisible shield. Aggravated chirping noises spurt from Charles's throat, his face twisted with rage. He adjusts his aim and pulls the trigger again.

*Bam*

He misses Aidan again.

But not Noah.

Charles was so fixated on Aidan that he didn't notice Noah stagger to his feet. Noah's body sways. He slumps to the ground, blood blossoming at his waistline.

Aidan doesn't take his eyes off Charles.

Charles wails like a wounded animal. Tears run down his red face as the gun in his hands turns toward him. The barrel digs into his belly. My head pounds with horror…

"*No!*" I shout, stepping away from the tree. "*Stop!*"

Aidan turns toward me, shocked.

His eyes glow blue. Like the creature's.

I run.

# Chapter 18

This is the end.

The end of everything.

I text Judy and tell her something unbelievably terrible has happened. She and Leo drive me to her house as I sob uncontrollably in the back seat. I'm grateful they don't push me to tell them why. They make reassuring noises. Judy wraps me in a blanket on the couch before the fireplace and lights a fire. She also makes me tea and gives me a box of tissues that I decimate.

"My folks are gone for the week. Just relax." She says. "We'll be in the library. The bathroom is over there." She points down to the left of what might be the entry. "Let us know if you need anything. Or if you need to talk. Okay?"

Leo quietly places a huge bag of peanut M&Ms on the coffee table. I manage a faint smile. "Thanks."

They leave me to the flames.

Judy's house has high ceilings and stylishly painted walls covered with abstract paintings. Bookcases are crammed with mystery novels, DVDs, and incredibly cool steampunk knickknacks. Someone artistic decorated this home. Maybe her mom. Or dad. There's no TV in this room. Just big worn leather couches, upon which sleeps a fat marmalade cat, and the fireplace. People must come here and talk into the wee hours. I don't know that much about Judy the artist. Now I want to know everything.

But it will have to wait.

An emotional voice mail from Mom and Dad says they are with Charles, who has been put into juvie with his friends for attempted murder. Noah is in the hospital, unconscious.

"Call me immediately. We need to have a family meeting. We'll talk to Aidan when he gets home from work," she says.

The tears return with a vengeance.

Michael texts me to say that he heard there was an epic fight between the jocks and crack heads, and that nobody won.

99

No kidding.

Everything is smashed up inside of me. Bleeding and screaming. I want to die.

Oh, Aidan. I love you. I can't live without you. But I'm terrified of you. I have to get the hell away from you. But what do I tell my parents? I would have to lie about why I'm afraid, to make up something believable. I can't bring myself to do such a thing, even if the ends justify the means.

Between sobs, I try to console myself with the knowledge that the carnage was in self-defense. That my brother and his friends would have killed Aidan. But. *But.*

What the hell did I see?

I pull the blanket tighter around myself.

I'm an engineer. A free thinker. A skeptic. A rational person. The details turn over in my mind. Can I even trust my own mind? My chest feels like it's full of razor blades every time I breathe. Every time I think of Aidan.

And those eyes.

The horror of finding Darren's body. The haunting of the photograph. The terror of encountering that creature.

Is Aidan the creature? No. He can't be. He was with Mr. Reilly when Darren was killed and with Dad when Judy, Leo, Michael and I encountered the creature. But clearly they're connected somehow.

They're both deadly. Although the creature couldn't throw people around like rag dolls. Couldn't? Or didn't? For now, I'll say couldn't. It seemed so feral, it would've lashed out any way possible, especially since it was injured.

My mind is racing as I grieve. If I don't accept what I saw at face value, I will go crazy. Maybe I *am* crazy. Mom and Dad didn't say anything about Aidan being at the police station. Maybe I imagined he was there and it was just a big fight between Charles' friends and the jocks? It wouldn't have been the first in history.

No, he was there.

From my phone, I write an email to Aidan that feels like a pick driving into my chest.

*Leave me alone. Do not speak or write to me. I don't know who or what you are, or how you did what you did, but I don't feel safe around you.*

I don't sign it. I just send it. And when my finger touches the send icon, my heart rips into a thousand bloody pieces. When will this nightmare end?

Aidan warned me. He told me about his father. But how on earth did he commit such violence without so much as a bruise on his body? There must be a plausible explanation.

If there isn't, the rest of my life is over. I'll have to admit to the BFJs that miracles do happen. That maybe even God exists.

How he did it doesn't matter as much as the fact that he hurt—even crippled—four guys, and might have killed my brother. Although, I'm not even sure about that. How could he make Charles point the gun at himself? How could he lift a two-hundred-pound jock into the air twenty feet? How could he throw a person against a tree without touching him? Wrap a chain around someone's neck with a simple gesture? It's impossible.

I think back to that morning on the bus when he startled those two students by knowing something about them.

That day when Mr. Spotty was in the driveway and Aidan raised his hand to a "stop" gesture just before Zachary's car stopped abruptly.

Yesterday with the butterflies.

My butterflies.

A knock on the front door. Judy and Leo emerge from the library, whispering. They open it and let in Michael.

"Where's the patient?" Michael asks.

The three file into the living room. Judy sits beside me. "I hope it's okay that I called Michael. We're really worried about you and we figured you'd have called your mom and dad if you'd wanted them."

I nod, wiping my nose.

"Hey, math queen," Michael says, sitting on the other side of me, putting his arm around me. It's the most physically intimate we've ever been. Two months ago I would have died of happiness. Now, I'm just dying. "You didn't answer my text. I figured something must be really wrong because I never have the last word with you."

My hand hurts. I've been throttling the phone. I don't know what to say to him. Or anyone. He hugs me and I hug him back. Long heaving sobs rack my body. I feel spikes in my lungs. I cough.

"You don't have to talk," Michael whispers in my ear. He just holds me. I have never let anyone do that except for Aidan and my parents. We sit like this for several silent minutes.

Judy brings out glasses of water. "Stay hydrated," she urges.

I take a long drink that turns to gulps. Leo sits on one of the couches looking miserable, but for me rather than himself. Leo, who saved my life.

*You got to trust someone, kid.*

Can I trust these guys? Probably.

But do I trust myself?

My perceptions? My judgments? My ability to reason? I can't possibly be objective.

Michael snuggles up to me. Leo and Judy curl up next to us. A group geek couch cuddle. Judy takes my hand. I must be really messed up or they would not be this sweet.

Also? I'm sweating. Blanket plus friends plus fire equals too hot.

After several moments, I struggle to sit up and shrug off the blanket. I still feel like crap. I accept that it's going to be that way for a while. In fact, it will probably get worse.

Michael looks at me expectantly. I realize this hugging stuff has been a tactic to get me to open up. Not a heartless manipulation. Just him hoping that, if he pumped enough love into me, I'd talk. Not so with Leo and Judy. They look surprised when I speak.

"I've got to come clean with you guys and tell you the whole story. I've been holding back some stuff, not to deceive you, but I had to have my own secret garden. Also, I don't really want to tell you what I saw today because I can't explain it. There are a lot of things, actually, that I can't explain. I just hope you'll believe that I'm telling the truth."

"CJ, I haven't known you forever, but you're one of the most credible people I've ever met," Michael says. "So clearly something's happened and those nunchuks need to fly."

"Yeah, but my nightmare right now is that you won't believe me because what I have to say is so outrageous and I don't have any evidence."

Leo shakes his head. "I bet there's more evidence than you think."

"Maybe," I say, looking at Judy. She squeezes my hand and watches me with watery eyes. It might be her allergies. But it also might be she actually cares.

"It's about Aidan," I start.

And I tell them everything.

# Chapter 19

When I finish, Michael stops pacing and stands with his hands on the couch back. Leo stares into the fire. Judy bites her lower lip, watching my face. She throws her arms around me.

"It's gonna be okay," she says. "The purpose of the Skeptics Club was to bring people together who don't believe things blindly. People who question and investigate. Am I right?"

I nod. So do Leo and Michael.

"Yeah, but it's become some kind of monster hunting club," I say.

Judy continues. "But you've had an experience that ties into something we've experienced together. We were eyewitnesses to the creature. We even have photographic evidence. I totally believe that something weird happened with Aidan because I can tell how much you love him and that it's killing you to be away from him. Why would you be afraid of him if he hadn't done something pretty monstrous?" She picks up the nearly empty box of tissues and shakes it. "Hello! And everyone at school can tell how much Aidan and you are into each other. It's so obvious."

"But he's dangerous," I reply.

"So is everyone when they're cornered," Judy says.

Michael laughs. "Oh, yeah. I bet you've got a mean right hook, Judes."

Judy rolls her eyes. "You know what I mean. But I understand how you feel. That thing about the glowing blue eyes. Oh, my god! That's creepy. Because, like, is Aidan connected to that creature thing? I can't even."

"Do you want us to talk to him?" Leo asks. "Do you think he would attack unprovoked?"

"I don't know on either count. I mean, what would you say? Hello, Charity just told us your whole history. Are you going to kill her? Yes/no?"

Michael sighs, his breath uneven. "Are you serious? Do you really think he's going to hurt you? Or your family?"

"I'm not sure. It's just that, after seeing him push that gun into my brother's—"

"You mean, after your brother shot at him? And then shot his best friend? And hey—maybe he decided to shoot himself!" Michael leans over the couch. "Look, CJ, even if Aidan is some kind of X-Men mutant—"

"Like Apocalypse!" Leo says.

"Seriously?" Judy says. "He's more like Franklin Richards. He's just a boy."

"What-*ever*, Team Marvel!" Michael puts up a hand for quiet. "All things being equal, CJ, I gotta say, if it was indeed Aidan, he did not act inappropriately. Well, maybe he shouldn't have let that dude drop. But even then." He pauses. "And you do realize that Jill Swain is a little bitch, right? They used her to get you away from him."

"But then why not just let me go home on the bus? I wouldn't have been able to interfere at all."

"I bet I know why," Leo says, his face darkening. "Those sick bastards wanted you to see Aidan in pieces. They probably had it timed so that Jill would bring you back and 'accidentally' stumble on the scene. Your brother said he'd make you pay. He knew seeing Aidan injured or dead would hurt you more than anything."

Judy shakes her head. "No. That's not it."

Everyone stares at her.

She takes my hand, a tear spilling over her cheek. "They were going to hurt you next, CJ."

I feel like I've been socked in the gut. I know she didn't mean to, but what Judy said has ripped open a black pit of ire. I hate my brother and I will never forgive him.

"Do you think any of those asshats told anyone what really happened?" Judy asks. "Or tried?"

Michael snorts. "I seriously doubt it."

A fresh wave of grief passes through me. "Talking to Aidan now would be like poking a wasp nest." My voice cracks. "Let's leave him alone and focus on the one thing we can do that will help solve the mystery."

Judy raises an eyebrow. "Which is?"

"Catching the creature," I reply. "I have a plan."

Mom very reluctantly agrees to let me stay the night with Judy. I ask her to text me when Aidan gets home, which she does. Another stab of pain. I've never felt about anyone the way I feel about Aidan, which means I've never broken up with anyone. It certainly hurt when Grandma Jones died, but we were ready for that, sort of. She'd been ill for a while. And it hurt when I lost Keiko. But this thing with Aidan—this is the worst that's ever happened to me.

This, and coming to this school.

In the morning, Judy drives me home. Aidan is at his job already, which is a relief. I stagger down the hallway to my bedroom like a dying person. His sweet smell wafts from his room like a ghost as I pass, causing me to break out in fresh tears. I don't know what I'm going to do when I see him. If I tell him to go away, he will, even if it means the authorities will be after him. He might already be planning to do so, but if he runs, he'd best run far and fast. And if he does, he'll take my heart.

Gotta stay focused. Yes, there's schoolwork. But more importantly, there's monsterwork.

Closing the door, I comb through Aidan's emails until I find the nagging detail that I need:

Peppermint.

# Chapter 20

Saturday morning, my computer hums with equations and Google searches for materials. Most of what we need can be bought dirt cheap at the hardware store. I text Michael and Leo about the parts. They confirm that they can get many of them from their own garages. Judy adds that she's got "loads" of mint from the local pharmacy. I'm not sure what that means, but I assume she knows what she's doing.

Aidan's gone to work. I survived the agony of hearing him just on the other side of the thin wall, my pulse loud in my ears as I curl under the covers.

Mom and Dad call me downstairs to sit on the couch. Mom looks hellishly tired and infinitely sad, a large mug of coffee in hand. In lawyer mode, she explains that police say Charles allegedly shot Noah in a group fight. He was aiming for one of the other kids but instead hit his best friend. The police not only found cocaine in Charles' bloodstream, they found gunpowder residue on his hands, face and jacket, as well as the gun with his fingerprints.

"Wait. It was a group fight? Who else was there?" I ask nervously.

She names Charles, Noah, and the other guys, including Zander, who is now in the hospital from his leg injury, but she says nothing about me or Aidan, who must have taken off right after Noah got hit. "There were no witnesses, then?"

"None that have come forward."

Of course, Charles wouldn't admit there were any witnesses. "So…what now?"

"I can only guess how the DA will go, but I suspect the boys will all be charged with attempted murder."

"But you said that Charles shot Noah. How can *everyone* be charged with attempted murder?" I ask.

"It's the felony murder rule," Mom explains. "Even if the boys only meant to beat each other up, they were all carrying deadly weapons, like bats and tire irons. If someone in their company kills someone, they become collectively responsible for that death, whether they personally pulled the trigger or not."

I wonder if they're in separate cells or all together. I hope they can't talk to each other. "How is Noah?"

"He's still unconscious," Dad says, grim. Eyes bloodshot. "Hospital says he's in grave condition."

The image flashes behind my eyes of Noah falling to the ground, blood blooming from his abdomen. "What does Charles say happened?" The burning question.

"Absolutely nothing. I've trained him too well." She smiles wryly at Dad.

"But if Charles and the other boys don't say anything, and there were no witnesses, how will the cops know what really happened?"

"They won't," Mom answers. "But the DA will prosecute according to whatever evidence they gather, even if they have no testimony. Unless Noah wakes up and testifies to the contrary, they have to assume that your brother was trying to kill him or someone else."

"Do *you* think he tried to kill someone?" I ask.

Mom's eyes find Dad's. "Charles is troubled, but I don't think he's a murderer. I think the police are wrong. I think they were all just fooling around. Boys…they roughhouse. They lose control." Dad nods in agreement.

"With a gun?" I ask, incredulous.

"Happens every day in this country with tragic results," she adds.

I can't argue with that, but I do think they're both in serious denial. "What happens now?"

"Monday, your brother will be arraigned with the other boys. A judge'll decide if they need to be appointed attorneys and then formally charge them."

"But we know how he's going to be charged."

Mom clenches her eyes shut. Tears streak her cheeks.

Aidan doesn't return from work. I thought he would return at some point to gather some clothing. Maybe he did when I was dead asleep. At dinner, I ask Mom where he went.

"He's staying with a friend of his."

I didn't realize he had any friends besides me. "A friend? Who?"

"I promised I wouldn't tell." She looks concerned. "Did you guys have a fight? Something's up with you."

I dodge. "He's probably freaked out. I don't blame him. I'm still pretty freaked out, too. Could I have some friends spend the night?"

"Like who?"

"Michael, Leo and Judy."

Mom frowns. "A co-ed slumber party? I don't know, Charity."

"*Please*. We're dorks, Mom. We're just going to play board games and fall asleep."

"Well…maybe." She sounds weak. Defeated. So unlike my mom.

"I need my friends now. More than ever. Please?"

"Tonight?"

"No. Maybe Monday night?"

I'm trying to sound like a normal girl, but I feel anything but normal right now. My family is in tatters. I'm dying every minute because I can't be with Aidan.

All I have is monsterwork.

Time to make a trap.

Monday. The construction starts in my back yard today after Dad leaves for work. Mom has been with clients since 5:30 a.m., having been called in early when someone's caregiver was found dead. They'll converge later at the courthouse.

Wearing heavy gloves, I empty out Dad's gardening tools and place them on a tarp under the deck. I push the lawn mower under there, too, covering it with another tarp to protect it from any rain. Dad will never notice. Since his back surgery, he's hardly been out here. The sun shines icy light on the trees. My heart breaks every time I look at the rose. It stands tall and strong. Fuller and brighter. A Christmas miracle, he called it.

*And I assure you, it won't be the last.*

His words replay in my head as I check and recheck shed measurements. I wish it didn't feel like someone was pulling my lungs out of my chest through my mouth. The design process calms me.

The hinge goes here.

The wires, there.

I considered a snare trap but the creature seems too smart for it, as Leo reports it had managed to evade detection on a another property this weekend before committing a gruesome attack on someone's pony five miles north of here. It had to be put down, it was injured so badly. So, I settle on a trap similar to the ones used for feral cats. The shed is the only place large enough to trap a creature of this size—at least, that we have access to. Judy's mom has a strong shed in the backyard, but it's crammed with heavy statues and fountains.

The doors pose the greatest challenge. They have to behave like the sliding cage door of the sprung trap, but that's not quite possible. So, I'm spring loading one of the outer doors. It will stand open until the trap is tripped. If I had more time and materials, I could have added an inner door that drops down, but the vinyl material isn't that sturdy and we would need to build an inner skeleton to support it. We don't need it, though. I hope.

Michael's car grinds into the driveway around 11:00 a.m. As he, Judy, and Leo unload, I hand them the plans I drew up over the weekend.

"Whoa!" Leo gasps. "You designed this?"

I hold up the power drill and pull the trigger. "Let's do this thing."

Reinforced door hinges with acorn nut tops. Spring installed. Slide lock snap bolted to the opening. Fishing wire strung through O-rings fastened to the inside walls feeds under a step latch at a shallow angle to the floor, similar to the feral cat traps, and out a wall to trip another hook latch holding the outer door open. I set the trap. The step latch spans the width of the shed, which means the creature can't walk around it, and it's long enough that the creature can't jump over it.

"Hey, that rose is something!" Michael says.

I sigh.

Leo draws the short match. We watch as he creeps inside. One. Two. Three.

WHAP! goes the fishing wire.

SNAP! goes the door.

"Jesus!" Leo shouts.

THUNK! goes the lock.

"Are you sure the creature is heavy enough to trigger the step?" Michael asks.

I nod.

"What about raccoons? Can they trigger it?"

Leo hammers his fists against the inside walls. "Hey!"

"Push it, Leo!" Judy yells back.

"I set the step for about sixty pounds minimum to trigger. Maybe a big dog could set it off or a child. But neither are likely to be on our property at night."

Leo throws himself against the walls. The tool shed rocks back and forth slightly, not enough to turn over.

"Do you think we need to anchor it?" Judy asks.

"Are you kidding? It would take six drunken frat boys to push this thing over. Or a bulldozer. Just keep the lawnmower and other crap in there," Michael replies.

"Otherwise, if you're feeling iffy, we could either dig out the earth underneath and pour concrete or create a wider base that we stake to the ground using concrete. Not only would that take time to set, but I suspect your folks are already going to be mighty unhappy with the current mods, so we shouldn't do it unless we really need to."

Leo throws himself against the doors. They hold tight. He presses his face against one of the acrylic windows on the side, puffing his cheeks. We laugh and call him "fish boy." Michael checks the lock. "You have the key?"

"Don't need it." I show him where we could have a lock if we wanted to, but the slide lock bar is strong enough to hold. Struggling mightily against the spring, Michael opens the door. Leo exits, smiling.

"Sweet!" he says. "You know, I knew what was coming and it *still* scared the hell out of me. This is brilliant, CJ. Nice work."

"It wasn't just me. You guys made awesome happen." I turn to Judy. "Hey, do you have the peppermint?"

She and Leo are looking goofy at each other the way I'm sure I did constantly with Aidan. "Yes!" She runs off to the car and returns with a bulging plastic bag. "They're already selling these. Can you believe it? God, I hate capitalism sometimes. Or maybe I just hate people."

The bag is full of candy canes. Big ones, small ones. Plastic wrapped, yet the odor of peppermint is already overpowering.

"I'm sorry I didn't get to the supermarket. I should have asked first. Will this work?"

My heart sinks. Aidan was pretty clear in his e-mail that he was on a peppermint farm in Washington, which means he had access to fresh peppermint, not this sugary, processed crap. I don't think this will work, but it's Judy's biggest contribution next to creating real camouflage for the interior shed and I don't want her to feel badly. Maybe she's right. Candy canes smell the same, don't they? They might bring ants, but that's not a huge problem. Perhaps this is the better choice. "We'll try it! Worst case scenario is that we'll have to change bait."

And who knows? Maybe I'm way off thinking that what I know about Aidan will also work with this creature. But it's worth trying.

As we sit peeling the plastic off of thirty or so candy canes, Michael says, "You know this thing is going to come at night if it comes at all. Are you going to be okay? What about your folks? How's this going to play out, you think?"

"Good questions," I reply. "Maybe we could have a sleepover for the next couple of nights. Safety in numbers and all that."

Michael shakes his head. "Not me. We've got houseguests and we're prepping for Thanksgiving. There's no way my mom is going to let me out of that."

Judy and Leo, however, are up for it. "But what are we going to do once we catch the thing?" Leo asks. "Thinking optimistically, of course."

"If we actually catch this thing, I'll call Detective Bristow," I say, licking the sticky sweetness off of my fingers. "Or just call nine-one-one. Provided there isn't anything more serious going on, the sheriff would be here in a few minutes max."

"Do you think it'll hold long enough?" Michael asks. He looks to Leo. "What do you think, beast boy?"

Leo shrugs. "He's got those badass claws but I'm not sure how powerful he is. I didn't have to hit him hard to take him out." He thinks for a moment. "How strong's the roof? We didn't test that." Michael helps open the door. Leo scurries into the shed and punches up against the roof. It doesn't budge but it does create a hell of a racket.

"Okay, okay!" I shout. "It sounds like the worst thing that could happen is that it could wake up my parents. But my mom's been taking Ambien and my dad's on medication for his back. So, I don't think they'd wake up immediately. And if they did, they'd call the police first. They're pretty cautious." Translation: they don't have a gun, so they don't take chances.

"And what about Aidan?" Judy asks softly. "Is he coming back?"

"I don't know," I say. I want nothing more than to feel his soft skin and hear the odd lilt of his voice. To look into those milky blue eyes and taste his lips. But that still feels dangerously wrong. Desire knots in my gut. "He's staying with a friend for a few days. I don't know who. My mom won't tell me. Maybe he won't come back at all." I press my lips together and look away. I don't want them to see the tears.

We seal up the candy canes in freezer bags and I store them in my room. Leo and Judy promise to return tonight as everyone piles in the car. Michael hovers at the open car door.

"I wouldn't worry about Aidan. I think we're on the right track." He rests his hand on my shoulder. "I've got a special ring tone for you. Just text me if anything happens. It'll wake me up for sure and I'll zip over."

As we hug long and hard, I wonder if I haven't made a mistake. Maybe Michael likes me more than I realize. Maybe I'm just trying to console myself.

When they're gone, I get the ladder and I tie a few pieces of candy cane on the higher tree branches swaying in the wind.

*Come and get it, you dog-eating piece of crap.*
*We're ready.*

# Chapter 21

"Charity? Come here, baby."

It's later that night. Judy, Leo, and Michael have gone home. Dad's eyes are still bloodshot and puffy. My heart hurts seeing him like this. He holds out his hand to me. His oversized 8-bit Batman t-shirt is wrinkled and stained with fast food. I slide off my bed. I take his hand in mine.

My hands ache from the work we did today but I hold on. I briefly worry that he's found the tool shed modifications, but he and Mom and have only been home a few minutes. They arrived bearing Chinese food. I can smell it from my room.

Mom lays out dishes and silverware as we sit at the table. Dinner feels funereal, but I'm starving.

"Your brother and his friends were arraigned today," Mom says. "It'll probably be in the papers, even if they don't use his name, so we should talk about it now."

"It's bad, isn't it?"

Mom looks like she's about to fall apart. "The DA is going for a series of felony charges, including attempted murder. All the boys might be tried as adults."

"Has Noah woken up yet?"

Mom shakes her head so she can get a mouthful of food. "Until he does, the judge has ordered that they continue Charles's detention. They'll have a pretrial hearing in a couple of weeks—on Monday, the eighth, I think—and then the adjudication hearing a few days later."

Tension drains from my muscles. Charles behind bars. I thought I would feel worse about this if it ever happened, but it's just the opposite. I feel secure. Like I have a normal family for once. No tantrums. No drama. Okay, maybe some drama, but no fighting or yelling. No door slamming. No simmering violence. Just quiet.

Just us.

"What's a pretrial?"

"That's where all the evidence will be shared between the attorneys," Mom explains. "If everyone is ready, they'll then hold the adjudication hearing, probably within the week. In fact, I think they've already scheduled it for the following Wednesday.

"Adjudication hearing?" I wrinkle my nose. "Isn't there a trial?"

Mom shakes her head again. She puts food on her plate but doesn't eat anything.

"That *is* the trial, baby. It's different for juveniles," Dad says. He eats standing up. His back must be hurting. "They don't get juries. Just a judge. Remember last time? It went so fast because he didn't have to go through that process of putting together a jury. If they wait, these kids could turn eighteen, and then everything changes."

"But just like at a regular trial," Mom continues, "the judge will look at the evidence and the charges, and decide if he's guilty." She wipes her chapped nose with a napkin.

"The legal fees are going to be hard on us," Dad says. "We'll have to make some sacrifices."

The air goes dead. I realize what they're saying.

"What you mean is Charles has destroyed my college fund." I want to shove the table the way Charles did the other night. Instead, I sit there, seething.

"You're going to be fine," Dad says. "You're extremely talented. Do you hear me? You'll get into any college you want on scholarship. You don't need us."

"Like hell!" I shout. "You act like just because I'm smart that I can do everything on my own. And you know what? I've been on my own now for almost four years. Ever since Charles started stealing and smoking and doing whatever else. And do I have a car or a license? You keep promising but you never have time. Do you care that the kids at school call me a beaner and send me death threats?"

The color drains from my mom's face. My dad starts to say something, but my mom shushes him. "Listen," she orders.

"You're always threatening to sue people for me. How about helping me actually grow up? You don't care about that. You only care about winning. Like it's a video game. Fix Charles and you win. Awesome! But you know what? I hate him. This whole family revolves around him and his stupid problems. Dad, you didn't take this job because we needed the money but because you thought it would be better here for Charles than Los Angeles. And you didn't care what happened to me. Oh, Charity will be fine. She's super smart. She'll be okay. Well, you know what? I'm not. And I hope Charles rots in jail. He's a miserable, worthless ass who ruins everything. I hope he's convicted and stays locked up forever!"

Mom and Dad look stunned. Dad starts to say something when the doorbell rings. Irritation clouds his face.

"I told Charity she could have friends over," Mom tells him, resigned.

Dad sighs. "We'll continue this conversation later."

My parents retreat to their bedroom while Leo, Judy, and I camp out in the living room. When we're sure they've settled down, we go outside and arm the trap. Judy does an outstanding job of camouflaging the step latch after we place the candy canes just beyond. We then put back the lawnmower and other stuff to make it look like the tool shed was left open.

Leo points to the car. "We smeared peppermint oil from my mom's pantry on the bumpers and tires, and we drove it up near where the last attack happened. We're hoping that it caught the scent and followed us."

"*I'm* not hoping," Judy says. "I hope it goes away. It attacked a horse. How horrible is that?"

"A pony, not a horse," Leo corrects her.

"And, hello, a *human being?*" I remind them. "I want it to go away as much as you do, but we need it alive. Maybe we can get some answers." I point up to the trees. "I tied candy canes to the branches. A little early Christmas decorating."

"I don't get it about peppermint. Does it have any real healing properties?" Judy says.

"It does, sort of," Leo says. "Peppermint has a lot of medicinal properties. It's an antiseptic. A decongestant. And it's really good for indigestion. It's been used for centuries to treat that.

"Let's just hope the creature eats up our candy," I say with dread.

The night passes quietly. Well, as quietly as it can with Leo snoring. I find cushy bright orange earplugs in the downstairs bathroom cabinet for Judy and I around 2:00 a.m. But I can't sleep because I'm thinking of Aidan. Feeling ripped open and ragged. Calculations move through my mind in waves as I double-check everything, a form of meditation.

What about the placement of the peppermint? Will the creature know it's a trap? How intelligent is it, anyway? Aidan is beyond brilliant. If it's connected to him in some way, there must be more to it than meets the eye.

*Aidan, if you are as brilliant as I know you are, please find a way to bring us back together.*

*Because I don't believe in magic.*

# Chapter 22

A shadow moves against the wall, vague and wavering. I'm at a school—not my school but another school. I scan the crowd to see who's making the shadow. It's Aidan. He walks toward me through the crowd. They push against him, jostling and shoving. But he only has eyes for me as he closes in. I'm transfixed by the sight of him. Dying inside. Wanting him more than my next breath. But I can't move a muscle. He carries something red, shining, wet in his cupped hands.

Is it blood?

After breakfast, I start texting Judy. I wonder, if her parents are gone, what's happening this week? So, I ask her.

> *What are you doing for T-day?*
>> Nothing
>
> *Just dinner at home, huh?*
>> No dinner
>
> *??*
>> Didn't want to say this because it sounds pathetic but my folks are in France
>
> *They left you here?!?*
>> Yes
>
> *No way!*
>> Yes way
>
> *So that's why they're not home.*
>> Yup
>
> *How long will they be gone?*
>> 3 weeks

I invite her over for Thanksgiving dinner and to spend the night without even asking Mom and Dad. Of all people, Judy deserves to have a family during the holidays. She agrees but cautions that she has to come home to feed the cats at some point.

Nice parents. Disposable daughter is a built-in cat sitter.

The monster box remains empty.

It's Thanksgiving. Thursday.

Mom sleeps in late. Dad and I brave the local supermarket for Cornish hens, potatoes and veggies. Two hours later on the way home, I ask Dad how Mom's doing.

He hesitates. "She doesn't feel good."

"She's depressed, isn't she?"

"A little."

The last time Mom was depressed, she transformed from Scary Lawyer Mom to Sleeping on the Couch Mom. It was just before she decided to change careers. She eventually had to go on medication. I don't think she stayed on it.

"The judge is going to try all the boys separately," Dad continues, "starting with your brother."

"And I care because why?"

He glowers. "For once, baby, the law is working as it should. I hate to say it, but normally they would just target your brother. His white friends had deadly weapons, every one of them. And did they get charged with felonies? Hell yes."

For sure, we've suffered plenty of race-related problems being a mixed family. Everything from hateful taunts to housing discrimination. The fact that Charles isn't being singled out isn't a silver lining, but it is promising that justice is working as it should.

I recall that hellacious scene. Of Charles shooting Aidan. I close my eyes, fighting tears. *You can't tell. You can never tell.*

When we arrive home, I help carry in grocery bags. Something catches my eye at the side of the house.

A rose.

I deposit the groceries inside and run back out. There's a new red rose to the right of the house on the pathway around the back to the tool shed. And another. And another…

Boldly blossoming where no flowers have ever stood before, eleven new, full-grown red roses wave in the wind for a total of twelve. These blossoms look as if they could withstand a hurricane. I crouch down and inhale their scent. Intoxicating.

There's no way these could have grown overnight. They weren't here last night when I last checked on the monster box.

And then I remember the dream.

It wasn't blood that filled Aidan's palms. It was rose petals.

A squirrel flits away from the shed with a candy cane in its mouth.

Crap!

Squirrels have stolen the candy canes I tied to the trees. I disarm the trap and check inside the shed. The candy canes have been munched and crumbled to pieces. Only a couple of canes remain.

When Judy pulls up, I jump straight into her car. "We've got to go back to the store!"

"Happy Thanksgiving to you, too," she says, amused. "Your Mom forget something?"

"Yeah. Candy canes."

Dinner is surprisingly fun. Judy entertains Mom and Dad with stories about the Himalayas and skiing in the Alps with her parents. Her freshly died magenta hair brightens the dining table. She seems comfortable, happy, bouncy. Judy must be very lonely, her parents dumping her whenever they have something more fun to do than being a family. I've seen her astonishing artwork online. Alien dragons. Superheroes. Dinosaurs that are half-human. She obviously gets a lot of mileage out of being alone, but it's clear she misses her parents.

After we devour apple pie and help clean up, Judy and I return to the monster box with our new candy canes and two bottles of fresh peppermint oil we bought at the drugstore.

"The roses!" she exclaims, agape.

"I know this sounds nutso, but I think they're from Aidan. I dreamed that he brought me rose petals last night. And here they are, like him. Defying the laws of nature."

We fasten a light mesh over the container with the candy canes and replace it in the trap. We then douse rags with peppermint oil and tie them to the branches.

Judy holds the ladder as I work. "Leo says he knows where Aidan is staying, but he won't tell me."

"He knows I'd try to get it out of you."

"And you'd probably succeed." Her voice changes. "Can I ask you a personal question?"

"I guess. I might even answer."

"Are you a virgin?"

"Duh." I laugh.

"Oh, come on. It's not always obvious. Can I ask you another question?"

"Sure," I reply.

"Were you ever worried you might go farther than you intended to with Aidan when you were alone with him?"

"No. Well, yeah. Kinda."

She looks uncomfortable. "So you *were* tempted?"

"Heck yeah, but I'm not ready and Aidan wasn't very aggressive. He likes to touch, he's affectionate, and I could tell when he was really turned on, but I think he still thinks he's in a Jane Austen novel. It's probably for the best."

Judy rubs a dirty spot on the ladder with her finger.

"Are you okay?" I ask.

"Yeah."

I climb down and sniff. Not enough peppermint. "There was that one day, though. The temptation was overwhelming. I don't know how far we would have gone if Charles hadn't caught us. But Aidan was definitely letting me decide how fast we moved." An almost crippling pang hits me at that last statement.

Judy looks relieved. "Thanks. I don't feel so slutty anymore."

I laugh. "Slutty? There's no such thing! Well, not according to my mom, anyway. I think she might have invented the term 'slut shaming.' She says whatever you like, want or do is fine. Don't let anyone tell you otherwise." I grab the bottle of peppermint oil and open it. "I want to die of embarrassment every time she mentions me getting the HPV shot."

"It's supposed to help," Judy offers, fidgeting with her hoop earring.

"At least she doesn't talk about this stuff in front of my dad. I would die and he would totally have a heart attack." I douse the inside of the monster box with the peppermint oil. "That should do it."

"I love this smell." Judy inhales deeply.


We go back inside for more pie and board games. Mom goes to bed early but Dad stays up to slay us at Settlers of Catan. He makes us a fire before we snuggle up in our sleeping bags amidst a sea of pillows and blankets.

"Do you need earplugs?" I ask.

Judy giggles. "You're not hiding Leo under one of these blankets, are you?" I laugh.

"He's pretty loud, isn't he?" She sighs and snuggles further into her pillows. "Something to keep in mind if you ever live together."

A big smile.

"At the rate he's going, that'll be when he's eighty. Right?"

Judy looks thoughtful. "Something must have happened that night when we were on patrol. When he called me the next day to make sure I was okay, I thought I would die of shock. And happiness. I just thought he was so adorable that day at the meeting, with his trumpet case and bushy eyebrows. And I'm a sucker for big noses." We giggle harder. Her face glows.

"So, he's changing?"

"Yeah. For the better! Definitely."

The fire crackles. We're silent for several minutes. "What do you want for Christmas?" I ask.

She doesn't answer immediately. "Well, two weeks ago, I wanted the latest version of Maya so I can do better animation, but now…" She picks at threads of her blanket. "I want to catch that monster and make it go away."

I think about my butterflies. My chest grows heavy.

Eventually our eye lids grow heavy and we slip into sleep.

*A shadow moves against the wall, vague and wavering. I'm at a school again. I scan the crowd to see who is making the shadow. It's Aidan. He walks toward me through the crowd. They push against him, jostling and shoving. He only has eyes for me as he closes in. I push forward into the crowd, struggling. Wanting him more than my next breath. Something cracks in the distance. A howl cuts through the air.*

*Aidan's eyes glow blue.*

I awaken, sit bolt upright.

The trap's been set off.

I fumble with my cell to text one word to Michael.

*SCORE*

# Chapter 23

Judy scrambles for her shoes and coat, using her cell phone as a flashlight. I do the same.

*Aaarrrooooooooo!*

A hollow battering follows.

"Shit!" Judy gasps.

Grabbing her hand, I lead her out of the house. If Mom and Dad aren't awake by now, they'll never wake up.

I tiptoe toward the shed, Judy close behind. The shed rattles from a blow inside to one of the walls. Judy stifles a scream. I pull her close.

"Remember, it's not getting out," I whisper.

The darkness is stifling as we approach. I hold the cell at minimal brightness to light our pathway. Past the roses.

*Crack.*

The acrylic shatters.

We stop. I aim the cell phone light at the long gray arm groping out of the tiny window opening. Claws swipe the air.

I hit the number in my address book. "Detective Bristow, this is Charity Jones. Come quickly to our house! We've got the thing that killed Darren! It's trapped in our tool shed." I give him our address and hang up. I then text the same number.

And I call 911.

A rumbling from the shed.

"Charity!"

I turn back to the spectacle. The creature hisses from the window. "Wicked! Wicked children!" it cries. "What have you done to us?"

In shock to hear it speak, I step forward, grasping at courage as it continues.

"Wicked! Torturers!"

I take another step, keeping the light to the side. I don't want to shine it directly at the creature and drive it into the shed. Not yet.

"Murderers!" it cries.

The creature's face appears in the opening as I draw closer. Eyes glowing. Round. Reflective like a cat's with a black slit for a pupil. Goatish snout and ears. Filthy jagged teeth jut from its gums.

Adrenaline hums between my ears as I speak. "*You're* the murderer. Remember me?"

The creature grows still. "I should have killed you after the boy. Cracked open your head. Licked the delicious blood from your skull." It makes a sucking noise.

Every hair on my body stands up. The cold night air pinches my face, but the true chill drives deep inside. I have no weapon. Only my engineering.

And then its clawed hands erupt from the window.

I reel back as it swipes at me.

"You know Aidan, don't you?" I ask.

The eyes shine. "The claws? You know the claws? I thought I smelled his stinking flesh here." It sniffs the air and rests its misshapen nose on the window's edge. "We smell him on you." The creature scans the yard beyond me. "Where is he? Give him to us!" Its arm shoots out again. Grasping.

Stall. Give the police time to get here. "Who is Aidan?"

"*He is the claws. The keeper of sin.*"

"I don't understand."

"Of course you don't! Ignorant, wicked, wretched…"

"Then explain. Tell me."

Its drool glistens as it drips down the side of the shed. Breathing labored. Eyes narrow. "First let us out."

"First tell me more about Aidan. Why do you want him?"

"He must come home! The father demands it!"

"Where is home?"

The eye blinks. "He has not told you? You do not know?"

"Maybe I do. He's from a very cold place."

I notice Judy is taking a video of the exchange.

"He's from up north," I continue slowly, buying seconds at a time. "Waaaaaay up north. Somewhere Russian icebreakers sail. With his library. And his siblings." The creature quiets, listening. "It's where you live, isn't it? You live in the north. With Aidan's cruel father."

The creature snaps away from the window. It hops around the shed on its one good leg, throwing itself against the doors.

*SLAM.*

*SLAM.*

*SLAM.*

I back away.

"Bad son!" the creature yells. "A very bad son. We must…*please*…the father!"

"CJ!" Judy grabs the ax and large hedge shears out from under the tarp beneath the deck. I shove the cell in my pajama pocket and she throws me the ax. I hold it in an aggressive stance. The shed rumbles fiercely.

But after a few moments of frantic bashing the creature quiets down. I guessed its weight pretty closely. Not enough mass to break the shed but enough to trigger the step latch.

I hear my dad calling but I don't see him. "CJ? CJ!"

Michael's car zooms into the driveway. "CJ! Judy!" He leaps out and rushes to the tool shed, a large hunting knife in hand. "Where is it?"

"In the shed. He's tired," I whisper. I tell him about "the claws."

"Called Bristow?"

I nod. I pull out my phone and discover the detective has already texted me back.

ON MY WAY

That was six minutes ago. I show the text to Michael. He approaches the shed. "Hey, in there. You like dogs? I got some dog meat for ya."

The creature says nothing. Crunching noises echo inside.

He must be eating the candy canes. Which means he'll start to heal.

Maybe soon.

Sirens bleed into the night. They're coming. We only need a few more moments.

*SLAM.*

*SLAM.*

*SLAM.*

The bolt cracks on the shed where it's attached to the door. I hold out the ax. Michael flanks, knife drawn.

*SLAM!*

"Charity?"

Dad's voice is drowned out by the wail of the police sirens. Flashing lights. Detective Bristow's Mustang and the sheriff's car screech into the driveway. They jump out, running toward us.

"*Police!*"

*SLAM!*

I stumble as I retreat, dropping the ax.

The creature explodes out of the shed. Rushing me. Teeth bared. Claws extended.

Those eyes.

Deafening explosions. Gunpowder scars the air.

An inhuman shriek. The creature falls. It tries to rise, reaching for me.

More shots. And then stillness.

Detective Bristow's gun is silent.

His eyes find mine. Haunted.

# Chapter 24

*He is the claws.*

*The keeper of sin.*

*A very bad son.*

*We must…please…the father.*

# Chapter 25

They shot and killed the creature as it attacked me. I'm both grateful and grieved. But it reminds me too much of the bullet that tore into Noah. The bullet meant for Aidan.

The back yard isn't even a crime scene.

Local news sites such as *The Mountain Republic* file breathless reports covering the story. My ingenious trap. The dead creature. Doctors trying to classify the body. The claws perfectly match the cut marks on Darren's body, the teeth marks on the dead animals. They determine it's some kind of mutated primate and forward findings to a prominent university.

Detective Bristow brags in every article. But hey, he and the other cops did save my life. He has my gratitude and respect.

My parents are both pissed and proud. I show Dad the mods to the shed. The damp ground shimmers with recent rain. Birds squawk overhead. We told investigators that we used candy for bait.

"You must've known this design was unbelievably dangerous." Dad leans against the shed, taking the strain off his back. "Anyone could have stepped in this thing and gotten hurt. Maybe killed. You see the flaws, right?"

I shrug. "Yeah. But now that thing won't kill anything ever again." The real story thuds in my ears.

*The keeper of sin.*

Dad makes me promise to tell him next time I feel compelled to play Daniel Boone. I'll have to Google what that means.

I promise, mentally crossing my fingers behind my back.

Michael, Leo, Judy, and I cram into a booth at Denny's.

"My fellow monster hunters," Michael says, raising his iced tea in the air. "Here's to us and to monster baggage!"

"Hear, hear!" We clink glasses and teacups.

"I've never been so simultaneously busted and praised in my life," I say, and sip my lemonade.

"I feel that," Michael agrees. "I predict that in a week the news will go viral. You think things suck now? Just wait."

A worried expression darkens Judy's face. Leo wraps his arm around her. "Any new thoughts about the creature's relationship to Aidan?" she asks.

I shake my head. "I've been obsessing over everything the creature said. It came here to bring Aidan home. That's all I can make sense of. And it kept talking about 'the father,' whoever that is. It sounded more like a title than a family relationship. Maybe a priest? Or minister?" Outside the window, a family of six slams the door of a van in the parking lot and heads to the restaurant entrance. Chubby kids, stout parents. Ski jackets. Faded t-shirts with football team logos and The Simpsons. So very normal.

"And the cops still don't know it talked?" Leo asks.

"I've told no one except you guys."

"Why not?" Michael asks.

"What would I tell them it said? All that crap about Aidan? No way. Now, what *I* don't understand is why it didn't kill me."

Michael clears his throat. "Not to split hairs or anything," he says, leaning toward me, "but it *hella* tried!"

"It could have but it didn't! Just as it was about to lunge at me, it hesitated. It could've taken me out in one swipe, but something happened. Something caught its eye..."

"The rose," Judy says, her eyes bugging. "Oh, my god! When it leaped, it saw the flower and hesitated. I swear! I saw it get distracted by the rose."

"What's distracting about that?" Leo asks.

"Aidan made it," Michael says. He directs the questions at me. "Do you think it knew that? Maybe it was afraid of Aidan?"

"It kept calling Aidan 'the claws,'" I remind them. "I think it's a term of deference. Like it was acknowledging Aidan's ferocity or strength." No one says anything. I lose it. "I can't even believe I'm saying this. Aidan is the gentlest person I have ever known! He's such an awkward, sweet, adorable dork."

"Who creamed a half-dozen dudes without touching them." Michael puts his hand on my arm. "Are you still afraid of him?"

"I don't know," I say. Restaurant noises drown out my thoughts.

"But you're still in love with him."

The answer catches in my throat. Heat floods my face. My body. Tears come. Michael hugs me.

Tomorrow is school. I have almost no homework finished. And Aidan will be there.

# Chapter 26

As soon as I shut my dad's car door, the school banter starts.

"Hey, monster hunter!" kids call out, waving. "Kick ass!"

I glance at the bike rack. Aidan's bike is there, this time complete with its front tire. My heart lurches.

People gawk. The haughty cheerleaders who rule the hallways, including Beth, clear a path for me as I approach the lockers. I'm too worried about my shoddy homework to enjoy my new status. I've got to win scholarships and my AP Calculus homework is shipwrecked on Aidan Island.

Knowing I will see Aidan, I keep my eyes down. Try not to look around despite the high-fives and fist bumps.

Leo basks in the attention, accepting congratulations and other encouragement with his usual grace. He knows how to take a bow. Judy, however, squirms whenever anyone tries to talk to her, pulling her navy toque down tighter. Leo draws her close to him, a protective gesture. It's sweet, but I wish she would own her success.

Then again, I wish *I* could own my success.

Meanwhile, Michael swaggers into calculus like an Olympian. It's faintly hilarious how he fends off the girls' attention, making a point of speaking only to me. His gestures to the guys are magnanimous, accepting their kudos and invitations to parties, dirt bike racing, and other things Michael doesn't do. Everyone asks us what it was like. I let Michael answer for us. "Better than a roller coaster," is all he says.

He pats me on the back as he leaves. I remain in my seat, waiting to be lectured by Mrs. Stewart for turning in a half-finished homework package. She asks him to close the door after him, leaving us alone.

She sits in a desk next to mine, cheek propped on fist, studying me. "I'm worried about you." She holds up my flimsy assignment.

I say nothing.

"Under normal circumstances, you should be getting nothing less than an A+ in this class, Charity. I mean it. An A+. And here you are with just about a

C+. You can't afford this. Universities are extremely competitive. Caltech and MIT are taking people with no less than a 4.2 GPA."

"I'm sorry," I squeak, apologizing to myself, not her. I want to fall through the floor.

"It's not your fault. I know you're going through a lot with your brother and what happened over Thanksgiving. In fact, I'm surprised you're here at all. You've got a lot of strength, Charity. You're brilliant. And I believe in you."

I say nothing.

"So, how about this: You pitch to me a project to make up your grade. If I like the pitch, you do the project and I'll give you extra credit points depending on the work involved. Does that sound fair?"

*Wicked! Torturers!*

"I have an idea," I say, cheering up.

"Go on."

"How about I show you the calculations I used when I built the monster box?"

I don't know what a real orgasm sounds like, but based on the noises she's making, I think Mrs. Stewart is having one.

100 points extra credit.

My triumph in calculus helps me hold it together through Honors Chemistry, French, PE, and lunch until I get to American History. Sliding into a back row seat near the door, I shield my brow from the stares. But when Aidan strides in, the bottom falls out of my universe.

He looks stunning. His hair's been cut in a trendy style, shorter in the back and longish on top. A bit of product tames the mop of curls just enough to take the edge off. His clothes are ironed and neatly layered. He wears Dad's black sweater over a blue button-down shirt with a clean pair of dark jeans. Someone's been dressing him. Or maybe he's learning. He sits in his usual seat. Girls raise a sickening chorus of "Hey, Aidan." He acknowledges them politely.

I'm suddenly surrounded by yammering Muggles who want to know more about the monster.

Mr. Reilly pushes up his sleeves, glaring at the students crowded around my desk. "We all appreciate what Ms. Jones and her friends did for our community, if not science itself, but it's time to settle down and talk about Friday's midterm. So turn to page 237, please?"

At that, Aidan's back stiffens. His head turns, scanning the classroom until he finds me in the back. Those eyes lock with mine. Troubled. Beseeching. Loving. Sweet. Forever.

Mr. Reilly asks Aidan a question, breaking the spell. Someone mentions the War of the Roses and *Game of Thrones*. The class is briefly hijacked by George RR Martin.

Terror and desire surge through me. Raw emotion chokes my thoughts. *Keeper of sin.*

As soon as class is over, I dash outside into the rain.

No one besides Mrs. Stewart brings up Charles today. Maybe because I'm not as behind in my other classes. I suppose if we hadn't caught the creature, Charles would be my only albatross.

Michael texts me.

> Need a ride home?
> *Can you?*
> Sure
> *See you at the car.*

Which isn't as easy as I thought. Once again, news vans choke the parking lot. Reporters are looking for us. The monster trappers. I pull up my hoodie the way I did Aidan's the day I hid him from the news cameras. We circle to the far end of the lot and move toward where the Honda is parked, slipping out with relative ease.

"I thought that was illegal," I say.

"What was illegal?"

"Interviewing kids without their parents."

"It's not illegal to ask kids to point us out," he says.

"This probably means we can't go home, either."

"They might be slow, but they're bulldogs," he replies, navigating the traffic. "I can't believe it's taken this long."

"They just released our names yesterday."

"One of them was a San Francisco news van."

"Dang."

It's quiet for a few moments. We're closing in on my street. "So, you going to that dance on Saturday?" Michael asks.

"I was supposed to go with Aidan." I no longer feel like talking. I just want to go home and curl up with headphones on. Maybe some Get Busy Committee. The Suicide Song.

"I think you should go. Have fun. Celebrate your newfound popularity. You deserve it, CJ. How often does someone get to go from villainous to victorious in less than three weeks? You're a phenomenon, doll face."

Still don't feel like talking.

"Why don't you go with me?"

I stare at him like he's from space. Who is this guy? My life has turned upside down.

"We won't go in this clunker, I promise. My dad has offered us the Escalade. We could double with Leo and Judy, if ya want."

"What are you doing?"

"I'm asking you to the Winter Dance. Do you want to go?"

I hate dances. But this is the closest I'll ever get to being homecoming queen.

Does Michael like me? I thought he had a girlfriend outside of school. Perhaps he doesn't. No, on second thought, that's just my ego talking. My hair is a disaster, my makeup smeared. He's just being nice. He feels sorry for me.

Then again, the last time I thought someone was "just being nice," it was Aidan. I smile. "Let's tear it up."

Michael lets out this mighty warrior holler and flips on the MP3 player, singing along with Michel Bublé on "Feeling Good." The horn section lets rip. I laugh.

"You don't want to know what the rejection song was!" he shouts and then continues singing.

What have I done?

# Chapter 27

I live with ghosts.

Mom rarely eats dinner. She goes to bed early. Dad comes home late. I fend for myself. Leftover Chinese food. Spaghetti. Almond butter sandwiches. She has just enough energy to scold the news people who come to our door. They want to hear about the monster. They even ask questions about Charles. She threatens them with legal speak. They leave.

Using some of my savings from tutoring money, I sneak out to shop for a dress with Judy. With much fuss I eventually find a sharp black dress that lengthens my waist and emphasizes my bust with straps that sweep up and hook behind my neck. I can pull it off with the strapless bra that's buried in my undie drawer.

Every day in History, he reaches into me with his eyes and I want to die. And I dream of him at night. In that crowd. Fighting to pass the bodies. Red on his hands.

Rose petals. Blood. It hardly matters which.

Thanks to the block schedule, I get a break on Wednesday, but it's a double-dose on Thursday when History is two hours long.

The blood of that creature is on my hands. I am ashamed of leading it to its death. Judy says I couldn't have known it would escape; much less that Detective Bristow would shoot it. And besides, it was a killer.

*It was also a person.*

Detective Bristow leaves a voicemail message on my phone to say the Sheriff's Department wants to give us a commendation for our help solving Darren's murder.

Friday puts up a fight by throwing quizzes at me in every class. I'm ready. I've not been able to sleep, so I've been studying for All The Things.

Sitting in Mrs. Hohlwein's class, I write about scorpions and butterflies, pigs' tails and Colombian history. Why does everything have to mean something? Why can't a thing simply be beautiful? I shudder as I think about Meme's bathroom full of scorpions. That has been my life the past few weeks. Secret trysts. Excitement. Scorpions and butterflies.

The bell rings. I look up. Aidan passes the window. We lock eyes for a moment. My heartbeat quickens.

I can't take it anymore. I race out of classroom after him.

I stand in the crowd of students, just like in my dream. Pushing against me. Keeping me from moving forward. But unlike the dream, he's gone.

How could I have forgotten the scorpions?

Saturday is consumed with hair treatments to tame the infernal frizz. Careful hours of hair relaxant produce sleek, glossy waves. Not as smooth as Keiko's but kind of astonishing. Thanks to online tutorial videos, I manage not to burn my scalp. Michael and I have agreed that we'll eat dinner at home, saving our outfits and pocketbooks the possible disasters of eating at a restaurant. The extra hours are devoured by meticulous makeup prep, watching tutorial videos for tips. Frustrated, I throw the box of lip pencils and eyeliners against the bathroom wall. How do I eyeliner? How do I lip line?

How do I girl?

I never worried about feeling beautiful with Aidan. I always felt gorgeous. One date with Michael and I've lost my mascara mind. The sobs well up as I sit on the closed toilet seat.

A knock on the door.

"Are you okay in there?" Mom asks.

"Fine."

"You don't sound fine."

I open the door reluctantly. Mom does a spit-take.

"Oh, my god! Your hair! It looks—different. Why did you do that?"

"I told you. I'm going to the Winter Dance. With Michael Allured." I face the mirror, examining the disaster that is my attempt at beauty. I shouldn't have tried to straighten my hair. Mom's right. It was prettier before.

"I didn't know you guys were dating. Does Michael's mom know?"

"We're not dating." I toss pencils back in the box. "We're just friends."

"Do you want some help?"

I need major help. Like, a S.W.A.T. team of MAC artists. My Mom, the Belle of Belfast City, never needs makeup. I don't see what she can contribute.

One of the reasons I hate makeup is because it's so hard to find what works on my skin tone.

"Here," she says. "Let's start with your skin, okay?"

Less is more, she says. Easy on the foundation. Powder applied with brush. A touch here. A dab there. She coaches me through the eyeliner and mascara. Even the shadow. It should be heavier than usual, since it's an evening event.

I melt. She's helping.

Helping because I need her help.

About an hour later, my face is transformed. I don't recognize myself—in a good way.

"You are gorgeous." Mom smiles one thousand kilowatts. "I'd kiss you but I don't want to muss you." Her fingertips dance around my newly relaxed waves.

Like butterflies.

I don't recognize the young woman I see in the mirror. I might enjoy getting to know her.

My shoes are surprisingly comfortable: strappy Mary Janes I bought last summer that were too big. Now they fit perfectly, with bandages protecting my Achilles tendon. The heels add about two inches, which is plenty.

Michael wheels up the driveway in his dad's gleaming black Cadillac Escalade. It's bigger than the Prius and the Camry stacked together. As I trod down the stairs, my parents appraise me like I'm from another dimension.

Dad clutches his heart and staggers back against the coat closet door. "Evelyn, I'm not ready for this!" Dad recovers and steps closer, beaming. A tear might be in his left eye. "My Little River." He plants a kiss on top of my brow. "Not so little anymore."

The doorbell rings. My nerves jump. Mom opens the door.

Michael stands in the doorway. Immaculate black suit and shiny blue tie. A dapper spray of mousey brown hair atop his head that defies gravity. He holds out a bouquet of white roses.

When he sees me, the penny drops. His mouth drops open. "I…who…" He slaps himself. "Wow!" He remembers his manners. "Good evening, Mrs. Jones." Then, to Dad, "Good evening, sir! I'm Michael Allured." Dad shakes hands with him, making pleasantries. He takes in Dad's girth, and his face takes on the appropriate mantle of dread. "Sir, I promise you. I shall not put a hand upon your daughter this evening except in utmost chasteness as we, you know, twerk. Ahem!"

Dad laughs. "That's okay. She's held her own against a bigger masher than you. You better watch out."

A momentary flashback to the creature lunging at me. I close my eyes. *Just keep breathing.* It's going to be okay. This is normality. Calm. Fun! Good.

"Mashers. Moshers." Michael sighs. "It's been a sincere pleasure to have formally met you, sir, madame. And now we have a dance to attend. My lady?" He holds out his arm.

I take it. And the roses, which I inhale. White. Not red. Calculated choice on Michael's part, no doubt. Mom helps me with my coat. I'm going to need it. Forecast of 50 degrees tonight.

"Have fun!" Mom says. "Michael, please say hi to your mom for me?"

"I will," he replies, helping me into the Escalade. "Have a wonderful evening! Wait up for us!"

"Be safe!" Mom says with a wink.

I can't believe she just said that. I crumple with embarrassment.

Unfazed, Michael climbs inside the cab and starts the car. It's spacious and luxurious. The perfect wheels. "You really are stunning, CJ. Um…you *are* CJ, right?"

I bat him on the head with the bouquet.

"Ow! Yup, that's you."

We take each other in. Eventually, I say, "Let's do this dance thing."

"As you wish," he replies, and the Escalade rips in reverse.

# Chapter 28

I forgot that the dance was to raise money for Darren's youth group, Inspiration International. The group's garish banner complete with golden cross is plastered on the wall outside the gym, as well as inside over a long table manned by church members collecting donations in jars and metal boxes. They tug at their ties, looking uncomfortable in their missionary haircuts and shiny shoes as the DJs thump out Avril Lavigne's "Hello Kitty."

Who needs chaperones? We've got Jesus.

On the other side of the door is a coat check. Michael and I exchange our wraps for a couple of tickets. A big donation jar sits on the coat check table with the Inspiration International logo. I would tip them but I know where the money will go. Michael tips for us.

The gym is a fishbowl of swirling green and blue light. The naked limbs of fake birch trees are wrapped in white lights and other ornaments. Couples and singles writhe to the music. Strutting. Turning. Flipping. Rocking. I've never felt comfortable in gyms and this is not helping.

It's too loud for conversation. Michael leans over toward me and shouts, "Let's walk the perimeter. Gotta show off the threads and find Judeo."

"Did you just combine their names?"

"I did," he says proudly.

I roll my eyes.

Boys in suits with discarded ties and open collars. Girls in tight dresses. Glittering jewelry. Tarted-up bullies. People congregate at the massive refreshment table. "Courtesy of the Jacobs Family" reads the golden banner on the wall above.

They really like their banners.

The DJ brings up a club version of Cage the Elephant's "Ain't No Rest for the Wicked." People race for the dance floor. Judy and Leo feed each other cupcakes at an empty table.

What happened to the cheap sale dress she bought? As we close in, the details of her ridiculously genius fashion makeover stand out. Judy has converted an otherwise unremarkable pale green dress into a Chanel masterpiece by adding new material and tucking the waist. She's now a vintage darling with her sculpted collar and an A-line silhouette heightened with an added chiffon overskirt. She wears her hair up a bit like Amy Winehouse, a tiny pillbox hat pinned to her magenta crown, and even wears a pair of smart white gloves. The not-as-fashionable Leo can't take his eyes off of her. He himself looks pretty slick in his black priest-collar suit and gold cufflinks. There's nary a trace of the boy in the forest who quivered at the thought of this girl.

Judy grabs his hand and tugs him toward the dance floor, but Leo balks like she's just invited him to jump into a piranha pool. Michael saves him with a salute. We cluster by the wall, leaning in to talk. Or rather shout. It would be easier to text.

Before we can even get through our greetings, adults descend upon us with serious looks, led by our principal, Mrs. Cartwright. The other adults are unfamiliar. Are they parents? Or just muscle? "Good evening, Charity. Michael. Will you and your friends kindly come with us for a moment?"

I don't like this. Judy and Leo seem annoyed but Michael looks the way I feel: downright hostile.

"We just got here," I say. "Are we in trouble?" Mrs. Cartwright has never before spoken to me directly. She congratulated our FIRST team when we won our last competition. But this is strange.

"There's someone who wants to meet you," Mrs. Cartwright says. "Please. It won't take long."

They then turn to leave, but Mrs. Cartwright's hand grasps my elbow. Michael intercedes. "If I may." Mrs. Cartwright releases me as Michael takes my arm. I look to my friends with resignation.

We're escorted out of the gym into an adjacent set of rooms. Offices where PE teachers and clubs meet. Members of Darren's church are gathered here, holding hands, praying. Bibles scatter the chairs and tabletops.

I am extremely uncomfortable.

Mrs. Cartwright leads us to a couple slightly older than my folks. Dressed conservatively, they appear more ready for a church service than a high school dance. "Mr. and Mrs. Jacobs? This is Charity Jones and her friends Michael Allured, Leo Donatti, and Judy LaHart."

"Hi," is all I can muster as a couple with bloodshot eyes enthusiastically shakes our hands. Mr. Jacobs is a tan, barrel-chested man in a gray suit. Mrs. Jacob wears multiple strands of pearls over her thick black dress. They both look like they could use at least a year of sleep.

"We," Mr. Jacobs says, indicating his wife, "That is, Charlotte and I just wanted to thank you for capturing and bringing our son's killer to justice. We prayed to the Lord Jesus day and night that He would deliver his killer swiftly. You are the answer to that prayer."

I want to tell them what a bastard their son was. The pain he caused me every day. And that killing isn't justice. The creature might have been vile, but death was not the answer. It was a tragic loss to science and humanity, too.

The words stick in my throat. I want to climb into a time machine and travel to another decade, maybe even a distant planet. The silence seems to unnerve Mrs. Cartwright.

"We are very appreciative for what you did," Charlotte says. "We were planning a more formal event with the Sheriff's office and superintendent, but when we heard you were here, we wanted to thank you personally."

There's only one thing I can say. It's what I feel when I remember what my family used to be like, before the troubles. And every time I see Aidan. The aching emptiness. The words for that feeling appear quietly in my mind. Words I've heard my parents say. Words I've seen on blog comments and social media. I take Charlotte's hand.

"I'm sorry for your loss."

Charlotte cries. We then each hug her. Mr. Jacobs shakes hands with Michael and Leo, tears streaming down his grief-worn face. I hug him, too. It turns out I've found something here I didn't expect.

The very last thing, in fact.

Connection.

We return to the insanity of the gym where the number of students has doubled. At full speed, I haul back to the refreshment table for a chocolate cupcake. As I wolf down the badly needed dose of chocolate, the DJ announces, "Hey, hey, hey, Oakwood High! Monster hunters are in the house!"

Oh. God.

The walls vibrate with a clubbed up mix of Lady Gaga's "Monster" as the crowd cheers.

No. No. No.

Like an amoeba, the dancers absorb us into a toxic swirl of twisting and thrusting. Those who cannot dance jump in place, hands in the air, shouting "Wooo!" Whiffs of whiskey and weed mingle with sweat. I'm caught up in the madness. My hand flings out for Michael. He plants his body straight up against mine. Just as I think I might have to knee him, he says in my ear, "Hold on. We're getting out."

Using his bulk, he squirms us out of the crowd, one "Woo!" at a time.

We slip out the back door. The cold air bites into my bare arms and legs. Michael gives me his jacket. Taking my hand, he brings me around the side that's exposed to the field beyond. The muted music tries to pound its way out.

"Wow." He shivers as he leans against the building, hands in pockets. "That was something." He hesitates. "You did good, CJ. I couldn't do what you just did with those people. None of us could. But you pulled through. That was awesome."

"Thanks." It's really damned cold. The sky is strewn with stars. Clear and sparkling. "Maybe we should just get our coats and leave."

"Mmmm," Michael says, knuckle to mouth. "Yes. But I have something to tell you first. I've kept a couple of secrets from you and the others. It's time to spill."

A riot of emotion. My teeth chatter. I do a little potty dance to keep warm. "But do we have to talk about it here? It's cold, and anyone could be listening. You can't hear it standing here, but sound echoes around the building."

"Nah, don't worry. Everybody's inside doing the stripper kick. Or the Nae Nae. Or whatever. It's time to come clean," Michael continues. He seems a bit anxious to get this out. "First, about me." His eyes mist as they look into mine. If he had a soul, I would be looking directly into it. "You've probably wondered why I've never asked you out before. Or any girl at our school."

"Yeah, but you're dating someone outside of school, aren't you? Some girl in community college? Why didn't you bring her instead of me?"

"It's not a girl."

The rumors about girls from other schools. Older girls. Invisible and impeccable. It makes sense now. Desperate attempts to stay in the closet. I put my hand on his cheek. "Thank you for trusting me."

We hug, long and hard. "I knew you wouldn't be upset or judgmental. Turns out maybe instead of medicine I should go into acting, huh?"

"Well, I hear there are lots of parts for straight characters," I joke. I hunch under the jacket. "Your parents know?"

"Oh, yeah. They're cool. They can't wait to get their first gay grandbaby."

I laugh. "So, you wanna hit me with Secret Number Two?"

"Yeah," he says, swallowing hard. "But I need you to trust me. Like, to the power of infinity trust me."

"Okay."

"You promise? You won't budge?"

"I promise."

His gaze trails over his right shoulder and fixes there.

Where Aidan emerges from the shadows.

# Chapter 29

"Hello, Charity Jones," Aidan says, hands in pockets. He is more stunning than ever. Curls escape from under the brim of a tall top hat to spill over his forehead. He wears a crisp black suit with a long, old-fashioned coat and a blood red cravat.

A storm of heat, desire.

Fear.

"He's been staying in our guest house," Michael continues. "Don't worry! He's not my type and I'm not his. He's definitely all yours. Although, I hope you don't mind my mom's been having fun styling him."

Dying inside as he approaches. But this time no one is in our way. Aidan sweeps off his coat and holds it open to me in one movement.

"As I was saying, um, I think Aidan has some 'splaining to do, Lucy. And I think it's good stuff. You should give him a listen. So, I'll let him do that."

Transfixed, I hand Michael his coat. He scurries out of sight.

Aidan wraps me in his coat. My heart rumbles like a volcano.

"Charity Jones, I am so, so incredibly sorry for the tremendous distress I have caused you," Aidan says. "I love you more than my life. I even thought of taking my life to prove it, but Michael convinced me otherwise. I would have done anything to end your troubles. And mine, as I mourn my sister's death."

I am no longer cold, and not because of the coat. There's something about his body, like we're in a bubble of warmth. Anyway, this sounds like the 'splaining. "You had a sister?"

His eyes are teary. "I have many brothers and sisters. As I mentioned, they do not look like me. We have a different mother. But we do have one feature in common: My father's eyes."

The creature. His sister.

Oh. God. Oh. God. Oh. God.

"My father must have sent them into the world to search for me. And astonishingly one tracked my scent. I had no idea it was she who was causing

142

the pain around us. Humans are so adept at creating pain on their own, you know. I'm devastated that my father sent them. He knows they'll die. Or be killed. They're too feral."

"Your dad must really want to find you," I say, feeling more ashamed and useless. I led *his sister* to her death. Aidan picks up on this with his weird guilt detector.

"You did nothing wrong, Charity Jones," Aidan says sternly. "It was not your fault. If anyone's, it was mine."

"How?"

"He's furious I ran away. He can't find me because I'm the only one besides him not on The List."

"You've said that before. *What* list?"

"*The* List. The one he checks. Twice."

I shrug, clueless.

Aidan's brow furrows. "Michael said my sister said something to you before she died. What did she call me?"

"Just 'the claws'." My fingers arch like a grumpy kitten and I *grrrr*. "Aidan, I don't want talk about lists or claws. What the hell happened that day you fought with Charles. *Did* you throw those guys around like dolls without touching them? *How* did you do that? By the end, it looked like you were trying to kill my brother—"

"Me?"

"Yes! I know he's a sociopath and that he was hopped up on drugs, but if you do have the power you seem to have—"

Tears fill his eyes. "My father's blood got the better of me when I became fearful. I never intended to hurt those people. They took the bike wheel and left a note saying if I wanted it, to meet them there. I thought it was just your brother. I was ambushed."

"I don't care about his jackass friends," I add quickly. "I mean what you did to my brother. With the gun."

"I tried!" Aidan's face flushes with surprise. "He wanted to die for killing his friend. But I wouldn't let him. He turned the gun on himself, but I fought his hand. I swear to you, Charity, with my whole being. I came to my senses and, with the power I used to control the others, I tried to stop him from pulling the trigger!"

I believe him, even if I don't understand the mechanics or lack thereof. I want to throw my arms around him, ecstatic and grateful. Instead, I step back.

"Don't get me wrong. I believe you. I'm happy you saved Charles. However you saved him. But…I'm having a hard time with this, Aidan." A little air. A deep breath. "You're saying that you lifted someone twenty feet in the air—with your *power*. That you threw a guy against a tree—with your *power*."

Aidan wipes at his tears with his hand. "I'm so sorry, Charity."

"But how is it even possible? It goes against everything we know in science and physics. Your sister?" I continue. "I captured her using two things: engineering and logic." I tap my head. "You gave me a clue in one of your emails."

"Peppermint. It's a tremendous healing agent for us. And we're drawn to it like cats to catnip."

"That's our shared reality, Aidan. The observable, measurable world." I knock on the cement wall.

Aidan studies the ground. "The Claws."

"Yes?" I repeat.

His eyes find mine again. "The Klaas." He says it a bit differently. A soft "s" at the end.

I frown, confused.

"I am the Klaas. The future Sinterklaas."

I can't speak.

He looks up to the sky. "When did it last snow in Oak County?"

"I don't know. Twenty years ago? I hear it snows sometimes up in Placerville, but our altitude is too low for snow."

He lifts his palms up. Skyward. And utters one word.

"Snow."

Within moments snowflakes drift down around his shoulders from the cloudless sky. The temperature drops another twenty degrees. The dark ground turns white. I shiver violently under Aidan's coat.

"I am the Son of Father Christmas," he says. "The original Sinterklaas. Also known as Santa. Who is, alas, *also* the Krampus. The two legendary companions—one good, one evil—are in truth the same person and always have been. These days, he's a frightful magical being who has hidden himself away in the Arctic snows. Once a great force for good in the world, he's rejected his goodness and is now a despicable beast that wants one thing: To control me, his one and only human son. He tortured me for my sixteen years. And I will never let him do so again."

No clouds. The snow is…falling. From nothing.

People in the parking lot shout with joy and astonishment. "Dude, *snow!* Yeah! *Wooo!*"

My heart does a double-skip as the voices startle me. Can they hear us?

"You said something about shared reality," Aidan says with a sly smile.

Awe demolishes every response. There is no response, really.

Just Aidan MacNichol. Son of Nicholas the Klaas.

He takes off the top hat and spins around, mouth open to capture the snowflakes on his tongue. "I've *missed* these! Have you ever tasted snowflakes? Try it!"

I hold out my hand. Snowflakes dust my palm. I turn my face up to the night, my legs cramping from the freezing air. I taste the delicate frost of snowflakes for the first time in my life.

Snow is thickening on the ground.

"You might want to stop that soon. I don't think anyone has chains."

"God, I hope not! How do you think I got those scars on my back?" He holds his hand out to me.

I take his hand and he pulls me close. I clasp my lips to his. We devour each other, clinging like people falling out of a plane, not caring if the chute opens. We seep into each other, our blood, breath, and sweat mingling. Images of snow flurries spin in my mind's eye.

Our lips part. I don't know how long we have kissed but anything short of eternity isn't long enough.

A smile like the rising sun breaks on his face. "I love you, Charity Jones."

"And I love you, Aidan the Klaas."

# Chapter 30

After we catch up with Leo and Judy, Michael brings us home along with Aidan's things, the bike hitched to the back of the Honda. It's almost midnight. Before we unload Aidan's belongings, we stand by as he visits the tool shed, the site of his sister's death.

"She was only doing what she was told to do. He surely threatened her with death. As he does everyone."

The crack of pain in his voice tears me up inside.

"Wow. Santa is one sonuvabitch," Michael says under his breath.

After Michael is gone, Aidan and I whisper in the sewing room. At last, the entire story unravels.

He paces, listening patiently until I finish. "I'm so sorry, Charity. I never dreamed I'd bring this on your family."

"You couldn't have known." My eyes grow heavy. "But what if another one of your brothers or sisters finds you?"

"It's unlikely," Aidan says. "This one happened to catch the trail of my scent, possibly from the blood I shed up north when I was injured. If there were another shadowing her, you would know already. But the trail is cold now. I've blended in. My scent is mixed with humanity, which is why it was nearly impossible for her to find me." He seems to sense my apprehension. Sitting on the bed with me, he kisses my hand. "I'm safe now. He'll never know. He's too cut off from the world these days."

"Why didn't you use your abilities to escape the authorities when they caught you?"

"I wasn't in physical danger," he says. "Besides, I wanted to know what it was like to be a normal person. It felt more like an adventure than anything. And look where it brought me. Here. With you."

Getting picked up by the sheriff and dumped at a family services camp doesn't sound like an adventure to me, but I understand. My eyes are closing.

"Why don't you go to sleep?" he asks. "I'll see you tomorrow night. Although, I'm going to surprise your mother tomorrow morning. Her reaction might wake you up."

"She's going to be super happy that you're back." I kiss him. I think I'm getting better at this kissing thing. "But I'm way happier."

I go to the bathroom to wash off the layers of makeup I didn't need. As I return to my room, light seeps from under the doorway of the sewing room. Silence. At last, I slide under the sheets, wishing for the day we can fall asleep together. I can't stand it. I get up and walk to the shared wall. I place my hand to the wall, imagining that he is doing the same...

"Go to sleep, Charity Jones."

*He knows when you are sleeping. He knows when you're awake.*

I stick out my tongue.

Almost as soon as I return to bed, I sink into a sweet, dreamless oblivion.

# Chapter 31

*My Dearest Charity,*

*My father can emerge only one night of the year, on Christmas, which he has sworn off since I was born. And even then, he would have to find me, a needle in the proverbial haystack of humanity. I'm undetectable to him unless I'm in his reach. He had placed powerful wards to prevent me from finding the doorways, but I mastered that magic without his knowledge, reaching into the books he thought so useless. He used my siblings as gaolers. They swarmed the inside of the fortress, advising him of every movement I made. After countless experiments, the secret to deceiving them revealed itself and I plotted my escape.*

*You don't want to know what I ate. I will spare you the menu. But you get used to prison food if you want to survive.*

*I often wondered why he kept so many books. I now believe it's because he envies humanity, secretly indulging in human life through the stories he collects. For since I have lived with you, I have tasted many of the joys I only dreamed of as I devoured those tales. The beauty of trees dripping with raindrops. The warmth of sunshine and the smell of morning dew. Family. Friendship.*

*Love.*

*For as I mentioned, the two legendary figures are one person. Half goat and half demon, the grotesque Krampus who whips and kidnaps bad children is also the jolly St. Nicholas. The vestigial part of him that is Nicholas craves these things.*

*You asked how Christmas songs have picked up on the details of who The Klaas is if we are so isolated. As I understand it, when my father made the rare excursion into the world, he occasionally answered letters children left for him by the Christmas tree. He loves those letters. They feed his ego. I don't know how but letters from all over the world appear in his vault by the thousands. And he reads them. His awful laughter fills the fortress as he reads children's letters. Begging Santa for dead mothers to come back from heaven. For siblings to live who are dying from childhood diseases. For money enough to buy food.*

*Nothing brings him greater pleasure than the suffering of others. That is why he stopped delivering gifts. He decided it was better to receive than to give. And the fewer dreams he fulfilled, the more letters came.*

*One of the letters he answered was from a young Mr. Coots, who went on to write an eerily accurate song about us. Father delights in the sinister undertones of that song. He mocks humanity for turning this time of year—the darkest and most deadly—into an occasion to make merry.*

*Honestly, I don't know everything about his past. I only know what he's told me himself and what my mother, Ciara, said before he killed her.*

*She died when I was 8 years old.*

*I've already searched online to find information about her. There's nothing. My mother said that he raped her on Christmas night and came back for us a year later. I believe she lived in Ireland, where abortion has always been illegal. My mother was Catholic. She never considered aborting me.*

*I wouldn't have blamed her if she had. Of course, my father would have killed her when he returned if he'd discovered she was not fruitful. I'm grateful she lived as long as she did.*

*My siblings are the result of the otherworldly creatures he mates with down in the dungeons. I call them "The Mothers." They disgust my father. He treats them like animals when he isn't rutting with them. I visited them several times, sometimes by force when my father threatened me with a cage. If the creatures have souls, they were extinguished hundreds of years ago. They have never seen sunlight. And they speak no human language.*

*Telling you these things must surely make you more anxious. No more tonight. Your true love,*

*Aidan*

Early Sunday morning. Dad and Aidan's chatter drifts up to my room. Laughter. I don't hear Mom. She's probably still sleeping.

I search online for images of Krampus. Image after image floods the screen of a goat-like being with enormous, twisted, gnu-like horns, goat hooves for feet, hands clawed like a Yeti, and a long, black tongue that hangs out of its mouth down to its chest. Its eyes bulge out of its head as it leers at Victorian women in provocative poses. In other pictures, crying children sit in the black sack slung over Krampus' back as he leads a parade of chained little ones to some undrawn hell. Modern drawings depict a Krampus that looks even more demonic. To my surprise, I find videos of "Krampus parades." The one in Graz, Austria is the most horrific, with countless people dressed in homemade costumes as astonishing and realistic as any monster movie. Growling horned beasts threaten watchers on the sidelines in the falling snow, scaring children, swinging scourges made of broom bristles. If I had never met Aidan, I would think this is cool. Instead, it's a chilling tribute to the creature that once terrorized someone I love.

A demonic creature that seems to be real.

Later in the day, I respond to Judy's texts ("OH, MY GOD! YOU'RE DATING SANTA!") by calling her to discuss Aidan's revelations. He'd done a few "parlor tricks," as Michael called them, for her and Leo that night that left them both totally floored.

"I'm really worried about his dad showing up," I confide. "He killed Aidan's mom."

"Someone should put a coal in Santa's own stocking," Judy says. "But I wouldn't worry. He's really far away and you guys can be happy now."

She's right. That evening, when Aidan returns home, I'm tormented again by his presence in the house, especially when he showers. My hormones are revving like a Harley. It's beyond wonderful to have him back.

Mom is up finally, making dinner, and seems happy to see him. Unusually happy. "Mr. Daniels says the best things about you. Mrs. Allured, too. I like what she did with your hair."

Rosy splotches rise on Aidan's pale cheeks. "Thank you."

She mauls him with hugs, and then asks me about the dance. Her face contorts as I tell her about the meeting with Darren's parents. "I'm so proud of you," she exclaims. "You're a grownup! How'd I make a grownup?" It's my turn to be mauled. And kissed. And mauled again.

Mom's maudlin behavior is embarrassing, but Aidan doesn't seem to mind. As I chop vegetables, he sets the table like a pro in seconds. For a moment, I imagine we're a happy family. Maybe even a young married couple having Sunday dinner with the in-laws.

"You seem awfully happy, Mom," I say. "What's going on?"

"I'm saving the news for dinner."

Dad emerges from his home office and leans against the kitchen doorway, taking in the activity. Mom and Dad are so simpatico that they can communicate without speaking, just a look. Will Aidan and I ever be that connected? Mom takes him in, waiting until he speaks.

"Looks like my last dinner home for a while," he says. "Got to go to D.C. tomorrow."

"Why?" I ask. Or, rather, whine.

"Congress is voting on cutting the defense budget. Likely we'll lose contracts. So they want an engineer there to meet with some of the lawmakers. Win over some folk."

"But Charles' hearings are this week." Mom's shoulders sag. "You can't go. He needs you. *I* need you."

Dad hugs her. He shakes his head. "I tried, babe. Having a black man on the team is too good a show for the administration. I'll lose my job if we don't get those contracts. And we can't afford that."

"Would you cut that 'black man' crap?" she says. "They want to send you because you're their most brilliant engineer. And because you can match your socks and talk to girls."

Dad grins. "You'll be okay without me from the sounds of things. That was some pretty great news we just got." He ambles toward the dining room, giving me a hard pat on the back as he passes. "Besides, I'm leaving our monster hunter in charge. Did they ever figure out what that thing was? Looked like something out of *John Carter of Mars*." He shudders audibly.

I dump the last of the veggies in the salad bowl and wince. Poor Aidan. "No, Dad. They have no idea."

"So what's the great news?" Aidan asks, grim. Can't blame him for changing the subject.

Mom opens the oven. Astounding smells flood the kitchen. A roast with garlic and potatoes. Mom's comfort food. "Your father feels like he can just traipse off to the White House because of the call we got earlier." Her voice cracks with tears of joy. "Noah woke up. He says it was an accident, that Charles wasn't trying to kill him. So, the judge might actually release Charles—and everyone else—on probation for a misdemeanor."

She and Dad hug. Aidan and I exchange a dire look.

# Chapter 32

Aidan needs to testify. And so do I.

But he won't. He loves my parents and doesn't want to hurt them. I can tell by the way he looks at them. They might second-guess their entire relationship with him, which would be too painful.

I will either have to tell the truth—and drag Aidan into it—or…have you ever wondered if you could commit perjury? It's a felony to lie under oath. If I wanted to keep Aidan out of it, I could lie and say Charles was shooting at *me* if I don't want the entire saga to unravel. There might be alternative stories, but nothing better comes to mind.

You can go to prison for committing perjury. If they catch you, anyway. The worst part is that, even if I get away with that lie, Aidan will know. I don't believe in heaven or hell, but I do believe in the sweet, mysterious boy I'm in love with. And I won't just get a lump of coal in my Christmas stocking.

He'll hate me. Or at least no longer love me. In those beautiful eyes, I'll be a criminal and a liar. Actually, he won't even know that. All he'll know is that I've done something very, very wrong.

But if Charles comes back, the peace we treasure will dissolve into chaos. Charles is changed. My parents have no idea how much. And that the violence is aimed at Aidan.

Possibly me, too.

Unless Aidan testifies.

It's Monday just after third period when Judy texts me.

> Going to shop for Christmas presents, we don't all live with Santa you know ;-) want to come?

*You chauffeur today?*

Yes, ma'am! :-)

*See you at the bike racks after 7th.*

Later after school, Aidan unlocks his bike from the rack and prepares his backpack. At least now I know why he doesn't need to wear a jacket in the cold. I stroke his arms, feeling the ripple of muscles developing in his shoulders and biceps. Girls stop to watch, commenting under their breath.

"What do you do at this job exactly?"

"I told you. I load trees into people's cars or tie them to the top." He hikes the backpack up over his shoulders. "And I unload trees from the trucks that bring them. Apparently, Christmas trees are swift business." A touch of pride in that last statement, I note. He holds me and brushes his lips against mine. "There is something wrong. What bothers you? Are you still worried about my father? Or maybe your own?"

My dad boarded the plane to Washington, D.C. this morning. I don't know if Aidan picked up on what my father was saying about the defense budget. I've never actually told him that my father builds bombs. He's a rocket scientist, but one who makes war machines. I hope Aidan never figures that out. "Neither, actually. I'm worried that Charles will get out of kiddie prison and ruin our lives. Or kill us in our sleep. That's all."

"Oh, he won't," he says, unlocking the bike. "I emailed the District Attorney last night and told him what happened. I even still have the note."

"*You what?!?*"

"It was the right thing to do. I wanted to confess to hurting all those boys, too, but as you have astutely pointed out, no one is going to believe me. So, I said nothing about that. I did tell a small lie. I told him that the fight was already in progress."

"You don't understand. It's not that it isn't the right thing to do. It's just that my parents are going to lose it! You're making my mom choose between her real son and her foster son. She'll send you away. To another family. And I can't stand the idea of being away from you again! Part of me will die forever."

His eyes soften. "It's not nearly as dangerous as letting your brother loose. Whether we are together or apart, it is more important that you are safe." He kisses me. "I love you more than my life. I will see you tonight."

And with that he rides off.


"Your brother confessed."

When I get home, Mom is sitting on the couch in her robe, one leg doubled up in front of her. She sips a glass of wine. The mostly empty bottle sits on the table. It's dark. The TV is off. An unopened stack of mail sits on the coffee table. Judging by the size and fancy stamps, they're Christmas cards.

My backpack slides off my shoulder. I shut the door. The house feels hollow. Stunned, I say nothing as I stand in the doorway, clutching the small bag of Christmas presents I got with Judy.

Tears gleam in her eyes. Her words are muddy with alcohol. "He confessed he was trying to kill Aidan. They're sending him to the detention center in Lake Tahoe until he's 18." She wipes her eyes. "My baby is going up the river. Or at least up the mountain."

"Why do you think he confessed?"

She shakes her head and swallows more wine. "I have no idea. When the DA mentioned Aidan had contacted him in the pretrial hearing today, your brother had an outburst and…he admitted everything. Why would he do that, honey? *Why?*"

I hug my mom as she sobs.

"I'm sorry, honey. I've been an appalling mom to you and your brother. And even worse to Aidan."

"No, you haven't, Mom. I love you so much."

Relief floods my body. For the first time in weeks, I can completely relax. I feel badly for not encouraging Aidan to come forward. It was his right.

Mom staggers to bed. Before she closes the bedroom door, she says, "Please tell Aidan I'm sorry." She then locks it. Not a good sign.

When Aidan gets home, I greet him in the garage. His face lights up when he sees me, wheeling the bike to storage. "Who would have guessed that such beauty and ecstasy could be found in the common American garage?" He takes my hand and kisses it chastely.

"You didn't even have to appear?"

"Appear where? Here?"

"No. In court," I explain.

"I'm supposed to hear back from the District Attorney, but I haven't yet." He clearly senses something is up. "Why?"

"Charles confessed."

"But why on earth?"

"He's more afraid of us than we are of him. Prison might feel safer than home."

I remember how frightened *I* was of Aidan. I can only imagine how my brother must feel. "Mom's devastated. She's locked herself in her room. She said to tell you that she's sorry."

The light dies in his eyes.

"I'm afraid of what she's going to do. She's never been this depressed."

"Don't worry. I know just the thing."

He kisses me. And he won't say anything more.

The bedroom door stands open as I do my homework. I sent a group text to the gang to let them know what happened today. Michael responded first:

*Thank the Gods of Snow. One more psycho behind bars!*

Leo was a little more compassionate.

*AWESOME!!!!!!!! Or is it awesome? It's kind of awesome, isn't it? :( I'm sorry.*

Judy was the most empathetic. She texted me a string of adorable emojis hugging, kissing, crying.

I listen at the door for sounds from Mom's bedroom. The rustle of bed sheets. Nothing more. At last, I call Dad on Facetime. He already knows the whole story, but he's not worried. "Your mom's going to be okay," he says, although he looks far from okay himself. "She just needs something good to happen. You know how she is."

Aidan and I risk kissing in the kitchen as we clean up after dinner. I half hope that we'll hear Mom's footfalls in the hallway upstairs but I revel in the freedom of loving him right here. Now. With no reserve. Rain falls steadily, splashing the deck, turning the redwood dark. Aidan's face shines. "It's the closest thing to snow I'm going to get without interfering again," he explains. "But that's alright."

My dreams turn frosty. A massive fortress of ice floats before me, blue shadows carved into the jagged walls. The freezing wind punishes my body with crippling blows. I plunge two rods into the snow to steady myself. Smokey goggles cover my eyes, yet ice crusts my eyelashes. Despite the extraordinary layers of clothing, my bones burn with cold. I shout into the wind until I'm hoarse.

Enraged. Dying with desire. I am shouting in a language I do not understand. The words baffle me.

Dream words.

A bloodcurdling scream yanks me from sleep.

5:30 a.m.

*Thunk.*

I kick off my blankets and jump out of bed. The house is freezing, which isn't unusual in the middle of the night. I'm not wearing my robe, and the heater isn't on yet.

I smell smoke.

Before I even reach the bottom of the staircase, I can see what Aidan's done to the family room.

Mom stands at the lip of the living room spectacle. The wine bottle she had taken to bed lies at her feet. She must have been taking it to the garbage.

The entire living room has been transformed into the ultimate geek Christmas jubilee. The top of a fat pine tree rises to the vaulted ceiling, bushy branches glittering with geek trinkets, including figurines of characters from popular science fiction movies, TV shows, and video games. An electric train races around the tree bottom. Mysterious boxes in shiny paper and perky bows peek out from under the lowest tree limbs. Three stockings lumpy with goodies hang from the lit fireplace. Flashing toy light sabers cross above the mantle. Most of the decorations had been stored in the garage, but some of it's Aidan's touch.

Each Christmas card stands open on the coffee table over its own envelope. A giant stuffed polar bear wearing a Santa hat sits next to the front door, mouth hanging open in a dopey grin.

Footsteps behind me on the stairs.

"Merry Christmas, Mrs. Jones!" Aidan announces.

"What have you kids done?" She comes unhinged. "It's totally inappropriate!"

"But…it's Christmas," I reply.

"Not in this house," she fumes, and stalks off to the kitchen.

# Chapter 33

Stifling a yawn in calculus, I focus on Mrs. Stewart's precise, even chalk strokes. Differentiable functions. Closed intervals. Relative extrema and inflection points. We're preparing for the midyear exam.

The bell rings. Two kids lean over their desks to talk to me.

"Um, Charity? Have you considered our applications to be monster hunters?" the boy asks.

Michael is behind this joke, pretending to take applications. I play along. "What's your name again?"

"Dylan Renke."

The girl looks hopeful. "Candace Saint Yves."

"I'll let you know if there's an opening," I say.

Beth Addison might be plotting my demise, the way she looks at Aidan, but she doesn't say anything. She's probably afraid I'll catch her in my monster trap.

At the lockers, I pick up the rest of my books as Judy waits. The din of well-wishers continues. Judy smiles and waves, her hand swathed in a cherry red leather glove. She seems more self-confident than ever before. I'm dying to know how things have progressed with Leo, but I don't want to pry. Judy's parents are back. The day they arrived, she finally sent a flood of texts after I had fallen asleep. *How are you? What are you doing? I'm sorry I've been AWOL. I really hate my mom.*

I'm shocked I've not heard a single word about Charles' arrest, although there've been rumors about the fight. Maybe my friends are hearing things and just aren't telling me.

It's just as well. I don't want to hear it.

At lunch, I tell Judy what happened this morning. Just as she's about to respond, she wrinkles her nose at someone behind me. A shy voice speaks.

"Hi. Can we talk?"

Keiko.

"Maybe she doesn't want to talk to you," Judy shoots back. "Maybe she should talk to her lawyer first, since you're the one who's been defaming her." Judy edges closer to me. "You can totally still sue her, right?"

I slam the locker door shut. "Maybe you should record this, Jay. Make a legal record."

"With pleasure." She whips out her cell phone, starts a voice memo, and holds it between us. "For the record, this is Keiko Mori making a statement to Charity Jones on December 10th." She shoves the phone at Keiko. "Speak."

Keiko stammers. "I just want to say…"

"I can't hear you," Judy says loudly into the phone. "What did you say?"

"I'm sorry."

"For what?" I ask.

Her voice is weak. "For accusing you of hurting my dog."

"So you promise to tell everyone in this whole *damn* school that you were wrong and that I did not hurt your dog? That, in fact, I would *never* hurt any pet if I could possibly help it? So help you not-God?"

She nods.

"Speak! For the record!" Judy says. I would laugh except that Keiko looks dead serious.

"I promise."

Whatever. Regret is cheap. "Can't believe I wasted an endangered gas on you."

"I'll make it up to you!" she says as we head toward the parking lot. "I promise that, too!"

"I'll let you know if that's even possible," I yell back, giving her a two-fingered military salute from my brow.

I realize it isn't fair that one reason I'm mad at her is that, if she hadn't destroyed our friendship, it would've taken me half the time to calculate the changes to the monster box. Her math skills are better than mine. She just doesn't apply them to anything. Theory is her gig. She'll make a great professor someday.

I glance at Keiko as I slide into Judy's car. She wipes her eyes with the back of her coat sleeve. Her image dissolves under the rain as it punishes Judy's windshield.

I would have to be in pretty freaking dire straits to let her back into my life.

My feet touch a paper grocery bag that's been rolled closed at the top. "What's this?"

"Open it," Judy says with evil glee.

"I don't trust that look on your face," I say.

"Oh, geez! Would you just open it?"

"Okay. Keep your hair dye on." I look inside the bag. Inside are dozens of green "bouquets" of a leafy plant with white berries. I sniff. There's no smell.

"My dad is a major douche bag, but he gets nostalgic for Christmas and smuggles home stuff like this on his trips. It's totally illegal. I think he's got a fake compartment in his suitcase so he can evade customs."

"What is it?"

"You don't know?" She throws me a look of pity. "It's French mistletoe. Take a bouquet! Not that you and Aidan need any excuse to smooch." She leans forward to peer through the windshield as the wipers squeak. "You guys're adorable, but I think Beth Addison is gonna have a seizure."

"Beth Addison has the hots for Aidan?" I laugh. "Damn!"

"Oh, yeah. Bad. But he never even glances at her. It makes her nuts. You should hear her complain about how he shouldn't be with a black girl."

"Awwwww! Poor boy has jungle fever!" Amused, I remove one of the bouquets from the bag and put it in my backpack. "Too bad. So sad."

"I predict that despite how cold it is, her outfits are going to get vampier. That's her pattern. Drop thread 'til he drops dead."

"Did you just make that up?"

"Yup!"

"Gimme some." We bump fists. "So, uh, speaking of dropping thread, how are things with you and Leo?"

Judy squirms. "Good. I think."

"Yeah?"

She nods. "Oh, god! He's super patient. I take that back. I think he's petrified. Like, even more nervous than I am. I always thought guys were pushy and demanding, but I guess not."

"He probably wants you to take the lead. If he really cares about you, he doesn't want you to feel pressured at all."

"True." She's quiet for a moment. "I think I want to move forward. A lot." She flashes me a grin.

I cover my mouth. "Oh, my god! That's awesome!"

She smiles even bigger. "I'll keep you posted," she says. "So…is Aidan your first?"

"First what?"

"Boyfriend."

"If you don't count going with Eron Vartek in 4th grade, yeah," I say, thinking of my string of torrid crushes that never went anywhere. "What about you?"

"No, but it feels like it."

"Do your folks know you're dating Leo?"

"They don't know much about my life," she scoffs. "And I plan on keeping it that way. They want to meet you, but I told them no."

"Why not?"

"They want to meet you because they don't think you're really my friend. My mom treats me like I'm autistic or something because I'm not Ms. Gregarious. You'd think she'd understand, being a famous artist, like, how it feels to be an introvert. But no. She thinks I have imaginary friends."

I don't know what to say. The car slows as it enters the driveway and idles for a moment.

"You're the best friend anyone could ever have," I say at last.

Judy beams. "I know," she says. "You, too."

We hug. I exit and the car peels out, Shonen Knife blaring from the stereo. I'm damned lucky.

# Chapter 34

*Dear Charity,*

*Do you think your mother will forgive me if I bake her a spinach frittata this morning?*

*Your love,*

*Aidan*

This email is already marked as "read," but I haven't read it yet. Maybe I read it on my phone and forgot about it? Not likely. He sent it in the middle of the night.

More likely? My email has been hacked. I quickly check past emails. I see nothing unusual.

Wait. A purple arrow next to one of Aidan's first emails. It was forwarded. I check to see to whom, but it's garbled like a spam address. I test other emails. If I forward an email, I can delete the forwarded email in my sent box, the purple "forwarded" arrow disappears on the original.

So, they might have forwarded every email I've ever sent or received. I only use email for Aidan, my folks and the occasional school project. I just don't think about it otherwise.

Boiling over with panic, I change my password to something even more secure. When I see Aidan in the kitchen, I tell him to change his password because my account was hacked. Maybe his, too.

"But I change my password every day," he protests.

That I do not doubt.

The previous password was good enough, I thought. It should have kept out most threats, although someone with sophisticated software can break any password. I just don't know anyone capable except Michael, but he doesn't have time or motive. Of course, there are hackers for hire. People use them when they think they're being cheated on. But who would go to such lengths?

"We're seeing your brother tonight. Be ready to go at three-thirty."

We're eating Aidan's mouthwatering frittata for breakfast when Mom drops the bomb.

"But I have homework!"

"Do it in the car," she says flatly, cutting another forkful of frittata. "Your brother has specifically asked to see you. So come home right after school and be ready as soon as I get here. It's going to be snowing. We need to get to South Lake Tahoe by six. Visiting hours close at seven."

Aidan takes this in, eating in silence.

"Aidan, just help yourself to leftovers when you get home. Or make something if you feel like it, sweetie. We won't be home until late."

Great. I have to visit my boyfriend's would-be killer. I'm grateful Mom is unaware of that one word in the previous sentence. I'm pretty sure it would give her a stroke. And we've already seen she can't even handle an early Christmas.

Well, from the real Sinterklaas, at any rate.

"What if I don't want to see him?"

"Your brother is going away for a long time and you might regret not seeing him again. Trust me. My friends have seen it in their clients. If you don't want to see him again after this, I'll respect your wishes."

"He's only going to Lake Tahoe, which is, like, an hour and a half away! It's not like he's going to Sing Sing or a Siberian gulag."

Picking up her empty plate and coffee cup, she then pulls out The Voice. "You are going. You will see your brother. And if you are not ready to leave and in the car with me when I say, there will be very harsh consequences."

I want to mouth off. *Look, lady, do you know who I am? I'm the one who caught the monster.* But I keep my mouth shut and eat.

I hope they have security cameras in the visitation areas. There's no telling what my brother will do. This could be an ugly visit.

Very ugly.

# Chapter 35

The higher the elevation climbs on Highway 50, the more mammoth the pines that line the highway, stretching up to the darkening sky. Placerville looks like a metropolis compared to the towns that follow. Pollock Pines. Fresh Pond. Pacific House. I've never heard of any of the places that follow Pollock Pines except maybe Strawberry, which gets pretty treacherous weather.

The highway narrows to one lane in each direction. My mom drives the speed limit, as always, but today she slows even more due to the icy road. Traffic thickens as everyone has the same idea. Mom put chains on the car tires before we left. We're in no danger of getting stuck unless there's an accident.

And I'm kind of praying there is. Not a bad one where anyone gets hurt. Just a bit of crunched metal and a couple of blown tires.

The slow drive gives me time to take in the scenery. Except for the occasional mountain man grocery shack, there isn't anything along the highway, just the awesomeness of nature rising before us. Snowy pines cover mountains that loom like fairy tale giants beyond the road, ancient and foreboding. I recall the nightmare. Standing before the floating frozen fortress. Shouting in a bizarre language. The rage and desire I felt in the dream briefly well up inside me.

On my smart phone, I search online for visitation rules. Siblings are not allowed, only parents and guardians. Mom explains that Charles' probation officer and the director approved the visit.

They are making an exception for me. I must be special. And for the first time in a couple of weeks, I wish that I weren't. I also wish I'd worn something "revealing," because apparently that can get you barred from visitation. Of course, Mom probably knows this and would have killed me if I'd even tried.

Not that I have anything "revealing" to wear.

I focus on my phone and pretend to do homework so that Mom doesn't engage me in conversation. Instead, I reread Aidan's email from last night. Every time I try to search online for his mother and what happened, I get the same results Aidan did. I wonder if she and the baby were even reported missing.

She might've been homeless. Krampy would have known where to find her no matter where she was because she's on The List.

My ears pop before we hit Echo Summit. A sign announces that we're over 7,000 feet in elevation. Banks of snow invite dog romps and snowball fights. Aidan would love it. Me, I don't like how this echoes my nightmare. The car is warm, yet my hands are icy. I slide the hand not holding the phone under my leg for warmth.

It's already twilight. Despite the darkness, the roadside reveals a spectacular view of the surrounding mountains. I try not to think about the drop over the edge. The vast emptiness is dizzying. Lake Tahoe sprawls lazily in the distance as we draw closer, but we soon lose the view.

The elevation drops a little. It's nighttime. We're heading into ski resort country. Snow abounds even when the roads turn civilized again.

The Denny's sign in South Lake Tahoe reminds me so much of Michael, Leo and Judy that I want to cry. Texting has been spotty due to poor reception. An avid skier, Leo has been to Tahoe more times than anyone. He warns me that I'm going to freeze my butt off when we get out of the car. I tell him about the dream. He responds: *Memory transfer? Making out with Aidan might be affecting your brain more than you think. Not joking.*

At last the car turns off the main road into a long, wide driveway flanked by towering pines. We follow the driveway until it winds up to the gates. A chain link fence topped with razor wire surrounds the property. My stomach tightens as the guards check us in and open the gates so that we can head toward the massive redwood facility: A log cabin on steroids surrounded by parking lots strewn with dirty chunks of snow.

Girls and boys live here who have been incarcerated or who are awaiting disposition of their case. Charles has been here since he was arrested, presumably with his cohorts, although it's possible they've been split up since Charles' confession to protect Charles. Mom said it was because Placerville Juvenile Hall was too crowded. I wonder what families do who can't travel this far when they have a child locked up here. They have no say where their child goes. And according to what I've read, they have to pay for the lodging regardless.

Even if Charles had been appointed a public defender, my college money still would have been spent on several years of three hots and a cot.

"Put your phone in your backpack and leave it in the car. You can't bring in anything," Mom says and noisily sets the brake. "Let's go."

I open the car door to the freezing air. My feet crunch in snow. The cold stings my face, slides under my coat and into the soles of my boots. Mom carries only a piece of paper in one hand and keys in the other. We pass through automatic glass doors and then metal detectors with the help of a kindly middle-aged white man and younger black woman in uniform. The bare halls scream: Rules! Regulations! Forever!

Mom tenses up as we approach the check-in desk, where a heavy-set, older white lady with short graying hair sits at a desk behind a thick plastic pane. The badge pinned above her shirt pocket says "Knox."

"I'll need a government-issued photo I.D." The lady frowns at me. "We don't allow minors for visits. She'll have to stay out in the car."

Rules! Regulations! Forever!

"It's okay. It was approved by Officer Blackmoore and Director Brackman." My mom stuffs a fax with signatures under the window. The lady takes it, reads. My mom slips her driver's license and my passport under the window into the tray. I never got to use that passport. We were supposed to go to Mexico for vacation when Charles got the flu.

The lady grudgingly approves our entry. We sign in on the roster attached to the wall. "Go around the corner. See Officer Parks to turn in your keys and any other personal items you might have. He'll go over the rules of conduct and you'll be taken to the visitor's room."

My mom thanks the lady, takes back our I.D.s and makes a restroom detour (thank goodness) before we head around the corner, where a tall, muscle-bound black man guards a door with a big clear window revealing a long hallway beyond. "Good evening, ladies. I'm Officer Parks. Welcome to the detention center. Who are you visiting today?"

"Charles Montgomery Jones," my mom says. Aside from our voices, it's eerily quiet. Not a lot of visitors today, probably, or everyone has already left. Visiting hours are almost over.

Officer Parks contacts someone with his walkie-talkie. They exchange information about us. He makes Mom check in her car keys, sealing them in an envelope and placing them in a secure locker. He gives her a claims ticket and then lays down the law.

"Are you the guardian of this child?"

"I'm her mother," she says pointedly.

I would be offended that he doesn't realize my white mom is my parent, rather than a guardian, but I'm too nervous to think. Anyway, Mom's used to it.

He continues. "Ladies, you will be escorted to the visitor's room. You must stay together." He directs the next bit at me. "Normally we don't allow minors to visit, so your parent must accompany you at all times. You cannot pass any items to the detainee. You will be monitored by detention center staff. Your visit may be terminated at any time at the discretion of our staff. Do you understand? Good. Officer Abbott should be here shortly to escort you inside."

And he is. The doors buzz and click before they open to reveal a bald white man with arms and chest that bulge with so much muscle that they threaten to tear his uniform. "I'm Officer Abbott. Right this way, ladies." We are headed into the belly of the beast.

*Maybe there's a beast. Maybe it's only us.*

The doors shut ominously behind us. Officer Abbott leads us into a maze of hallways, past staff offices and other facilities. Officers pass with walkie-talkies, wearing utility belts. Everyone has handcuffs and pepper spray.

We enter a large, drafty room with circular tables and smaller circular seats. It's like a space age cafeteria with a high ceiling and bright lights but no food. The glossy walls say new building. Or at least new paint job. Officer Abbott leads us to a table with one seat on one side and two on the other. The seats are set back from the table.

He indicates we should sit. We do.

Officer Abbott stands by as a door at the opposite end of the room opens.

Charles emerges in a yellow sweatshirt and blue sweat pants. Hands handcuffed in front of him. Feet manacled.

If I could bust down those doors and beat it out to the snow, I would.

Another officer escorts Charles to our table. My brother snarls at me.

*You twice stood up to a monster that tried to kill you. You can take your brother's anger.*

"Hey, Mom," he says, his voice flat. The officer returns to the doors and stands before them, feet spread, at attention. "Sis."

I can sense Mom holding back. I know she wants to throw her arms around him, as if she could put him back in the womb. "Hi, honey. How are you?"

His sarcasm is searing. "I'm great. Things are great here."

"Do you want any books? I can bring two. Just say when."

166

"No, as long as I behave, I can watch TV," he says. "And I like having time to think. Thinking is good. Planning is better. But I do need more stamps."

He sounds mechanical, his words cold and rehearsed.

"You're writing your friends. That's great. It's good to stay in contact." Mom rests her hands on the table, but she's not relaxed.

His gaze scalds me. "Well, you know, my friends send me letters. They keep me up to date on stuff going on. I can receive one ten-minute phone call a day, too. With supervision."

"That's right. I forgot." Mom looks wistful. She seems to notice him staring at me. "You wanted to talk to your sister."

"I did," he replies with a smirk. "Yesterday I sent a special letter. A letter to Santa."

"Aren't you a little big to write to Santa?" Mom asks.

"Nope. I needed to send the big guy a letter. Especially after what I learned about Charity's new boyfriend."

The world falls out from under me.

"Honey, I don't know what you're hearing, but Charity and Michael aren't dating."

"Of course they're not. Michael's a fag."

"Knock it off! I didn't raise you to be a bigot," Mom barks.

I stay silent.

Charles is still smirking. "You know how I know? Because Charity was right. Voices echo around the gym."

My heart races.

"I know because, like Santa, I have friends everywhere. But you know, I've never believed in that fat bastard. Not since I was a little shit. But based on what I've seen, heard and read in email—" he levels a dark look at me, "other people's email, that is—I might have changed my mind. So I'm really excited about Christmas this year. I can't wait for Santa to visit. In the letter I sent to him today, I made a special request."

Oh. God.

That maniacal grin tears up one side of his face, his voice pregnant with triumph. "I asked for Aidan's dad to take him home on Christmas." He chuckles.

*Oh. God.*

Mom is agitated. "Charles, it's the last time you'll see your sister for years—"

"What's the matter, Charity? Worried everyone's going to find out you believe in Santa? Or are you worried Santa might not be a nice guy. That he might hurt you and Mom if Aidan's not there?"

"Charles!" The Voice.

He ignores her, hissing. "Santa's coming. And if Aidan runs, your life is over. *In more ways than one.*"

Officer Abbott approaches the table. "*Visit* is over, Mr. Jones." The other officer is already on top of Charles, dragging him away.

"Merry Christmas, Charity!" Charles calls out and laughs, "*Ho ho ho*" The officer threatens him with "segregation" as they disappear through the doors.

Charles laughs again. That terrible laugh.

# Chapter 36

Nausea overpowers me as I stumble past the sliding glass doors. Vomit scalds my throat and mouth. I double over, retching onto the pavement.

No ambition. Bad friends. Even worse grades. I've always assumed Charles was a loser because he wouldn't go along with society's plan. Madness may have ultimately gotten the best of my brother, but everyone has seriously underestimated him.

Especially me.

He might not really believe Aidan's story, but he knows that I do. He knows how to hurt me the deepest. I think he does believe it, though. After what happened, it would be hard not to.

As I try to recover, taking deep breaths and willing my body to relax, Mom scoops up a little snow from the perimeter of the building to clean out my mouth. I refuse to go back inside the building. In the car, she finds a half-finished bottle of water. I splash water on my face and clutch the bottle for when my stomach finally calms down.

She doesn't say much until we're on the road. "I'm so sorry, honey."

My seat inclined back as far as it will go, I reply faintly, "It's okay." My mind is in overdrive. My teeth chatter violently. Thank goodness I can't see out the windows. I'd probably get carsick.

She drives in silence for a bit. "Do you have a boyfriend?"

"He was just being mean about Michael," I lie. "You knew that Michael was gay, didn't you?"

"I did. I didn't want to out him to you. I figured he would tell you in his own time. And who knows? Maybe he's bi? He's still growing." More silence. "I'm sorry I made you come. I should have known it would be upsetting to see your brother like this. I should have known he'd be angry and take it out on you." She falls quiet again and sniffles.

I don't lose it until the "text not sent" message appears when I try to text Michael. It's an emergency! Why can't satellites tell when it's an emergency?

I was afraid people could hear the conversation between Michael and I that night. And if we were being followed, it's certainly possible a couple of people working together could've managed to eavesdrop.

My email is another story. I've had no brain since Aidan arrived. I should have taken extra precautions. But how could Charles have known what was in the emails? He must have friends who did the hacking and they relayed the information to him.

We were incredibly stupid. And now we're paying the price.

My immediate concern is for Michael. I don't know when Charles got his last phone call, but the news must be out there. And there are kids who will tear Michael apart. At my old junior high school in Simi Valley, the boys ganged up on a skinny, short guy they had decided was gay. Not someone who was out in any way. Just a guy they *thought* was gay. At first, they just tore his backpack. Bruised an elbow. Or his ego. But eventually they put him in the hospital.

My texts get through to Leo and Judy. Hopefully they'll reach Michael and Aidan.

By the time we get home, it's almost 9:30 p.m. We get out of the car and Mom hugs me hard. Once inside, she opens a bottle of wine and takes it to bed. I worry this is becoming routine. As she heads up the stairs, Aidan emerges from his bedroom.

"Good evening, Mrs. Jones. I pray the visit went well."

"As well as could be expected. You okay? You eat?"

"Yes. I'm fine." He doesn't sound fine. I've never heard him sound this bad. Leo or Judy must have reached him. I wish Mom and Dad had gotten him a phone.

"Good. Good night, Aidan." She hugs him, holding him close for a moment, and kisses him on top of his head. Like a real son. Her door shuts a moment later.

As Aidan descends, we exchange dire looks. We hold each other tightly in the living room, mourning in the midst of the Christmas cheer. After a bit, he whispers with tears choking his voice.

"I should have known my freedom would have a price. A gruesome price that would be exacted on those I love most."

"Stop blaming yourself." I wipe my own tears soaking his dark blue t-shirt. "Charles was headed down a bad road. He would have gotten there sooner or later. I just can't believe how much I underestimated his ability to track his prey."

"I'm also worried for Michael," Aidan says.

"Have you heard from him?"

"No. Just Leo and Judy."

For the first time, I consider my brother's reach. If he and his friends were selling drugs, he might be more popular than I ever imagined. With his crew locked up, a segment of the school might be not only desperate but enraged to have their supply of molly, hash, tweak, or whatever else cut off. A whole school jonesing as winter exams draw near. He could turn some dangerous people against us.

Who am I kidding? They are already against us.

Aidan considers the situation.

"But you just captured the…the *thing* that was terrorizing them. Wouldn't they still be grateful? They have short memories."

"Welcome to the human race."

My phone buzzes. It's Michael.

You there?

*WORRIED*

No kidding

*ABOUT YOU*

Had to give my folks and Ricardo the low down on the Nazi zombies. Circling the wagons at Denny's. Pick you up in a few.

Michael's face is red and puffy when he shows up. He doesn't say much as we drive. Aidan sits shotgun, sliding a hand back to me.

At Denny's, Michael sits like the Commander-in-Chief at the end of the table with each couple in a booth. Judy is on the verge of tears. Leo wraps his arm around her. Everyone slouches over something sweet (Aidan insists on treating) as I recount what happened. I leave out the barfing.

"So, you're sure he's outing me?" Michael asks.

"He looked like The Joker when he said you were the f-word. The only thing missing was the white grease paint."

"He *is* like The Joker," Leo says, gaze grinding into the table. "He's totally insane."

"The difference between him and The Joker is that he's not operating on chaos. He wants revenge," I reply.

"So, what's going to happen?" Judy asks. "Michael, are you going to be okay at school?"

"Dunno," Michael says. "Based on the latest horrors in the news, I predict verbal humiliation, physical assaults and vandalism of my locker, car, and other personal effects. And, of course, let us not forget online harassment, including text bombing and social media campaigns encouraging me to kill myself."

"Familiar with those," I mutter. Aidan squeezes my hand and kisses my cheek. "So, basically, you have nothing to worry about," I say with sarcasm.

"Yeah," Michael says. "And I expect these cats will spread the love to those nearest and dearest." He smooches the air at me.

"Aidan, you're not leaving, are you?" Judy asks.

"I can't. If I leave and my father shows up at Charity's house on Christmas, he'll kill everyone there."

The table falls silent.

"I'm sorry," Aidan continues. "But I wouldn't put it past him to hunt down Charity that night and hurt her. That's just who he is. And he can do it easily."

"But we can't just sit and wait for your dad to show up." I gulp down some water. My stomach has finally settled and I'm super thirsty.

"I'd rather be taken by him than endanger your life," Aidan says. "I know you don't like that answer, but it's the truth."

He's right. I don't. I push the glass to the edge of the table for a refill. Aidan is really frustrating me.

Everyone looks as shell-shocked as I feel.

My phone rings. I check the number. "Crap. I never called him back." I answer the phone. "Hi, Detective. I'm sorry I couldn't get back to you. It's been kind of crazy." Understatement of the century.

"No worries," he says. "We—meaning, the Sheriff's Office, the Superintendent and a few others—we were just wondering if you and your friends and your families would like to come to the Sheriff's Office to receive the award on Friday evening. It'll just be a small ceremony. Really informal. We didn't want to cut into your school nights, so."

"Let me ask my mom tonight. My dad's in D.C. It would just be me, my mom and Aidan."

"Let me know by tomorrow?"

We hang up. No one seems excited about this latest development except Leo. "Hey, at least it's not all bad news today."

"I'm not saying we're *not* doomed," Michael says, setting his spoon in the empty dessert dish. "But this feels pretty doomed. Or at least doomed-ish."

Leo checks his phone calendar. "Nine more days of school including three days of semester finals," he notes. "Two weeks total until Christmas Eve."

We have some time. But is it enough?

# Chapter 37

The war starts Friday as we leave Honors Chemistry.

Michael's phone blows up with the hate as soon as he takes it out of his pocket. *Die fat faggot. Fudge packer. Shit stabber.* Sweat trickles down his temple. "I can't block these asshats fast enough."

"The cray-cray has started, huh? You need a whitelist app, stat." I suggest the one I used. "You only care about us and a few other people, right?" I catch myself before I say "and your boyfriend." I can't believe how hard this is to keep secret. It's like containing an airborne virus. Who was it that said two people could keep a secret if one of them is dead? I can only imagine the toll such secrecy has taken on him. How painful it must have been to take me to the dance and not the guy he loves.

*Bam.*

Michael lurches forward and spins to the side of the hallway.

Two senior guys ram into him as they pass by. "Sorry. Heard you like it from behind," one says. I forget his name. They laugh. I recognize them. Customers of my brother and his friends, no doubt.

Cheeks red, Michael buries his gaze in the ground. "I gotta hit the loo. Catch you after school at the car."

He disappears down the hallway en route to the guys' restroom. I wander, unsteady. I've been feeling sick, worried I might lose Aidan to his father. I remember my Aunt Bellina pinching my cheeks the summer before I started high school and chirping, "These will be the *best* years of your life!"

*Aunt Bellina, if these are the best years, I should make out with Smith & Wesson at graduation.*

The day continues without event. Until the end, that is.

As I approach the parking lot, scornful laughter blisters my ears. People yell, "Come here! You've got to see this!" My legs wobble.

People gawk at Michael's car, joking and talking. Pointing. Spitting. A single word is sprayed in white on the decrepit Honda's windshield.

FAG.

Oh, Michael! I turn back to catch him before he sees, but he's already at my shoulder. Shaking. I've never seen Michael addled. Not even when the creature was slamming around in the shed, sirens wailing and guns blazing. His eyes mist.

"Be cool, Em. Don't let the bastards get you down."

We wait until more cars leave and the crowd disperses before we wander into the lot. The tires are slashed. Michael kicks the floppy tread. "I wonder if AAA gives discounts for hate crimes." His voice wavers. He's probably imagining that this could have been him damaged rather than his car. I know I would.

"We can give you a ride."

Keiko. She gestures to her Mom's car that idles at the curb.

Michael doesn't answer. His eyes check mine.

"What do you think?" I say to Michael.

"I appreciate it, Keiko. But I gotta stay and call the cops. And my folks."

She smiles sadly. "Okay. Let me know if you need anything."

Maybe there's a chance for us to be friends again. We'll see.

Unlike the hit party my brother threw for Aidan, these tormentors don't hang around. The police arrive shortly, but AAA is delayed and Michael's parents don't show until almost 5:00 p.m. By the time I get home, I've barely got enough time to do my hair and slip into a dress.

Mom moves like she's sleepwalking. She puts our dinner dishes in the sink and lets the water run for what sounds like hours.

As I'm dressing, I hear Aidan's door open. He knocks on mine. "Charity, I want to know if I look acceptable."

He has no game, and it's completely adorable. "Just a sec." I zip up and open the door.

There he stands in a black sweater and gray slacks, dress shoes polished to a gleam. The sweater's half-zip collar is open, the tender flesh of his Adam's apple exposed. Curls spill over his forehead.

"You're trying to kill me, aren't you?"

He tilts his head, confused. "What do you mean?"

I kiss him. He sinks into me, pulls away to glance down the stairs for Mom, and kisses me again.

We gather Mom, who sleepwalks through a change of clothes, and head to the Sheriff's Office in Placerville. Judy texts me.

It's crazy!
*What do you mean?*
Everybody is here, news people and the mayor
*THE MAYOR?!? Don't think we have one.*
I don't know, Leo says it's the mayor

I text Detective Bristow.

*Hey, I thought this was a small event?*
Sorry. :( City council got carried away.

The film crews we've been dodging swarm our car like zombies. Jabbering, stomping, pressing faces to the windows. Part of me wants to boast, to show off for once, but the desire dies in my throat. I can't put Aidan through that. It's bad enough he's now on camera.

Then again, it's not like his dad doesn't know where he is.

Sheriff's deputies help us out of the car and lead us to the Oak County government building, a wide, white building with arched windows that reminds me of a Spanish mission. I want to take Aidan's hand but I can't. He sticks close to Mom and me as we're ushered up the steps and through the glass doors. We move through the metal detectors before proceeding down the scuffed hallways. Brass lettering on the redwood doors that swing open indicates we're entering the Oak County Sheriff's Office.

A chattering crowd greets us.

"This way, please," says the young deputy with freckles, leading us into a big room with a podium at the front, flanked by flags for the U.S. and California. A giant green and yellow emblem of the Sheriff's Department is mounted on the wall behind the podium. Rows of packed seats. Standing room only. It looks like cop church. Journalists pepper the congregation with black microphones and heavy cameras. I think I even see Darren's parents in the audience.

Detective Bristow sits in the front row next to Michael, Leo and Judy, with an empty seat between them. Parents, families, and officials fill the next rows. I recognize Michael's mom and dad. A slouchy man with Leo's profile sits wide-eyed with his highly attentive, bleached blonde wife. A very handsome, lean, well-dressed couple with sharp dark haircuts sits behind Judy. They've saved two seats by draping coats over them.

When we approach, they and Leo's parents eagerly shake hands with us in introduction. I miss the names because the crowd din rises, people craning their necks to get a better look at us. Judy's dad holds up a sophisticated video camera. He tells my mom, "I'm getting it all. I'll put up a copy for your husband." Judy's mother then takes away the coats and says to my mom, "These are for you and Adrian."

Ugh. At least they're trying. And maybe now they believe Judy.

Detective Bristow moves over one seat and motions for me to sit between him and Michael, who still looks ill. Judy and Leo are both dressed in dark suits. Judy would never wear something like that. Her mother must've forced her. The couple is somber as if they'd been arrested rather than getting an award. The detective's aftershave warms my nose, his moustache crisp. He looks slightly less haunted than he did that night. "I'm so sorry," he says in my ear.

"No worries," I reply and lean against Michael.

Michael buries his shoulder in mine, whispering. "Get ready for the big sleep. *Zzzzzzzz*."

I swat him.

A parade of officials mounts the podium. One after another, city council members and other officials bore us to tears about Darren's death and the impact it had on the lives of citizens and law enforcement alike. The terror. The grief. The mystery.

And then the breakthrough.

At last Detective Bristow stands to speak. He describes the investigation and directs his gaze at me. "Little did we know we had a team of high school geniuses creating a unique animal trap in their back yard. I had interviewed Charity Jones along with many other students when Jacobs was killed. She'd impressed me then as a conscientious, intelligent young lady with a bright future ahead of her. I had no idea what she was capable of, although I later learned that her father is a lead engineer for a high-level national security firm."

He pauses. His face darkens for a second. Why is he looking at me that way?

"Like a great leader, she enlisted the help of her friends to realize her vision. In an age when we doubt the moral integrity and industry of the young, we have shining examples of extraordinary intelligence, application, and cunning in the service of humanity."

Cunning? I feel like I'm being accused rather than congratulated.

An official who might be the Chief Sheriff himself moves to the front of the room and stands beside the detective. "Ladies and gentlemen, it is with great pleasure I'd like to introduce to you Charity Jones, Michael Allured, Judy LaHart, and Leo Donatti." He motions to us. "Please stand."

We rise and turn to the room. The applause swells. A standing ovation. The rapid clicks and blinding flashes of cameras.

Another official approaches the podium. Detective Bristow introduces him as George Richards, the Representative of District Four, and then steps back. Rep. Richards presents a certificate to each one of us "for outstanding service to our community."

Detective Bristow's eyes scald my face as he claps. Is he angry?

Rep. Richards shakes our hands and thanks us for what we did. He then says, "So, Ms. Jones, what sort of thing does a young lady like yourself ask Santa to bring you for Christmas?"

Is this guy for real? To hell with anonymity. The Klaas knows where Aidan is. And who I am. "That's between Santa and me, sir," I say confidently, looking directly to the lens.

Aidan's eyes are damp with what looks like pride. And hope.


Outside, deputies escort us back to our car, but Detective Bristow and another detective catch up to us. "Mrs. Jones, may I have a moment with Charity?"

"Sure," Mom says.

Aidan looks wary.

Detective Bristow and the other man—whom I now recognize from the Thanksgiving raid—lead me back down the sidewalk toward the building. "This is Sergeant Mathers, Charity. We just have a couple of questions."

I say nothing.

"Charity, why did you use candy canes to attract the creature when you knew it was a carnivore?"

I shrug. "Everything likes sugar."

"But why candy canes? Why not chocolate? Or cookies?" Sergeant Mathers asks.

"They're cheap?" I say. "I don't know. Judy bought whatever she could afford in bulk."

"You also used mint oil," Bristow says brusquely. "The smell saturated the area. I thought at the time that it was unrelated, but not anymore. Not given how smart you are and the fact that your father works for a secretive government defense agency. I think you're holding back important information about the creature. You might even know what it is."

"I'm an aspiring engineer," I reply. "Do you honestly think I'd hold back anything from science?"

"If you had reasons? Yeah."

They aren't going to let up. "Okay, here's what I suspect. I think it's from the North Pole. It might be part human."

"The North Pole?" Mathers laughs. "This kid is bullshitting us."

"That's what it told me before *you killed it.*"

Detective Bristow's face drains of color—what little it had, anyway.

I change my tone. "I'm grateful to you for saving my life. I wouldn't want to see this turn into an officer-involved shooting instead of a monster hunt."

They say nothing.

"Are we done?"

Detective Bristow nods.

I return to the car. Faking holiday cheer, I wave before I slide into the front passenger seat. "Thanks, Detective! Merry Christmas!"

# Chapter 38

By the time we get home, I no longer feel like I'm #winning. After Mom goes to bed, Aidan and I kick off our shoes and curl up together on the couch, staring at the cheerfully decorated fireplace.

"You're sure he would kill us. My mom. My dad. Even me."

"Without a doubt," Aidan says. "I can't bear the thought of being without you. And I can't return to all that pain and suffering." He falls quiet and kisses my head.

"Do we need guns? Please tell me we don't need guns," I say.

"They would only work on my siblings, anyway. Besides, do you even know how to shoot?"

He's right. None of us knows anything about guns. My gaze falls miserably on the fireplace mantle. "You need a sock."

"You mean a stocking?" he asks.

"Yeah."

"Don't be grotesque." He kisses my head again.

A distraction presents itself. "Oh! Judy gave me something the other day I've been meaning to show you. It's the one thing missing from this room." I taste his lips—luscious, sweet, incredible—and leap off the couch. "B-R-B!"

I run up to my room. After a moment of digging in my sock drawer, I find the carefully wrapped sprigs of French mistletoe. The bright green leaves droop. Their shape reminds me of kelp. White berries bud like pearls from the stalks. Before I reach the bottom of the stairwell, I pause, mistletoe behind my back. "Close your eyes."

"Very well." He squeezes his eyes shut.

Bubbling with excitement, I tiptoe towards him. His smile fades. Leaning over the couch back, I hold the mistletoe over his head. "Open your eyes."

Aidan wails. He flies off the couch, scrambling away from me. "Are you trying to kill me?" he gasps, flat against the wall by the fireplace. "*Put it down!*"

"But it's just—"

"*Mistletoe!*" His face is twisted in terror, sweat bathing his brow. "European mistletoe. Very deadly."

"Yeah. If you *eat* it." I hold it up over my head. "I thought you knew every Christmas tradition, Aidan *the Klaas.*"

"*Mistilteinn.* It doesn't ring a bell? Haven't you ever read The Poetic Edda?" he asks, knuckles white.

He's not joking. I lower the mistletoe. "I don't even know what that is."

"It's a collection of Norse poems about their myths. Except they aren't entirely myths."

Rewrapping the mistletoe in the tissue, I set it on the far end of the mantle. "I can't throw it away. Judy's parents smuggled it from France." He relaxes a bit, wiping tears from his eyes. I start to throw my arms around him, but he backs away.

"Please wash your hands. I mean it."

Riddled with guilt, I march to the downstairs bathroom and wash before returning. He looks infinitely relieved as we hug. "I love you so much. I'm sorry I upset you. I didn't know. I thought you were kidding."

He leads me to the couch and wraps himself around me as if protecting me from the thing on the mantle. "You must understand. The god Odin and goddess Frigg—well, what humanity might call gods and goddesses, anyway—had a son whom Frigg loved more than anything. His name was Balder. Now, Frigg had the power of prophecy. My father is descended from her, or so he says. But Balder she wished to keep from harm. So, according to the legend, she made everything in the world swear to never harm him. The mistletoe was too young to take an oath and thought to be harmless, so it never promised. Balder seemed invincible. The other gods enjoyed trying to kill him for sport, but he merely laughed as every weapon failed. Loki noticed this. You know who Loki is, right?"

"I've seen the movie."

He arches an eyebrow. "Okay. Well, for reasons that are unclear, the mischievous Loki decided he wanted Balder dead. He therefore crafted an arrow made out of mistletoe and gave it to Balder's angry blind brother, Hod, who shot it at Balder, slaying him."

*Slaying him.* "So, if mistletoe can kill you, can it kill your siblings?"

Aidan nods. "My father perhaps, too. He hated it." He swallows.

"Are you sure? Have you ever been hurt by it? Has anyone in your family been?"

"My father has, if one believes his rantings. He says he stepped on some in a house somewhere on the Continent and that his foot burned for ages. It's one of the reasons he never ventures out anymore."

My hands burrow under Aidan's collar to feel the soft skin and stray hairs at the base of his neck. "Aidan, I know what to do. I have to be my dad."

"Which means?"

"He builds missiles for the U.S. military. We have to build our own."

The business of death. That's what I've always thought of my dad's job. He helps Americans kill people of other nations. But I can no longer afford the idealistic notion that I can avoid violence. Aidan's father is coming to take him and probably kill us, too.


We crowd in Judy's car in the parking lot where Aidan works for a conference while he's on break. Not many people are buying trees in this weather, anyway.

"Where are we getting the material to build bombs?" Leo asks.

"Yeah, *without* getting put on some Homeland Security list," Judy points out. "We're going to get thrown in jail before Christmas. We can hang out with Charles. Build snowmen in the prison yard."

"We're not building *bombs*, you guys. We just need—okay, *I* need to develop a delivery system for the mistletoe. This is the best weapon we have."

"Is it just the French mistletoe?" Judy asks. "Or can we use any mistletoe? 'Cause we don't have that much. Especially if we need to experiment."

"I'm not certain," Aidan says. "*Viscum album* is deadly but the California mistletoe might not be. It's an entirely different species and I'm not up for experimentation on that point."

"Christ, you guys," Michael curses. "We can get tinctures of it online and have it overnighted. My parents say desperate people use it to treat themselves for cancer."

Aidan blanches.

"Supersoakers?" Leo says.

"Good thinking, Leo," I reply. "The tinctures are probably too expensive for that, but it doesn't mean we can't dilute the mistletoe we've got and deliver it in a diffuser."

Michael searches on his phone. "Sixteen ounces would set us back one hundred and fifty smacks. That is, if we haven't already spent all our dough on Christmas presents."

Every face in the car darkens. Except one.

"I have the money," Aidan says. "Mr. Daniels pays me every day in cash."

"Wait! Concentration?" I ask Michael.

"One to four to twenty-six dry."

"Is that strong enough, Aidan?"

He nods. "Should be. You might be able to dilute by ten. But no more."

Michael frowns. "We can't order online. We don't have—"

"I have a credit card!" Leo announces proudly. The whole car seems to light up. "Actually, I'm on my mom and dad's account. But they'll be cool with it if I give them cash to cover the purchase. Send me the link. I'll order it today."

"Let's save as much of the actual mistletoe for direct delivery as possible," I say. "It just has to hit the skin. Right, Aidan? Eyes are the targets."

He nods, looking uncomfortable. "Where will I be in this?"

"Dad's office," I say. "It's on the first floor, but it's the most defensible and doesn't have a window. It can also shield you from mistletoe dust. You'll wear goggles and other skin protection."

Turned backward in the driver's seat, Judy rests her face against the headrest. "I am really scared, Charity."

"Just wait until you see him," Aidan says. "I hate to upset everyone, but you have to be prepared. You must purge every image you have of him and brace yourself for something more frightening than you can imagine."

"Krampus," I say. "We've seen the drawings. They're accurate?"

Aidan nods.

"Weapons," I say to Aidan. "What will he bring? And how can he attack?"

"He's terribly old-fashioned. Back home, he carries an enormous scourge made of chains, but I don't know if he will bring it," he says, his face reddening. "He has my abilities and more, but I can protect you to an extent. It's hard to say because I've never encountered him outside the fortress. I definitely can't do much hiding in a room. Your best defense will be me and I have to see what's happening."

"All right, then," I say. "We'll just rig the room for a hasty retreat if you need it and you can remain in the hallway. What about your siblings?"

"My siblings can only attack as you've seen, but I guarantee he won't bring any lame ones."

"How many?" Leo asks.

"The sleigh can carry about a dozen and maybe one per wind climber."

"Wind climber?" Judy's eyes brighten, her imagination clearly engaged.

"They're like goats," Aidan clarifies, "but they fly."

"*The sleigh?!?*" Michael wails. "Pulled by *goats?*" Of all things, this unhinges him.

"Get a grip," Judy says. "We know it's creepy."

"This means my childhood was worse than a big fat lie!"

"Everyone's parents lie to them about Santa," I say.

"It's not that my parents lied to me. It's that they were telling the truth! There are elves! But they're not cute little people wearing felt hats. Oh, no. They're dog-eating monsters. *That are real!* (No offense, Aidan.) And Santa! Holy crap! He's not a jolly, fat nice guy. He's a giant goat-thing that rides *a sleigh* and sneaks into your house on Christmas to rape your sister!" Michael flops back against the seat, horrified.

"Oh, stop it, already!" Judy says. Then, to the rest of us, "We need help. Just the five of us? Even with our secret ingredient and Aidan, we're outnumbered."

"I can get Ricardo," Michael says, calming down. "I'm pretty sure, anyway. I'll have to show him Judy's night photos in the Dropbox. He'll totally break up with me after this, but he can help. He's a semi-professional fighter."

"What about the cops?" Judy asks, looking at me. Just as I'm about to speak, Aidan answers for me.

"He'll kill them first. Just for the joy of it. Trust me. But us…if we're in the house, we have a chance."

"And I know one other person who can help me design," I say.

"Who can help *you*, Ms. Genius?" Judy asks.

"It's not a matter if she can. It's if she will."

# Chapter 39

Every moment counts. But do I spend it making love? Or war?

Or studying? Finals are Wednesday, Thursday and Friday. No matter what happens to Aidan, I need those grades. But to say I don't need Aidan is a lie. What kind of life will I have if I lose him to his father?

Then again, if Krampus kills us, I'll have no life at all.

Saturday night I stay up researching possible delivery systems and land on our best option.

Les Femmes Nikitas.

The drones could be operated and reconfigured to drop payload on K and the Goat Riders.

But it's futile. If Krampus has some form of telekinesis—or, as I like to think of it, an ability to manipulate gravity—then he could throw the Nikitas into a wall. I need to interrogate Aidan further about this.

It's 3:00 a.m. when I knock softly on Aidan's door.

He answers, eyes creased with worry, and lets me in.

I keep my voice low. "Aidan, I assume your dad can do to people what you did to Charles and his friends."

"Yes. He can overwhelm anyone by manipulation of gravity and other natural forces."

Despair sets in.

Aidan continues. "But once he's inside someone's house on Christmas, there are rules that may or may not be relevant."

"Such as?"

"He can't damage or otherwise hurt your gifts."

I didn't see that one coming, but yeah. Useless. "Okay. Anything else?"

"He can't hurt animals, as much as he would like to."

"Well that's something, I suppose." It's extremely unlikely that we'll be able to recruit an army of chimps to fight for us. "Any other rules you can remember?"

Silence as he thinks. "It's unlikely that your mother would awaken, even if she weren't taking sleeping pills. He induces sleep paralysis in those who are already asleep. But those who are already awake, he cannot incapacitate in the same manner. That's everything I know."

Just as I want to sink onto the floor and curl up to sleep, a powerful idea ignites. My head feels full of bees. "Aidan, does it matter whose present it is? Say, if I give *you* a present, he can't hurt it, right?"

"Correct."

"I'm giving you Les Femmes Nikitas. And Mr. Spotty. And any weapon we create. Every weapon, every payload delivery system I create, they are gifts to you."

He leaps from his desk and kisses me passionately, lifting me off my feet. "I told you it's your magic, but you didn't believe me. The best part is that they will just be toys to him. Unpredictable toys. He won't have any idea what they're going to do, much less that they will hurt him. And even when he realizes what's happening, he won't be able to do anything about it."

I finally relax and crumple under the weight of my exhaustion. Aidan carries me to my bed and tucks me in.

"We will be together forever, Charity Jones. Sleep well. And trust that amazing mind of yours." We kiss. He then touches my forehead with those silky lips before he leaves.

The next day, after hours of deliberation, I sit on my bed and make a phone call to a number I had deleted but could not forget.

"Hey. It's Charity. Yeah. I'm okay. Can we talk?"

# Chapter 40

The wind punishes the leafless trees as Keiko and I huddle by the lockers at lunch. The daytime temperature has dropped almost ten degrees since Thanksgiving. My teeth chatter with more than the cold, though, as we hurtle toward Doomsday.

Christmas, that is.

Some students cram sandwiches in their faces as they seek refuge under building eaves while others eat in the cafeteria with freshmen despite the shame. I constantly look over my shoulder, monitoring who is close, who might be listening. We couldn't meet yesterday and I didn't want to wait until the end of the day to talk to her. Aidan already ate his lunch and is helping Mr. Reilly with some project.

"So, Aidan's Dad is coming to take him away and you're building this defense system? Why don't you call the police?" Keiko asks.

I couldn't tell her that Krampus would just kill them. "They won't do anything until it's too late. It's happened before. It was almost a disaster when we caught the creature. I'd be dead if they'd gotten there a moment later. Don't worry. We'll definitely call them once he shows up, but we have to take care of ourselves in case they don't. It's the only way."

"Does your mom know?"

"No, not yet. Besides, Aidan's dad has threatened to kill her if she or my dad finds out." Not entirely untrue. So far, I've mostly left out things she's less likely to believe. "This guy is one thousand percent evil and powerful. There's no telling what he'll bring. Aidan has scars on his back from where he's been beaten. We've got to defend ourselves against this guy and send him a message that he can't hurt kids anymore."

Keiko thinks for a moment, her eyes focusing on where the stream of rain forms a puddle in the crabgrass by the walkway. "I don't know. You seem really wrapped up in Aidan. Is he worth it?"

The air changes. Male voices rise behind us as several guys gather around the guys' restroom. Michael is stopped at the entrance by a senior gorilla named

186

Burke Wasnowski AKA Burke the Jerk. He used to date a girl everyone called The Snow Queen—thanks to her coke habit—until she got expelled. He's probably one of Charles' angry ex-customers.

"We don't let girls in our bathroom. Especially not girls with dicks."

Michael moves to leave, but another musclehead steps in his way.

"I'm not fighting you hyenas," Michael says.

"Sounds like fighting words to me," the musclehead says.

Burke notices me watching. "What are *you* looking at, Oreo and banana?"

"A pile of feces, that's what *I'm* looking at," Aidan says behind me. He steps past me, stopping in front of the musclehead. The crowd mutters.

Burke shoots Aidan a look of white-hot hatred. "Hey, it's Sherlock. Gonna tell me what I want for Christmas?"

Everyone laughs as Burke brushes past his fellow gorilla and grabs Aidan by the collar, his backpack falling to the ground. Burke pulls Aidan up on his toes, shoving him against the wall. I silently beg Aidan not to go Bad Santa on these guys. I can't take a repeat of that. Bracing myself to push Keiko out of harm's way, I watch the encounter closely.

"You know what I want for Christmas? To smash your face until it's mushy like cookie dough," Burke says.

What is Aidan doing? I worry he's about to blow up.

"I'll make a bet with you," Aidan says. "If you can flatten my nose in one punch, then you can beat us both into said cookie dough. But if you can't, you have to let us go and never bother us again."

Michael's red, frantic face sweats even though it's 45 degrees outside. Through his gritted teeth he says to Aidan, "What. Are. You. Doing?!"

Burke grimaces. "I don't need no bets. I'll just take you out right here."

"Afraid you'll lose?" Aidan asks.

Burke throws him against the brick wall again. "I'm not gonna lose."

"Take the bet, then," Aidan says with infuriating calm. "Punch me hard. You get one shot."

Apprehension gleams in Michael's eyes. I can't believe Aidan is doing this.

Everyone gasps as the musclehead explodes with a hook punch to Michael's head. His hand collides with a sickening *crack* against an invisible wall just inches from Michael's ear. The musclehead curses loudly, doubling over.

Aidan holds a hand at his side in a subdued "stop" gesture like when he stopped Zach's car.

Burke throws a meaty fist at Aidan's face. Aidan closes his eyes. Another crack echoes in the hallway as Burke breaks his knuckles on an invisible surface. Burke howls. His mangled hand bleeds. Tears streak his face. Enraged, Burke drops Aidan and drives a foot into Aidan's leg, but Burke's foot bends at an odd angle on contact. He shrieks, cursing and limping away to lie on the grass in the rain.

"What's the matter?" Michael yells at the musclehead. "Can't aim, dickhead?"

Is there such a thing as a whole-body exhale? Because I totally do that. Every ounce of tension drops away as the attackers and crowd disperse.

Aidan says something to Michael I can't hear. Michael enters the restroom without resistance, smiling. The bell rings. Aidan shakes off the encounter and kisses me. "Subtle enough?"

"Yes," I say. Then, with joy: "Aidan, this is Keiko."

Keiko gapes, mouth open.

"Nice to meet you, Keiko," he says with a bow. "Charity says lovely things about you." Then, "Right. Off to class! See you, my love." He kisses me once more and scuttles off.

Keiko regains her ability to speak. "What just happened? That guy punched him! How did they not get hurt?"

"Aidan is like a guardian angel. He has the power to protect people. He saved Charles' life once, even though he didn't deserve it. But he can't protect himself from his dad. He's more powerful."

"Count me in," Keiko says. We hug and my heart lets go of the hurt.

# Chapter 41

The next morning, my eyelid twitches from lack of sleep as I try to apply mascara. At 6:00 a.m., Michael picks me up and we go to school. He brings me back home to study at 3:00 p.m. At 8:00 p.m., I switch to artillery design until midnight, feeding Keiko calculations and drawings so that she can figure out the algorithms I need to make the Nikitas fly inside using the GPS.

She has no idea what we're really up against.

And despite her help, it's clear we don't have enough time to do everything if I'm also going to do well on my finals. Because the reality is this: if we win, nothing changes and I need the highest grades possible to get into the schools I want. If we lose and I'm somehow not dead, I'll need everything in my power to move forward. I don't know how I'll survive without Aidan, but I'll have to try.

I refuse to believe that anything is going to happen to Aidan. Or us.

I focus on mods to the Nikitas, including the drop function so that each quadcopter can release a payload. It can't be big, though. Each quad can only carry a few ounces at a time. The big hits will launch from a simple air cannon. I found a design online that won't take too much garage time to make. I shanghaied Leo into helping with the power tools.

Leo also found powerful water pistols in his older brother's closet, the one who's at Yale. The pistols can shoot up to 20 feet with some accuracy and not drip. Judy is drying the French mistletoe in her mother's fruit dehydrator. She found goggles and filtered masks in her mother's workshop supplies for us to wear during the melee so that we wouldn't get ill or blinded from the dust and liquids during the fight.

Michael's boyfriend, Ricardo, studies Krav Maga, a military style of fighting. Apparently, Ricardo was beyond impressed with the photos. They are outside in the backyard, where he is training Michael. In his YouTube videos, Ricardo is an absolutely ripped hunk of Latin teenager tearing through a room full of guys in fatigues. With his bare hands.

In the backyard, Ricardo attacks Michael with a wooden knife. Michael dodges just barely. "Like this." He stabs Michael in the neck, holding a buckler shield in the other hand. "Now do this to me."

Aidan watches with curiosity as he periodically checks the laptop. Judy made a series of absolutely incredible animations, recreating the creature's anatomy, how it maneuvers and especially its attacks. The guys have been playing each animation, Ricardo imitating the creature's movements as he trains Michael how to defend and attack them.

"Maybe I should be in charge of the water pistols," Michael says.

"No way," I say. "We need your muscle."

Ricardo agrees. "He's done this before. We met in this class. He's just rusty. Rotate from your core!"

Michael does so, swinging his own buckler at Ricardo to bash away his "claw" to shoot water at his face and neck with a water pistol.

"Better," Ricardo says.

"Where did you get the shields?" I ask, noting some bigger shields stacked by an open duffle bag on the deck.

"The SCA," Ricardo says, sending Michael to the ground with a kick to his unguarded leg. "The Society for Creative Anachronisms. It's a medieval recreation group I'm in. We fight in big tournaments that go all weekend."

Aidan shakes his head, indicating the current animation. "I don't think your attack is quite proper. You still need more reach."

"You're right," Ricardo says. He drops the knife and buckler in the duffle bag and dons gloves that have a giant aluminum claw sticking out of the tip of each finger. A Freddy Krueger costume glove just like in the movies. "We use this from now on." He then scurries around after Michael in a squat, swiping at him. Michael barely stifles an "Eek!" before he regains his cool and works to protect his legs and crotch.

Ricardo must have steel calves and thighs. "I've got shin protectors if you need them," he chides his opponent.

"Much better," Aidan says, rocking on his heels, hands in pockets.

I turn to Aidan. "Since Krampus can't hurt gifts, the Nikitas will be wrapped lightly as a gift to you under the tree here," I explain, "ready to burst from the tissue."

"You don't even need the tissue," Aidan says. "Just a bow on everything."

Michael interjects as he successfully dodges a claw swipe. "We're assuming he'll come down the chimney."

Aidan confirms. "The only other way they can enter the house is the front door if it's left ajar or someone opens it for him."

"Like vampires," I add.

"I suppose. Yes." He calls to Michael. "You and Ricardo will flank from the kitchen with pistols and shields, then?"

"Aye, captain!"

During a training break, we continue to plan our defense and offense while Michael and Ricardo guzzle water from the refrigerator dispenser between smooches. Despite the circumstances, it thrills me to see Michael happy and just being himself. "We've got to secure the first floor. Put safety latches on the kitchen cabinet doors. Stuff like that," Michael says. "Those sibs of yours could start throwing dishes. Turn anything into missiles to use against us."

"Should we all use shields or armor?" I ask.

Aidan moves under the archway of the downstairs hallway. "Perhaps I should remain in this opening, obscured by shadows but with a good view so that I can do my worst. Judy and Leo can be stationed above. I'll bind and injure as many of my siblings as possible as they emerge from the chimney."

"And you'll be putting Mr. Spotty to the right of the fireplace," Michael adds, indicating me.

I don't say anything.

"What's wrong?"

"We don't have time to alter Spotty."

"*What?*"

My cheeks burn. The whole room narrows to just Michael and me.

Michael fumes. "He was going to blast mistleballs! What are we going to do without that?"

Our nerves are frayed from finals topping the horrendous stress of the last month. Things could get ugly fast. "Look, the air cannon is easier to build," I explain. "It'll take only a few hours."

"*What* air cannon?"

"Hey, sweetie. Relax. Hear her out," Ricardo urges Michael.

"I've got plans I found online for a PVC air cannon. It can launch a mistletoe cannon ball up to three inches in diameter."

"We don't have that much mistletoe!" Anger twists his face. He's losing it.

"We have enough!" I catch myself yelling. "Judy's coming over tomorrow and we're making cannon balls using the extract and a form of maltodextrin as a base. Plus a binder. It'll hold together."

"I love this woman," Ricardo says to Michael. "Air cannons? Quadcopters? This is insanely cool!"

Michael takes a deep breath, closes his eyes, and puts his head in his hands. He sits with Ricardo on the couch. Ricardo plants a kiss on Michael's cheek and asks the question I was hoping he'd ask. "How'd you come up with that?"

"Judy did. It's a cooking thing her mother taught her."

"I thought she was this sensitive punk artiste."

"She is. But she's finding her inner mad scientist. It's awesome."

Aidan sits with me on the adjoining couch, pensive. He takes my hand in his. Warm. Amazingly soft. "Sorry to change the subject, but it occurred to me that I might have misled you about my father's appearance."

"Oh?" Michael guzzles more water. "He's not a big chain-slinging goat muncher?"

"Don't be ridiculous. Of course he is," Aidan replies. "But he might appear differently to you than he does to me. He can do that. At home, he hasn't much occasion to change his appearance, but I recall him seeming far more human around my mother when I was younger. He breaches the chimney by changing his shape, after all."

"Does it affect how he'll respond to the mistletoe?" I try not to sound annoyed. But I am.

"No, but it could affect you psychologically," Aidan says. "And that might be his greatest weapon."

# Chapter 42

"I'm so proud of you, my Little River."

I sit on the floor of my bedroom, back against the bed, exhausted on a Wednesday morning. Mom is overwhelmed with work. Everything that can go wrong in her eighty-five cases has. Aidan is helping Michael, Ricardo, Judy and Leo downstairs.

I hold up my phone. Dad's face is in a hotel room somewhere in D.C. Judy's parents sent him a link to the video. "Are you okay, baby?" he asks. "You look beat."

"Finals kicked my butt," I reply. "You look kinda tired, too, mister."

He rubs his eyes. "I'm okay. I'm sorry your visit with your brother didn't go too well."

Ah, Dad. Deflecting my concerns. Changing the subject from him to me. "Yeah, I think it's going better in the Middle East."

"I'm sorry you went through that, baby. I'll make it up to you when I get home."

"Which is?"

He shakes his head. "No idea. But I promise to jump on the first plane out of here as soon as they give me the go. Even if it's today." He looks wistful. "You taking care of your mom?"

"Trying. She's on autopilot." She sleeps all the time and her temper is on a hair trigger. Yesterday morning she mumbled something about seeing the doctor after the holidays. It's killing her to have Christmas without Charles. "After work today she's supposed to go to the detention center to visit Charles. She said to expect her late."

A sound from downstairs. "Aidan! Stop!" A crash. Huge laughter. Everyone is punchy with stress and jitters. At least it's an improvement over all the bickering.

I close the door and sit down again. "So congress is buying? Or will you have to open a BombMart on the Mall?"

"Shop smart! Shop BombMart!" Dad says in a jolly Bruce Campbell voice. "We might have to," he says. "No one wants to invest in defense these days except the usual suspects. And they're so busy fighting everyone here that they ain't gonna get their way on anything else."

My eyes heat with tears. Is this the last time I'll see Dad? "I love you, Daddy."

"I love you, too, baby. Don't be sad. Give Aidan a hug for me, too. Okay? I'll see you all soon."

A dozen sharpened pencils hover in the air at the hallway arch. Michael and Ricardo stand off to the side of the fireplace. Everyone wears goggles and holds SCA shields, watching the giant stuffed polar bear sitting in front of the opening. Standing by the tree, Aidan holds up a finger and then drops it suddenly. The pencils launch into the polar bear. *Shut shut shut shut.*

Ricardo points at Aidan, his mouth hanging open. "Holy shit! You just shot—with…Did you see that?"

"Yeah. I told you he does that," Michael explained. "He did lots of parlor tricks for me when he was staying in the guest house. You'll get used to it."

Upstairs, Leo madly pumps the air cannon as Judy shouts, "Fire!" She hits the foil covering the back of the cannon with a padded mallet. The test "snowball" explodes out of the PVC pipe and ruptures against the bear's chest, crumbling in a not very satisfying hit. Like the pencils, the test snowball doesn't have the extract. Once finished, the cannon balls will be transferred from the garage freezer to an ice chest. The maltodextrin ensures that they stay in a solid ball shape yet not freeze hard. Judy has numerous pre-covered back ends for the cannon that seal it shut before the pump sucks out the air in the pipe.

"I hope the snowballs are enough." Aidan lifts his goggles to survey the damage. He walks over to the bear and digs a finger in its belly to withdraw a pencil buried deep inside. "I don't like the pencils. My father can use them against us." He looks to me. "Charity, are the Nikitas ready?"

"Yup!" The controller is set up in the loft.

"Aidan!" Leo calls down as I scramble upstairs. "What exactly happens to you when you're hit by mistletoe?"

The room dims as Aidan speaks. "It's a poison that penetrates the skin and mucous membranes to enter the bloodstream and curdle the blood. The effect is quite gruesome."

"You've seen it?" Michael asks.

Aidan's mouth thins to a grim line. "Yes," he replies.

"What's to keep him from blocking the attack?" Michael asks. "Like you did with those douchebags when they punched us?"

"The element of surprise." Aidan looks up to me. "Ready?"

"Ready!" I direct a symphony of talcum terror. The copters buzz as they rise from under the tree. Everyone seems just as riveted by the copters as the pencils. Number 1 soars over Michael's head and unleashes a payload of baby powder. Ricardo laughs hysterically. Simultaneously Number 2 zooms high up into the rafters and drops another payload on Leo's head as he tries to dodge, arms covering his head.

Judy squeals with delight. "I love this!"

The two copters return to base immediately.

Number 3 flies up to Aidan. He doesn't flinch but watches with amusement.

"Hold out your hands like you're catching something," I say.

He does. Number 3 gently drops an origami heart into his palms. He looks up to me, his face glowing with happiness. A blue flame flickers in his eyes.

"Awwwwww!" Judy says, stealing a kiss from Leo's floured face.

Number 3 droops. She ascends back to the loft unsteadily.

"She's broken?" Judy asks, wiping powder off of her mouth from kissing Leo.

The copter lands on her pad, which is surrounded by small plastic baggies full of mistletoe dust barely stitched closed. I pick her up and carefully pop open her panel with a screwdriver. The problem is evident. "I need to resolder a wire. It'll only take a second."

Carrying the copter to the garage, I throw on the light and tear into the tool kit. Should I start up the soldering iron? I don't want to waste time. Instead, I dig into the box looking for the blue cigarette lighter. No dice. Charles must have stolen it.

Aggravated, I march back into the house and upstairs to my brother's room. The voices of the others fade as they continue to plan and question General Aidan.

"Most likely, my father will want me alive," Aidan says. "But he doesn't have much personal power over me. Therefore, I suspect he will send in my siblings first to subdue me and won't make any appearance whatsoever if they are successful. But if there's a problem, he will enter. And it'll be horrific."

I lose track of Aidan's voice as I step into Charles' room. The faint odor of boy sweat and cigarettes dusts the air. It's like walking into a tomb. Dark. Silent.

Forbidden. Dirty clothes are strewn about the room. Guitar magazines lie in a rumpled stack. His guitar and amp are tucked into the corner like abandoned toys. Mom and Dad haven't touched anything since Charles was arrested.

The closet stands halfway open. His leather jacket hangs inside. Mom probably hung it up and couldn't bear to deal with anything else. I fish in the pockets for a lighter. Nothing. I flip on the light and scan the room. A morass of metalhead boy stuff. The dresser drawers sit at various degrees of openness. I start yanking them open, digging for my lighter.

I should have just started up the soldering iron. He probably used up the lighter fluid some time ago. But now the urge to snoop sinks in.

As I'm searching through the bottom dresser drawer, I see a shoebox under the bed. I yank it out and pull off the lid. A pair of brand new Nikes that he never wore. Just as I'm about to slide the box under the bed, I spot another shoebox farther under the bed.

Drug paraphernalia? Porn? More shoes?

Flattening myself on the carpet, I reach as far as I can underneath. My fingertips brush the box. I flip over on my back. Straining harder, reaching farther. My fingertips hook the lid.

At last.

I drag the heavy box out from under the bed. Whatever it is, it sure as hell ain't shoes.

When I pry off the lid, I'm shocked to find the pistol inside. So Charles had a second gun. It must also belong to Palmer's dad.

I feel oddly relieved. A gun. I probably pissed off Detective Bristow. No cavalry will come to our defense tonight should the encounter turn deadly and the mistletoe proves ineffective. Putting my hand in a clean sock, I lift the black gun by its wooden handle. It's so heavy that it must be loaded. A box of brassy bullets packed in the gun's cloth bedding is missing exactly six.

Spellbound by the sight of the weapon, I don't hear Mom's car enter the driveway or anything else until Michael says, "*Mom!*"

A car door slams outside.

Startled and shaking, I gently pack everything back in the shoebox and shove it under the bed as the front door opens.

"What the hell is going on here?" Mom yells. "Charity! What the fuck are you doing? *Who made this goddamn mess?*"

By the time I reach the bottom of the staircase, Mom is having a full-on rage attack. The living room furniture and carpet are covered in white flakes and talcum powder. Two lamps are knocked on the floor. Dirty plates and glasses are piled on the coffee table. SCA shields are scattered by the doorway. The stuffed polar bear "bleeds" fluffy white stuffing over the rug. Everyone withers from her as she continues on her tirade.

"How dare you kids come here and destroy my house! And who the hell are you?" She looks accusingly at Ricardo. Everyone starts speaking at once in a chorus of apologies.

"Mom, I'm sorry—"

"Mrs. Jones, I deeply apologize. We had planned to—"

"I don't care!" she yells. "You kids should be ashamed of yourselves. Now, get the hell out of here. Not you, Charity, Aidan. You better clean this shit up. And you are both grounded. That's it. As for the rest of you, I never want to see another one of you in my house ever again. I'm calling your parents right now. I'm letting them know how deeply disrespectful and destructive you are to other people's homes and property."

"*Screw you!*"

I'm shaking with fury. Mom is stunned. So is everyone else. But I've never seen her this angry before over so little. And I've had it.

"It's not fair that you come home early and freak out on us just because you're having a bad day! Guess what? I'm having a bad *life*! Charles' jerk friends are torturing us at school, and all you can do is get drunk and feel sorry for yourself? Screw you and your drinking and your feeling sorry for Charles who is a total effing sociopath. I'm sick of you! And I'm not cleaning this up until I damn well feel like it!"

Can't. Stop. Erupting! I thought we'd have time to plan and test more in the precious few hours before nightfall. And what if, now that everyone's in trouble, they can't get out of the house tonight? Pretty much everyone had planned on sneaking out except Judy, who had gotten permission to spend the night. Now everyone's parents will be on alert and Judy will probably be grounded.

"*You are grounded this minute! Up here!*"

"*No!*" I cry. "Why don't you just get drunk and leave us alone?"

She throws a dangerous look at everyone. "Get out! All of you!"

Ricardo reaches for the shields. Michael intervenes. "Leave two," he whispers, taking two of the four water pistols.

Everyone files out, looking like losers in World War III. Once they're gone, Mom goes into her room and slams the door.

I'm still shaking and crying. Aidan holds me. Tears run down his face, too.

"I'm so sorry. I couldn't take it anymore," I say, sniffling. "What're we going to do? I've never been this terrified in my life!"

"Me, too," he whispers. "Let's clean up. When she leaves, we'll strategize. We can't give up hope."

# Chapter 43

It's 11:38 p.m.

Thunder rumbles over the crash of rain on the roof. Aidan and I pace the loft, checking and re-checking the ammunition, weapons and tactics. Aidan wears goggles, a filter mask, protective clothing, and rubber gloves to protect his skin. He looks like either a beekeeper or a scientist during an apocalyptic plague.

A fire hisses in the fireplace. The odor of charred wood comforts me, as does the idea of Aidan's father singeing his evil butt on the flames.

"This is the most defensible position we have," I say. "As they emerge from the fireplace, we can hit them with the cannon. If they charge up the stairs, we can nail them one by one. If they climb up the walls, we have mistletoe water. And from here you have the best view so that you can do what you do." I falter.

"As they say, we won't go down without a fight," he says.

I wrap my arms around him. We're both shaking. "I love you, Aidan the Klaas."

"And I love you, Charity Jones. More than you'll ever know."

We kiss. An eternity between our lips.

Mom sleeps after what seemed to be a rough visit with Charles. The only thing we've heard is a text from Michael.

*Ricardo says his mom went crazy after one of his brothers was incarcerated. He says try not to hate your mom.*

Ricardo's shields are stacked in the corner of the loft.

I say nothing about the gun.

A burst of light at the windows. Two seconds later, thunder rips up the sky.

My phone lights up, too. A text from Leo.

> It's Judy on Leo's phone! We're almost there!
>> BEST. FRIENDS. EVER! How come you didn't answer my earlier texts?
> Sorry I didn't message before. Mom took my phone.

And then Michael.

> Parental units in bed. ETA 00:15.
> Roger that. Door is unlocked.

Elated, I show Aidan.

"My father can't arrive before midnight," Aidan says.

"But what if he comes *at* midnight? Or three minutes after? Can we last fifteen minutes by ourselves? Can we last even five minutes?"

Aidan places a loaded water pistol in my hand. "Let's hope we don't find out."

A knock at the door.

I jerk toward the noise, startled. Aidan turns toward the staircase.

"No!" I grab his arm. "We can't leave this post."

"But what if it's Leo and Judy?"

Doubt suffocates the moment.

Another knock.

"Come in!" I say. If it's Aidan's father, he won't be able to enter unless we open the door.

Nothing.

"*Come in,*" I say, louder, worried I will wake up my mother.

No response.

It's 11:49 p.m.

Aidan and I look to one another. Maybe the person outside can't hear us over the rain.

Or maybe it's his father.

In eerie silence, Aidan makes his way down the staircase. I crouch behind the loft wall, clenching one of the pistols. With the other hand, I text Judy.

*You here?*

No answer. Of course! She doesn't have her phone. I text Leo instead. I then reach over and flip on the quadcopter controller. It whirrs to life. The armed Nikitas are ready under the tree.

The windows shudder like it's an earthquake, the rushing wind howling through the eaves like a pack of ghosts.

I peek over the wall. Aidan madly motions to someone at the door through the window by the Christmas tree. Outside, people scream.

A bone-chilling crash and clatter on the roof.

12:00 a.m.

Christmas.

The front door flies open. Judy and Leo burst through, soaking wet. Aidan flings the door closed behind them. They pound upstairs. I leap up to greet them.

"Charity! Jesus, it's horrible!" Leo yells.

Pale and trembling, Judy throws her arms around me. "It's worse than you can imagine!"

The sting of adrenaline drives me to pure action. I pump the first cannon as the noises on the roof get louder. Pounding. Crunching. Cursing and shrieking. Leo and Judy quickly fall in line and take over the weapons.

Aidan remains downstairs. He must be assuming his original position now that Judy and Leo are here.

"I'm so sorry," I say to them both as I pass them goggles and face masks.

"Don't be," Leo says, confident. Driven. Changed. He puts on the goggles. "We've got this."

I text Michael.

*KRAMPUS*

We hear an explosion of bricks and metal. Wild chattering and baying. He's probably tearing off the chimney cap. A horrible smell wafts into the living room as fluid rains down, extinguishing the fire. Everyone gags. Ammonia.

Elf piss.

"We're locked," Leo says, voice low as Judy readies the mallet.

The mistletoe pencils are hovering, ready to launch. So unnerving. Adrenaline spikes my nerves.

"On my word," I say, aiming steady.

Ash dribbles down the chimney walls into the fireplace for several moments.

A small wooden windup toy drops down onto the grill. Playing a child's tune, it whirrs and twitters as it climbs out of the grill and rolls onto the hearth on miniature wheels.

It stops at the hearth's edge. So cute! So sinister.

The toy spews black smog that rapidly billows into the living room.

Black. Blind. Terrifying.

I wait until I hear the half-burned wood scatter.

"*Go!*"

The cannon blasts a large ball of mistletoe dust into the spreading cloud.

The darkness rises to the loft, tendrils of midnight creeping over the wall's edge. Dual beams of blue light flash in the smoke. Judy and Leo duck, but they keep loading. If the smoke is poisonous, we're not suffering. Yet. The filter masks might help.

"*Go!*"

Another blast. Agonized cries tear through the expanding darkness.

Aidan says nothing. He doesn't give away his location.

"*Go!*"

I pump the largest water pistol and spray the room. More cries. The stench of burning flesh and fur overpowers me. I gag. A loud *crash* against the wall and fireplace. And another. And another. Great tearing noises as claws slash the couch fabric, the couch and other furniture overturning. Lamps smashing.

"*Go! Move around!*"

I fall back with the water pistol, grabbing another as I dash to the staircase. The blackness unfurls around me from behind. I crouch, aiming. Waiting.

The wails of Aidan's injured siblings rise in a bloody chorus. We're hurting them. Killing them.

But where is Aidan?

"*Aidan!*" I shout.

One of the pencils floats up the staircase, pointing at me. Before I can jerk out of its trajectory, it turns sideways and…bends. Into a smile. The pencil returns to him as we're enveloped in blackness.

My heartbeat thuds in my ears. I hear shrieks of pain. Claws raking into the walls as they climb to the loft.

I stumble into my room and throw open the window. In the bathroom, I do likewise, opening every window except Mom's and Charles'.

Charles.

The gun calls to me.

And then something awesome happens.

A downstairs window smashes open. And then another. And another. At last the front door explodes open, the smoke escaping into the windy night.

"*Fuck you, Santa!*"

The inky smoke dissipates to reveal Michael and Ricardo blasting through the living room with mistletoe water, shields up, sometimes bashing them into the snarling, slashing elves. Bodies are piling up, the dead and dying mutilated by the poisonous plant. The freezing wind carries away both the smoke and the stench that stabs at the back of my throat.

Fireworks in his eyes, Ricardo clobbers the last standing elf. It staggers back against the trashed polar bear. Three pencils dart out of nowhere—*phht phht phht*—straight into the elf's chest.

Dead and dying creatures litter the room, many clogging the fireplace, their cries of suffering creating an eerie chorus with the wind.

Everyone is panting. The roof creaks ominously. Hooves stomping. They sound like they're just inches from our heads.

Motioning to Leo and Judy, I point to the cooler. One? Two? How many left? Leo makes a "zero" with his hand.

Crap.

And Krampus is still up there with no telling how many more elves. He sent his children in first to take whatever we had to dish out, exhausting our resources. The tree has fallen on the Nikita. There's still too much smoke to see clearly if any of the quadcopters can get free.

There is one weapon left.

The box is where I left it under Charles' bed. I heft the gun. Heavy.

Deadly.

More creaks on the roof.

Aidan hovers in the archway of the downstairs hallway. He looks bereaved as he surveys the bodies of his siblings.

Gun at my side, I rejoin Leo and Judy in the loft. Freezing winds tear through the living room. I shiver. Sweat drips down my neck into my collar. I scan the area for more elves, pointing the gun at any movement on the floor or fireplace.

"Holy crap! Charity!" Michael says, backing away when he sees the gun. Shield up. "You've gone L.A. on us."

A figure steps into the broken window frame.

"Charity? What *the hell* is going on here?"

It's Dad.

He stands in the broken window, wide-eyed, exhausted, staring at the living room carnage in disbelief. He steps through the window and over the frame, glass crunching underfoot.

I aim at him and pull back the hammer.

# Chapter 44

"Don't move!" I command, bracing for a shot.

Dad puts up his hands, eyes even wider. "Baby, what the hell are you doin'? Put that goddamn thing down!"

Tears pour down my face. I miss my dad so much. It's Christmas. We're supposed to be together. We're supposed to be a family. But this isn't my daddy. Or is it? "Where's your suitcase?"

"My *suitcase*? The *fuck* are you talkin' about, girl? We've gotta get out of this mess! *Now*. Where's your mom?"

I feel myself breaking down. I've just been through hell. Stinky, horrible dead things litter the floor. The house—my *home*—is destroyed.

Everyone watches him and then looks to me, questioning. If it's my dad, I don't even need the gun. And if it's actually Krampus, it's useless, as Aidan so kindly demonstrated weeks ago...

Or is it?

"Mom's in bed. Asleep."

I so, so love my dad and want him here right now. He's smart and cool, and knows What The Doctor Would Do. I'm just his Little River. The resemblance twists me up inside. I'm paralyzed with love, longing, pain, fear.

Aidan loves Dad, too. This must be hard for him.

As my eyes scan Dad, I spot a bright blue sticky bow. One quadcopter is partially visible beneath the fallen tree.

Judy moves confidently to the console. I forgot that she games. She's seen me work the console and it looks like she knows what to do.

He walks further into the living room. "Asleep? With this shit goin' on? Baby—*put it down*. It's gonna be okay. Just come here and give Daddy a hug." He opens his arms.

The Nikita rises behind him.

Aidan disappears beneath the loft.

"Hey! Where you going?" Dad calls after him.

"Not with you," I reply.

I pull the trigger.

His hand extends in front of him. The bullet stops in midair, hovering before his face. As he's distracted, the Nikita soars over him, releasing the powdered mistletoe payload.

A hellish roar reverberates through the house. Where the mistletoe powder hits, my father's skin boils off his body. A hideous hide of thick silvery fur emerges from his flesh. Hooves burst from his shoes. The rain of dust seizes midair.

I'm thrown against the back wall. Stars explode behind my eyes. Pain singes the back of my skull and spine. I fall forward, landing on the loft carpet.

"*Charity!*" Judy scurries to me.

I crawl forward, waving my hand at the console. I can hear a quadcopter struggling to rise under the pine branches. Leo dives for the console and takes over as Judy helps me up.

Through the wooden slats of the loft wall, I see the tree rise by itself—Aidan!—freeing the remaining quadcopters. Michael and Ricardo rush Krampus, pistols splashing, before they, too, are thrown clear, smashing against a wall.

"Idiot children. Should never have opened the windows." The Krampus rises to his full height, twisted horns spiraling from his massive, goatish head. Thick nostrils flaring. His muscled chest spans at least three feet, covered in white, scarred flesh. His shaggy silver fur is streaked with dirt and soot. A long, black tongue lolls from his mouth surrounded by fangs jutting from his bottom jaw. The legendary black bag hangs like a backpack from his shoulders. His glowing blue eyes narrow as he scans the house. He strikes the Nikita, but because it's a gift, he can't hurt it and his claws pass through, leaving it unharmed. Snarls of rage and agony. The dust that hit him is burning the skin of his head and left shoulder, leaving a stretch of charred, raw flesh.

"Such clever friends, Aidan," the Krampus bellows, his voice *basso profundo.* "Come here before I kill them all."

The Nikitas swarm him. He bellows again, trying to move his hooves. They seem glued to the floor. Aidan holds him, no doubt.

Leo clutches at his throat as his body lifts into the air, passing over the loft wall up to the vaulted ceiling. Judy screams.

"*What will you do now, Aidan?*" Krampus shrieks, his voice fanning into a demonic chorus. "*Where is Charity?*"

I then realize what I have to do. When the Nikita lands in the loft, I pluck the baggy from her payload and stuff it in my jeans pocket.

"Come and get me, you bastard!"

My body rises. In one "empty" hand, he holds Leo, whose face is turning purple. In the other, me. An invisible force squeezes my waist. I feel my ribs ready to snap.

"*Let them go!*"

The house groans. Wood from the banisters splinters off. The kitchen cabinets open and the dishes hurtle out, smashing around Krampus.

In this moment as I hang in the air above the carnage, over the death and rage, all I can think of is how much I love Aidan and how much I hate his father. I don't care for my life. Or my death. I just want this monster dead.

Krampus throws Leo through the sliding glass door. A sickening crash. He lands on the deck. Blood from a gash in his neck quickly soaks the planks. Judy wails with grief.

"You had to make this difficult, didn't you? I need to get a good look at the girl who would defy me for my worthless son." Krampus leers at me and his long moist tongue whips around the opening of his mouth. He clutches me and brings me closer to his face, his claws sinking into my waist. Blood soaks into my shirt. He steps out from under the rain of mistletoe dust, letting it continue to the floor. His rough tongue runs over my neck and face, leaving slime in its wake. His breath smells like rotten eggs.

"Delicious. I see why my son wants you. Too bad you must die."

Blinding pain in my chest as a rib snaps. I shriek but I don't hear myself as the pain obliterates everything. White light explodes behind my eyes.

"*Stop!*" Aidan shouts. "I will come with you, but only if you don't hurt her. Or anyone else."

My eyes meet those of Krampus. Alien. Hateful. Where is Nicholas? He is lost. Forever. His foul breath rushes over me.

"Here I am. Now release her."

Aidan is behind me, but I don't look. I'm losing blood.

My moment has come.

Hand plunging into my pocket, I withdraw the baggy and smash it against Krampus' chest. His eyes widen as he shrieks. Inhuman. Wounded. His skin blisters against my hand. The mistletoe eats into him, but it's not killing him quite as I'd hoped. I push it deeper into his flesh. He drops me as he convulses in pain.

Ricardo breaks my fall, quickly dragging me away with his one good arm. Tears pour down his face. "Don't look!"

But I do.

Aidan walks obediently to his father who shakes with pain and rage.

"Don't hurt anyone else," Aidan says. "Please."

The house shrapnel rises up, jagged edges pointing toward us as they hover in mid-air. Ricardo covers us with his shield. Michael crawls over to join us, raising his shield, me between them.

The bag on Krampus' back opens and swallows Aidan.

"*Aidan!*"

Krampus whistles "God Rest Ye Merry Gentlemen" as he limps to the fireplace. He throws the dead elves clogging the opening aside. Then, with a twinkle in his eye, he disappears up the chimney. The frightening clatter of hooves. His voice calling into the night.

"*Aidan!*"

I scream until I taste blood in my throat. Tears burning my face. My body. Screaming.

Bleeding.

Everything goes black.

# Epilogue

*Nine months later.*
*Reconnaissance mission. Geographical North Pole.*

The Russian ship's nuclear-powered engine hums a mechanical lullaby beneath me. I awaken to the sharp, guttural exchanges between crewmembers.

Propped up on an elbow in my bunk, I blink with exhaustion. The dreams started haunting me immediately after that hellish Christmas. I've gotten used to them now, but it can still be hard to rest. As Leo said once, maybe physical contact with Aidan has affected me in more ways than one.

The dreams have been a homing beacon leading me to the exact coordinates of the fortress where Aidan is captive. There's the geographical North Pole, the magnetic North Pole, and the "magical" North Pole. Filled with tourists and scientists, this Russian icebreaker is headed toward the first. It's just a reconnaissance run courtesy of Volertech, the company contracted by the State Department where I'm an intern. They build drones and other high-tech machines of war. I'm designing one that flies in subzero temperatures. The Arctic is getting warmer, which means Russia is on the move. The U.S. wants to keep an eye on them.

Like father, like daughter.

And like Leo, I died, too. For a minute, anyway. The paramedics brought me back. Judy was dialing 911 on Leo's phone as Krampus tried to kill me. I saw no lights, experienced none of the typical near death phenomena. Just the delicate darkness. Silky, like Aidan's skin. Warm. Peaceful.

I woke up screaming. I'm not sure when I stopped.

Every minute since that hour I've planned to avenge my friend's death and the kidnapping of the one person I love more than anything.

That night changed not only me but also the world. Science. Anthropology. Biochemistry. Zoology. And much more.

We didn't tell anyone it was the Klaas. We told them Aidan's father—an enormous, incredibly strong guy—brought the creatures to attack us. He murdered Leo, tried to kill me and everyone else, and then took Aidan away. They asked us about the dust. We answered that Aidan had told us mistletoe was toxic to the creatures.

I doubt they believed us, but the evidence supports it.

After Detective Bristow saw the destruction, he visited me in the hospital. "You're incredibly brave. Why didn't you call me for help?"

"You would have been killed outright," I replied. "I couldn't be responsible for that."

He said, "I'm sorry" and nothing more after that.

My brother mysteriously disappeared from the detention center that Christmas night. The FBI is still looking for him. Maybe that was his deal with Krampus, if one can make any kind of deal with that monster. Trading Aidan for his freedom. There's no telling where he is now. Probably far from home. In hiding. My brother will be fine.

Our family is shattered. My parents are divorcing. I haven't heard much from my mom. She crashed emotionally after Aidan was kidnapped and the house destroyed, unable to forgive herself for letting it happen. She's living with her cousins as she struggles with alcohol and depression. I worry about her constantly. My dad says *I* worry him, but he loves me and knows how capable I am. And I love him very much. Shortly after the battle, I told him the truth about Aidan, about our relationship. I've not told him about the mission I'm planning next April, but I did confess that I wanted to save Aidan.

"You'd throw away your life on a boy?" he shouted.

If there's anyone in this world worth saving, it's Aidan. Judy, Michael, and Ricardo all agree. While my dad doesn't want me trying to save Aidan myself, he's heartbroken over Aidan going back to his horrible dad and very much wants to rescue him. But I don't want him to jeopardize his career—his entire life. I'm young. I don't have as much to lose at this point in my life in terms of reputation and money.

As I recovered from my injuries, I graduated early from high school. Aerojet offered me a full scholarship to Carnegie Mellon, but I used the offer as a negotiating chip for a full scholarship from Volertech. Dad was mad at first, because Aerojet is the company he works for, but he eventually understood that I have very specific goals.

Maybe he was right about my talent, though. I might not even need to graduate from CM. I'm already developing drones and other tech that would make Tony Stark blush. Ricardo says I should go into business for myself. Maybe I will someday.

Michael graduated early from high school, too. He came with me to study programming but dropped out to become a hacker for hire, mostly working for shady business ventures, but also for me. I'm not sure what Ricardo is doing, but he has black belts in various martial arts, is an expert marksman, and even trains tactical teams in Krav Maga with one of his brothers. Plus, he's hella smart. I wish he'd go to college, but he refuses. He's mentioned possibly going into business with his brother, but I don't know that business would be. Whatever he chooses, he'll be great help in my plans, tactically if not financially.

Judy is taking her considerable artistic skill to study anthropomorphic animation at Stanford, writing more about The Elves than anyone. (Everyone calls them The Elves, not because they know their origins, but because the attack happened on Christmas.) She draws an insanely popular web comic about them. She also has a vlog with over a hundred thousand subscribers.

She still grieves Leo's death. I don't know if she'll ever recover. But I do know she's all in on the rescue mission once it forms.

As much as I want to save Aidan, I need to destroy Krampus. In addition to the drone, I'm developing the weapons to do just that...

A scruffy Russian crew member stumbles into the bunk room to retrieve some breakfast supplies from the lockers. "*Dobroye utro*," he says.

"*Dobroye utro*," I reply, dour. I don't want to encourage him. He watches me with shark eyes. I wish I could have brought a Taser. As I've tinkered with the Taser at home, I've toyed with some ideas about how I can interfere with Krampus' power over gravity. It's all experimental, of course, as I didn't get to study Aidan's powers. But I have theories.

I'm obsessed with this plan to save Aidan, but I have work to do first. And money to raise.

This morning, we're moored at an outpost not five hundred kilometers from the fortress. The icebreaker is to stay a day so that the scientists on board can take some climate measurements.

I'll be conducting my own tests with a prototype I call Ghost.

It's only 5:30 a.m. Before layering up, I make a trip to the bathroom and pull my ever-unruly hair into a huge ponytail. Thick bands of hair turned white that night. I dye them purple like Judy's. I love my hair these days. Fully clothed and coated, I tiptoe out of the bunkroom and close the door behind me.

The Russian crew watches me as they go about their business. My face, even my teeth, ache in the freezing air. It's only 28 degrees. This one trip to the Arctic Circle won't be enough to acclimate me to prolonged exposure to cold. Hopefully when we save Aidan the exposure won't be for that long, though. Just a couple of days.

I climb the mast of the great red ship. The winds are calm this morning compared to last night. Actually, this time of year it's twilight all day.

I wear goggles to protect my eyes from the winds racing around me. I hold steady, hunkering against the ladder to keep my balance. The height is thrilling as I overlook the surrounding bluish-white sheet of ice. Sea ice is at its lowest in the past century, which is evident by the ghostly gray pools of water pock marking the glacier. It's part of the reason our ship can get as close to the Pole as it has.

When the winds die down, I pull off my glove and let it dangle from my lanyard. I wear a second, thinner glove beneath so I can work in the freezing weather. The Arctic winds are underscored by the muffled purr of the ship's engine far below, peppered by the crewmember's voices. Withdrawing a piece of paper and duct tape from my coat pocket, I clumsily affix the piece of paper to the mast. It's symbolic, as the tape won't really stick to the icy surface.

Perhaps we shouldn't advertise, as Keiko once said. Keiko is literally saving the whales these days. She lost interest in mathematics entirely and has plunged into environmental causes, majoring in marine biology when she starts UC San Diego in the fall. We don't talk a lot—not because we're not friends, as we totally made up, but because we've both been ridiculously busy. I miss her more than I can say.

The paper on the pole is a simple letter to someone very special. Soon, I will see him. Before I let go, I read it once more in the Arctic twilight through my goggles.

*Dear Santa,*

*I've been a very good girl this year. I want two gifts for Christmas more than anything.*

*Aidan.*
*Your head.*

*See you soon.*

*Sincerely,*

*Charity Jones*

As I climb down, the winds rip away the paper from the mast and carry it off.
To Krampus.

# Acknowledgements

There is so much for which I'm grateful. Due to hand disabilities, I couldn't have written this book without Dragon NaturallySpeaking running on VMware for my Macbook. Nuance Communications has saved me more times than I can recall, and this was no exception. Merci mille fois.

I'm also grateful to have had such kickass teen beta readers. Many thanks to Miri, Hannah, Livi, Kate, and Jonathan for helping me see Charity and her world through their eyes, and for their relentless excitement about this book. (Holy crap, you guys are awesome.) I'm in debt to their parents, too, especially Betina and Judy. Their enthusiasm, love, and support for both me and the story kept me away from many a ledge during the darkest hours.

Not that I ever got too close to ledges. My wonderful agent, Alex Slater, has been my rock. His belief in this book meant everything to me, and still does. Ditto to Jennifer and John at Raw Dog. I'm so proud to be part of their literary family.

As for the crime drama, the story wouldn't have been so painfully accurate without my consultations with retired homicide detective Derek Pacifico. He even went above and beyond to get me necessary details about the juvenile court system. (Any procedural errors are my fault, not his.) I also consulted an open online support forum for parents who have incarcerated children. Their posts broke my heart. I wish everyone in that situation blessings and brighter days.

Last but not least, I'm entirely thankful to my friend Neil Gaiman for writing Nicholas Was lo those many years ago. When he later read my short story "Coming Home," he said, "This is the story I should have written." Bless! Published numerous times, "Coming Home" went on to be adapted to various formats, and it was stolen more times than I can count. Now it's a novel. This novel, to be precise...

Merry, merry, merry Christmas.

# About the Author

Maria Alexander is a produced screenwriter, published games writer, virtual world designer, award-winning copywriter, prolific fiction writer, and poet. Since 1999, her stories have appeared in publications such as *Chiaroscuro Magazine*, *Gothic.net*, and *Paradox*, as well as in acclaimed anthologies alongside living legends such as Clive Barker and Heather Graham.

Her debut novel, *Mr. Wicker*, won the 2014 Bram Stoker Award for Superior Achievement in a First Novel. *Publisher's Weekly* called it, "(a) splendid, bittersweet ode to the ghosts of childhood," while *Library Journal* hailed it in a Starred Review as "a horror novel to anticipate." She's represented by Alex Slater at Trident Media Group.

When she's not wielding a katana at her local Shinkendo dojo, she's being outrageously spooky or writing *Doctor Who* filk. She lives in Los Angeles with two ungrateful cats, a Jewish Christmas caroler, and a purse called Trog. For more information, visit her website at www.mariaalexander.net.